THE
WINGED
HORSE

Center Point
Large Print

Also by Max Brand® and available from
Center Point Large Print:

**This Large Print Book carries the
Seal of Approval of N.A.V.H.**

THE WINGED HORSE

—A Western Story—

MAX BRAND®

CENTER POINT LARGE PRINT
THORNDIKE, MAINE

This Circle Ⓥ Western is published by Center Point Large Print in 2015 in co-operation with Golden West Literary Agency.

First Edition
August, 2015

The text of this Large Print edition is unabridged. Printed in the United States of America on permanent paper. Set in 16-point Times New Roman type.

ISBN: 978-1-62899-665-4 (hardcover)
ISBN: 978-1-62899-670-8 (paperback)

Library of Congress Cataloging-in-Publication Data

Brand, Max, 1892–1944.
The winged horse : a western story / Max Brand. — First edition.
pages cm
Summary: "A young man with a bad reputation and many aliases helps a rancher in his battle with a clan of rustlers"—Provided by publisher.
ISBN 978-1-62899-665-4 (hardcover : alk. paper)
ISBN 978-1-62899-670-8 (pbk. : alk. paper)
1. Large type books. I. Title.
PS3511.A87W56 2015
813'.52—dc23
                                        2015015424

THE
WINGED
HORSE

Chapter One

He was an inch over six feet, and yet he looked light enough to ride a small horse and strong enough to break a big one. He was not a pretty man, because his eye was cold and his jaw was grim. Since he was without a coat and one sleeve had been torn out of his shirt, an arm was visible. It showed a white dazzlingly pure skin, contrasted with the sun-blackened skin of hands and face. A student of anatomy would have been entranced by that arm. It was not bulky, but it was not sleeked over with a layer of fat. On the contrary, every muscle was a separate string that could have been picked out between thumb and forefinger. The sheriff had been regarding him.

"I'm gonna soak you into the hoosegow, stranger," he said.

"All right," said the stranger. "I need a rest, anyway."

"You're gonna get one," said the sheriff. "A good long one."

"That depends on the way you feed," said the stranger. "What kind of chuck you throw to the boys in the hoosegow?"

"Frijoles," said the sheriff.

"Well, they'll hold me for a day or two," said the stranger.

"We'll hold you the rest of the time," said the sheriff.

The other smiled. The hardness vanished from his face and the sheriff found himself looking into the twinkling eyes of a boy.

"Aw, I dunno," the stranger said.

This was a challenge, and the sheriff sneered with anger. He jerked a piece of paper toward him and stabbed his pen into the inkwell.

"What name or names have you got?" he asked.

"That depends," answered the other.

"Depends on what?"

"On where I am."

"You're here, now."

"I dunno what this place is," said the prisoner. "It ain't on the map, is it?"

"Stow your jaw," answered the sheriff, growing very hot of face. "Ain't on the map!" he echoed fiercely.

"Maybe I'll put it on," the prisoner said cheerfully. "But I dunno how it is . . . some places are pretty hard."

"You'll find this place hard enough," the sheriff assured him with satisfaction.

"I mean hard to wake up," said the other.

"You heard me talk. What's your name or names?"

"In Montana they call me The Kid."

"They do, do they? Is that all they think of you up there?"

"They spell it with capitals like a headline," The Kid informed the lawman.

"It's kind of terrible the way you despise yourself," sneered the sheriff.

"They found me pretty young," said The Kid. "I grew up in a week."

"Tall enough to see, eh?"

"You couldn't miss me," the boy assured him.

"What other name have you got besides The Kid?"

"Over in Wyoming they call me Slippery Elm."

"Why?"

"Because I was sort of hard to hold."

"*I'll* hold you," said the bitter sheriff.

"You'll hold trouble then," said the prisoner, and yawned in the face of the officer. "And maybe I'll give you trouble to hold," he added blandly.

"What other name, or names?" asked the sheriff, breathing hard.

"Once in Nevada I was traveling pretty light and pretty fast. It was winter . . . kind of bleak and miserable. I hit a cow camp. I hadn't no horse and only but one shoe on. They call me Lonesome, over Nevada way, right up to now."

"That don't mean nothing."

"Yonder around Denver way, they call me The Doctor."

"Because of the way you could handle a sick horse, maybe?" glowered the sheriff.

"Because I was pretty handy with a knife," said the prisoner. "That was all."

"What other kind of names might you have, Kid?"

"Why, down in Texas, they call me Montana, and up in Idaho they call me Texas."

"They call you pretty near anything, it looks like," suggested the sheriff. "Do you always come?"

"Sure," said the prisoner. "I come anywhere. Even into a joint like this town."

"You'll stay a while, too," said the sheriff.

The prisoner yawned again.

"What's your real name?" asked the sheriff.

"Alfred."

"You?"

"Sure. My mother liked the name."

"What else?"

"Percy."

"What?"

"She thought that I looked that way."

"What's your last name?"

"Lamb."

"That's a lie."

"Sheriff, don't say that again."

"Alfred Percy Lamb . . . that's a moniker to be hung onto a bird like you?"

"It rests pretty light," said the prisoner, "and don't bother me none at all."

"There's some mules," said the sheriff, "that

dunno when they're carrying a load or not."

"I hanker for that rest to start," said the prisoner. "Lead me to that hay pile, Sheriff, will you?"

"Lemme fill out this record. You never been arrested before, I s'pose?"

"Me? Oh, never. I never been this tired before."

The sheriff snorted like a seal. "I bet you been in every hoosegow betwixt here and Frisco," he said.

"You got a kind face," said the prisoner, "but you left school young."

"What kind of a face have you got for describing?" asked the sheriff. "Start with the hair . . . what color is it?"

"I never stopped to think," said Alfred Percy Lamb.

He ran his hand through it; the links of the handcuffs jangled with a delicate sound like silver bells. It was ordinary blond-brown hair, but faded by the sun at the edges, and with a broad streak of gray that ran back above one eye, so that at times it gave oddly the effect of a single horn.

"How would you say?" appealed the sheriff.

It was dusk, and the lamp was lit, but at this moment there was not enough lamplight to replace the day, and not enough day to withstand the night. The sheriff, by raising the lamp, merely dazzled his own eyes. He put the lamp down

11

hastily, for the prisoner had leaned quietly and quickly forward and his eyes became like the eyes of a cat. The sheriff shrugged his shoulders. A chill ran up and down his spine, and his blood was only warmed again by the honest touch of the handles of his revolver.

"I'd say average brown, or medium brown, maybe?"

"Medium brown," the sheriff agreed, and forced his hand through the labored writing, his head cocked over to one side, his eyes looking blankly at the prisoner, as though he were composing a poem that far exceeded the subject matter. "Now your eyes. What say?"

"I dunno . . . gray, or green, or blue, or something."

"That's a help. Don't you know what color your own eyes are?"

"I dunno. Look for yourself."

The sheriff impatiently snatched up the lamp and rose to approach his man, but suddenly he seemed to remember something, and halted far short of his mark. He merely leaned over, holding the lamp high, and squinting.

"Why, they're hazel," he said.

"Put down hazel, then," said the prisoner.

"No, they're gray."

"Make it gray, old-timer."

"Or blue, is it? Say, I never seen such changeable eyes. Medium, I might say."

"Yes, you might."

Eyes, medium, wrote down the sheriff with somewhat less care. "Lemme see . . . the nose?"

"I dunno."

"Turn your head, will you? It ain't very long. It ain't snubbed, though. It ain't got a hook onto it, either. It ain't big and it ain't small. How would you describe that nose of yours, Lamb?"

"I dunno that I ever thought about my nose."

"Medium, I might put."

"Sure you might."

Medium, wrote down the sheriff, toiling over his pen work. "Now take your whole face like a map, what might I say about it?"

"Pretty," suggested Alfred Lamb.

"Huh?" said the sheriff, puffing like a seal again. "Pretty! Pretty? Huh! Face . . . lemme see . . . Western-looking for a face, I'd call it. Face . . . er . . . medium, say. Any kind of distinguishing marks?"

"Not that I know about."

"Where you get that streak of gray in your hair?"

"There was a greaser come up Tucson way that thought that he had a grudge ag'in' me. He was pretty near right about it, too. But he was just a fraction high . . . afterward the hair all grew in white, the way that you see."

"That's a mark. Now, I got something definite on you. This is better . . . and how did you lose that bite out of your left ear?"

"There was a little argument in Denver, one night, over some cards. The fellow had his gun slung under his armpit. He tried over the table at me, while I tried under the table at him. He removed part of this here ear."

"And you removed a part of him, I suppose?"

"He began to scream something terrible," said the prisoner. His eyes grew soft with reminiscence. "There was a fine sunset . . . all gold . . . outside the window. Says one of the boys to him . . . 'Joe, you couldn't've picked a better time for snuffing out.' Funny how little things like that sticks in your mind, ain't it?"

"Sure it's funny," answered the sheriff. He tipped back his head. He, also, had apparently grown absent-minded, so fixedly did he regard the prisoner. "What's that mark down the left side of your face?" he asked presently.

"Pal of mine got to arguing. It was up in Alaska. The point was what share we each was gonna have. He'd done more work than me. I didn't have the same kind of a liking for the handle of a pick that he had. But I'd stood off a couple of tough nuts that wanted to clean us out, when my friend could think of nothing but running all of the way to Dawson for help. However, when it came to standing up for his rights, he wasn't no four-flusher. He waited till my back was turned, and then he come for me. I turned my head and got the edge of the axe here." He sighed. "It hurt like fury," he said. "You just got no idea how that edge of an axe can hurt. It's kind of broader and more ragged than the edge of a knife."

"It is," the sheriff said sympathetically. "Did he change his mind after he'd laid you out?"

"I had a lot of luck that time, and just as he heaved up the axe for another swipe at me, I shot him through the heart while I was falling. That was a pretty close one," said the prisoner, shaking his head pleasantly, as though reproaching fate—or luxuriating in it, perhaps.

"Ain't that another scar that dips down into the inside of your collar, there?"

"Sure! This was down in Mexico City. They sure love a knife, down there. And a family . . . it all sticks together. I met up with three brothers. They was all high class, and they liked poker too well to play it straight. We had a little argument, and while I was getting two of 'em, the third one got me here and pretty near croaked me."

"But you got away?"

"Yup. There was a gendarme handy that seen a chance to get the stakes from the table. He took them, and beat us all up, and turned us loose, and there you are."

15

Chapter Two

Finishing his record, the sheriff said: "Alfred Percy Lamb, alias what shall I call you for short?"

"Why, I dunno."

"Lemme see. Oh, damn these 'mediums' . . . because they make hash out of this here report. Why not Medium? Kid Medium!"

"It ain't much of a name," said the prisoner, "but I might stretch it and make it do."

He was taken to his cell.

"I want to see those beans," he said. "I want to see those real frijoles that you was talking about to me."

"Sure," said the sheriff. "It's suppertime, now. We got a pretty full house tonight."

"What a lot of mangy bums," said the newly named Kid Medium.

The sheriff nodded at this uncharitable statement. "Here's a corner cell for you," he said almost respectfully. "You see, you ain't got no neighbors here. There's a pretty good couch in there, too."

"Now, that's mighty kind of you," said the prisoner. "Dog-gone' hospitable, and everything. Only, I'd like to say that the chuck is what makes the big difference to me, partner. It don't make much of a change to me, no matter what the company and the sleeping is like. But I lived long enough in Mexico to want a pretty good dish of frijoles."

The door closed behind him with a gentle but ominous clang.

The sheriff went home to his supper, through the quiet streets with the scent of frying bacon issuing from every house. He was silent at his table, scowling at the hot cornbread that his wife placed before him, and forgetting his coffee while he pulled at his long, saber-shaped mustaches. Those mustaches had elected him four times to the sheriff's office. Without them, his face looked too thoughtful and gentle, and his stomach had been pounds overweight for years.

A hand knocked at the front door and the sheriff sang out.

"It's me," said an answering voice.

"Who's me?" grumbled the sheriff, uncertain.

"How you talk!" exclaimed his wife. "Don't you know Colonel Pete Loring's voice?"

"Hey, come in, Colonel!" the sheriff called.

The front screen banged and jangled. The colonel strode into the dining room and sat down, leaving a stir of acrid alkali dust in the air.

"How's little things?" the colonel asked.

"Why, kind of fairly stirred up."

"I heard there was a racket last night."

"There was a pretty good racket."

" 'Punchers off the range on a party?"

17

"*A* 'puncher," said the sheriff, "if he is a 'puncher."

"*A* 'puncher?" the colonel said, mildly surprised. "And did one man work up a ruction here?"

"By keeping on moving," said the sheriff. "He didn't stop to let them hit back. His idea was to keep reaching out . . . and most of the things that he reached, dropped on the spot."

"What name?"

"By name of The Medium Kid, or Kid Medium, or something like that. Are you gonna feed with us, Colonel?" he said.

"I ain't going to feed. I sat down in the hotel and got outside of some chuck, there. Now, regarding this wandering 'puncher, what you done with him?"

"Slammed him in the hoosegow, of course."

"Did he fight?"

The sheriff smiled. "Did he fight? He did fight, Colonel. He fought like a wildcat. But we got a rope over his neck and choked him down like a wild horse. Then we toted him to the jail."

"How does he look?"

"Like a mustang."

"Where'd he get that name?"

"Because it's pretty hard to fasten onto him and say why he looks so wild. Y'understand? Everything's just medium about him till he gets into action."

"Would you be needing him long in that jail?"

"He says that I won't."

"He says so?"

"That's the kind he is. He says that it depends upon how things size up in the jail . . . the chuck is what interests him, and if the chuck's good enough, he says he'll stay and rest for a while."

"Look here, Bud . . . did you search him?"

"To the skin."

"Then what's he got that'll bust his way out for him? Friends here in town?"

"It ain't likely. It looks like his first visit to the place, it seems to me."

The colonel was silent, biting his lips in the profoundest thought. He was a fat and smiling man, with a dark skin and a very large mouth. His thick hair was worn away in front, leaving his forehead vastly high. After much thought he said: "You want that fellow pretty bad, Sheriff?"

"Why, I dunno. I wouldn't, except that he told me first that I wouldn't want him for very long."

"What you intend to do about that?"

"Why, it's pretty simple. I'll go up to my office, after a while, and sit there in the dark."

"You think that he'd come on through the office?"

"Why, I dunno. I think that he would."

"Why for? To find trouble?"

"He seen me hang up his guns on the wall."

"What's the difference? Ain't there other guns in the world?"

"Not with such pretty notches on 'em."

"Ah," the colonel said, and his yellowish eyes opened and gleamed with light. He asked bluntly: "How many?"

"Just five on one and six on the other."

"Eleven!" exclaimed the colonel.

"Exactly that."

The colonel sighed. "I'd like to see that young feller, Sheriff, if you got no objections."

"I got no objections at all . . . as long as you want to see him in the jail."

"I'll go up there and sit in the dark with you."

So they went back to the jail, and there they lit two lanterns, which could be closely shuttered.

"Put yours on the floor at your feet, and keep one foot on the catch. If anything stirs, open up wide with that light. I'll open up with mine, too, and here's a sawed-off shotgun that we can use on him. One for you and one for me."

"You don't want to blow him right to glory," Colonel Loring said pleadingly.

"Not nacherally, I won't, if he'll play fair and square with me."

"Give him a chance, give him a chance."

"Is he a friend of yours, Colonel?"

"No, but I got hopes that he will be. Look here, Bud. You know that I need good men. If you could see your way to turning that gent loose, there's five hundred in my wallet that ain't working very hard, just now."

The sheriff smiled, and his saber-like mustaches fanned stiffly out to the side. He had the look of a walrus, suddenly.

"Look here, Colonel Pete," he said, "I like you fine. You're my friend. But I never took coin, and I never will."

"No harm meant," the colonel said hastily.

"Sure not," answered the good-natured sheriff. "I don't mind you getting this gent, if he busts loose, and if I don't have to kill him. Only . . . I won't have money for him."

They closed their lanterns, and they sat for a long hour in utter darkness, their shotguns across their knees. The window was closed. It was very hot and breathless. But the sheriff remained fixed in his place. There was no noise in the jail. From the town they heard merely high-pitched notes, now and again—a shrill cry of anger, or a pulse of laughter, foolishly thin and high.

Then the door opened from the cell room. It could not be seen. It could only be sensed, by the soft, quiet wave of air. Then, by the movement of another wave of air, the sheriff knew that it had been shut again.

Chapter Three

He still waited for a moment, and then from across the room came a flash of light. He snapped on his own torrent at the same instant and he saw his prisoner, Alfred Percy Lamb, as active as a Punch and Judy show. Without a sound, with wonderful surety and swiftness, the man had crossed the floor in that utter darkness and reached his guns. He whirled with them in his hands, and fell toward the floor, with a double click of the weapons.

The sheriff leveled the shotgun and the shaft of light at the fallen man.

"It's no good, Kid," he said. "It's no good at all, Medium. You can't ride dummy horses, even with the longest spurs in the range."

"You pulled the teeth of these dogs," The Medium Kid said, rising alertly to his feet, "and nobody can bite without guns. Am I talking straight?"

"Why, straighter than a string, by a whole lot. Set down and rest your feet, Kid."

The Kid sat down.

"You might introduce me," said the colonel. "When I saw those guns wing, I pretty near introduced myself with both barrels."

"Colonel Pete Loring," the sheriff said. "And this here is Alfred Percy Lamb."

"I didn't quite follow that recitation," said the colonel.

"You ain't been to church for a long time," the sheriff said dryly. "Which your mind is out of practice on texts, and such-like things. But you might know him as The Kid, or The Lonesome Kid, or The Doctor, or Montana, or The Medium Kid, or Kid Medium, if any of those names sort of sounded to you, Colonel."

The colonel smiled his capacious smile and showed a wide range of broad, white teeth. He seemed full of the content of good living. "Glad to know you," he said.

"Glad to know you," said Kid Medium, alias Alfred Lamb. He turned to the sheriff. "It was the way that cook done the frijoles," he said, "that got me all restless. You know how it is when beans is cooked with only one kind of pepper?"

"I know," said the sheriff.

"They ain't satisfying."

"No," agreed the sheriff, "they sure ain't."

"But I'll try 'em again," said the youngster, "and see if I can get used to 'em."

"Do you think you can?"

"I'm kind of afraid not. Frijoles I'm special particular about, having spent some time in Mexico."

"I don't want to be prying," said the sheriff.

23

"But I'd like to know who you talked into opening the door for you and unlocking your irons."

"I talked to the irons first," said the prisoner, "and then I talked to the lock on the door."

"What kind of talk?"

"Sign language."

"How old are you?" the colonel, interrupting, asked suddenly.

"Twenty-two."

"Like fun you are!"

"Sorry you don't think so."

"Ain't you on the far side of twenty-seven or eight, maybe?"

"Thanks," he said. "But I grew up fast."

"Now," said the colonel, "I want to talk business with you."

"Sure," answered the boy. "I love to talk business. The sheriff will tell you that."

"I'm serious. The sheriff, here, is a pretty doggone' good-hearted gent."

"He is," said the boy, "or otherwise he would have plastered me a minute back, just as I was about to plaster him." He added gravely: "I was shooting for your legs, Sheriff. Y'understand?"

The sheriff nodded with the utmost cheerfulness. "You just wanted me out of the way. I never had a better thought in my life than taking the salt and pepper out of those lunch boxes. But listen to what the colonel has to say."

"You ever hear of me, son?"

"I don't know. Lemme think. Colonel Pete Loring? Are you him that has a Montague every Sunday for breakfast?"

"Perhaps I might have run into the Montagues, now and then. But it was them that first run into me."

"I've heard something about it," said the boy. "I don't know what."

"Trouble!" exclaimed the colonel. "There's been nothing but trouble since I ran into the Montagues. You take my record. Clean as a whistle. But when I come onto this range, where there was room for everybody, the Montagues started to make trouble. Dogs in the manger. They couldn't use all the range . . . but they didn't want anybody else to use it. You'd despise to know how mean those gents can be, those Montagues."

The boy nodded, watchful and intent. He glanced aside at the sheriff.

"Yes, ask the sheriff," Colonel Pete Loring said.

The sheriff shook his head, however, and grinned, his mustaches furring out in the peculiar way they had, which always made him look like a walrus.

"I don't take sides," he said. "Colonel Pete has been a pretty good friend to me, and so he has to most of the boys in this here town. But I don't take sides. There's some that say that the Montagues are all right, and I don't take sides.

Thank heaven that the fighting ain't been in my county, or I'd've tried to round up the whole gang, all around."

"If it had been in your county," said the colonel, "the trouble would never have got fairly started, but being where it is, with the sheriff bought up by the Montagues . . ."

"They say that he's bought up by you!"

"Sure they do. Why, it'd made a man tired, the way those low-down skunks will lie about a man. Bought up by me. Bribery! Why, rather than bribe . . ."

The colonel caught himself. The sheriff was looking straight at him with a quizzical but not unfriendly smile.

Then he said: "But I'll get right down to business. You guess what I want with you?" he asked the boy.

"I dunno. I could guess."

"Well, then, I want you to help me to protect the range to which I've got a good right."

"That sounds reasonable. You got a pretty good outfit?"

"The best gents in the world. Some of 'em are kind of rough, but a mighty good set, take 'em all the way through."

"Some of 'em get pretty sick, all of a sudden?"

"Why . . . some do, and no mistake."

"Too quick for the doctor to get to them?"

"There ain't any denying of that, either."

"What sort of a price?"

"Sixty bucks, and a bonus for trouble."

"Why, I dunno. I might think it over."

"In jail?"

"This jail is kind to me," said the boy. "It wouldn't ever hold me, to tell you the truth."

"Talk up," said the sheriff. "Do you want this job?"

The youngster hesitated. "No," he said. "Not at sixty."

"Well, what's your figure?" the colonel asked.

"I'm worth a hundred. I'll take ninety. That's only three dollars a day."

"It's a lot," growled the colonel. "If I paid you that, you'd have to keep your face shut about the money that you get."

"Talking after hours," said the boy, "is what I chiefly hate, Colonel."

"Done, then," said the rancher. "What about it, Sheriff?"

"It's kind of a funny business," said the sheriff, "that a gent that gets jailed for a street fight in my town should be promoted to a good fat job over on your side of the fence, Colonel. But I got nothing ag'in' him. He didn't punch my nose, and he couldn't get loose from my jail. So I call it an even break. Take him away if you want him."

"Pronto," said the colonel. "Are you ready, Kid?"

"Ready now to step."

"Have you got a horse in town? If you ain't, I brought in an extra one. They's no sense in going fishing if you don't take a basket."

"I've got a horse already, but I'll take a look at yours."

"This'll make you some trouble, likely?" said the boy to the sheriff as they parted.

"No, it won't. The judge don't mind me settling cases outside the court. He knows that I never make a penny out of these here deliveries, and so long as I keep turning the right kind out and keeping the wrong kind in, what's to complain of?"

This free and somewhat extra-legal viewpoint was heartily applauded by the colonel, and he took his protégé down the front steps of the jail, a free man.

They crossed to a side street to the stable attached to the jail from which, at a message from the sheriff, the horse of Alfred Lamb was being led.

The colonel walked about it with a keenly critical eye. "This horse set you back something," he said at last.

"It did."

"Money or trouble?"

"Both," the youngster said noncommittally.

"Has she got enough under the cinches?"

"She won't say no if you ride her all day."

"She'll do, then. I've got a good thing for you, but it's five hundred dollars cheaper than *that* nag."

They passed up the street, leading the mare behind them, and as they turned a corner, the colonel laid a sudden hand upon the shoulder of his protégé.

"Young fellow," he said, "I want to put the cards on the table. If you're what I want, I'll make you rich enough to buy a whole stable of horses better than that one behind you."

"Try me first," said the boy, "and see if I can take any tricks."

Chapter Four

On the colonel's place they were rounding up weanlings. They were in the last camp before they made the ranch house. Therefore, good cheer should have been strong among the cowboys, but good cheer hardly fitted in with such weather as they were having. The fall was ending and winter was beginning to show its teeth. The wind came straight across the mountains, well chilled from the upper snows, and at all things it struck with a fierce lunge, and drove its spear point of cold far home. Many days of riding in wet clothes, on wet saddles, with water squelching in their boots, had worn out the cowpunchers, and their tempers had gone before their strength. But above all they were tired of the wind; its weight leaned continually against them, cutting their faces red and raw, and making balloons of their mouths when they attempted to speak.

It was good food that the cook gave them. The Dutch ovens were filled with excellent beef, with roasted potatoes, richly browned and covered with juicy gravy. There was a sort of stew in which tomatoes were the chief ingredient. All these delicacies steamed and gave forth their fragrance when the cook shouted—"Come and get it!"—and the hungry cowhands swarmed in and lifted the lids. But with all this, and the supreme charm of the perfume of the coffee streaming through the air, still the men went stolidly, grimly about their supper. The cook himself scowled; he was disheartened by such lack of appreciation and swore silently to himself that he would make these cowboys rue their glumness the following morning at breakfast time.

The attack upon the food had barely started when through the wet and the wind a horseman rode in and dismounted on the verge of the firelight, where it gleamed vaguely on him, and more brightly on his horse.

"This is the colonel's outfit, is it?" he asked.

Heads turned toward him. They nodded.

"Where's the cavvy?"

They pointed to the rope corral that made its location known, at the instant, by a sudden outbreak of squeals and whinnies. In that direction the stranger disappeared and returned with considerable speed, carrying his saddle and a small pack. He went through the circle of feeding men, produced his own plate, cup, knife, and fork, and helped himself generously to everything. This was not at all unusual, of course, upon the range. But there was something about the assured air of this youth and the size of the portions to which he helped himself that irritated the wagon boss.

He said: "Who might you be, stranger?"

"I'm a new hand," said the other hurriedly.

"What's your best hand?" asked the boss.

"A left hook," the stranger answered as he settled himself in a strategic position where the wind snarled and snapped a little less than in other places.

The wagon boss felt that he was set back. Also, he saw the men lifting their heads a little. They looked upon the stranger with anger because, though strange, he was not abashed, and yet they smiled a little—faint, semi-secret smiles, for it soothed their very souls to have the wagon boss put down even with words.

For the wagon boss was a bold, bad man, and though every one of these hand-picked warriors

31

of the range would have qualified in the same category, yet they acknowledged him as their master. He was made of iron. There were two hundred and twenty pounds of that metal in him, and he had been heated with liquor and hammered with bullets and tempered in gore, so to speak. He rarely had occasion to lift his voice or his hand, once he was known.

Now he raised his head stiffly and stared at the newcomer. "What's your name?" he asked.

"What's yours?" asked the stranger.

"I'm Muldoon."

"Muldoon what? Or, what Muldoon?" asked the cheerful stranger.

At this, a deep, grim chuckle passed around the crew. They knew that destruction was rushing down upon this glib youth, but they could not help enjoying the badgering that he was giving to their man of might.

"Muldoon," rumbled the wagon boss, "of the street of Muldoon, in the town of Muldoon, in the county of Muldoon, in the state of the same name, and Muldoon is the name of the country, too. Have you heard of it?"

He had suspended his eating operations—which were conducted upon a vast scale—and he let his eyes wander a little over the group. He was proud of his speech. It was not the first time he had made it, as a matter of fact, but it was pronounced for the first time here.

"I've heard of it," the stranger said, continuing to eat with an unabated appetite. "I've heard a lot about the country of Muldoon."

"You read about it in your geography, maybe?" Muldoon said. "Then maybe you know that the kids are born with teeth, in that part of the world, and suckers starve to death, and four-flushers have their heads beat off."

This last he said with a good deal of scowling point, for he was working himself into a rage. He enjoyed being in a rage. He reveled in the deeps and darknesses of fury. He began to pant, and to make his chest heave, and to clench his hands, and to roll his eyes like the eyes of a maddened bull, for he knew that if he went through all the appropriate gestures, it would not be long before he was actually in the state that he simulated.

The wind, at this point, took control. It leaped off the nearest mountain and flattened the flames of the fire to flickering, blue-rimmed tatters. The light was nearly extinguished, so that every man became for an instant a stranger to his nearest neighbor, and the pencilings of rain were visible, and the face of the night and the storm pressed down and breathed upon that little human company.

Having stamped upon this spot, the storm wind leaped away again. The first voice to be audible was that of the stranger, remarking, as he drained his coffee cup, that he had heard these things before, and he had also heard that all the winds that blew in the country of Muldoon were composed of blasts of hot air. He stated, also, that he had learned in school how to bound the country of Muldoon, and that he had been taught that it was bounded on the north by a heavy frost, on the east by a flood, on the west by the big rain, and on the south by the 4th of July.

He stated his conviction with perfect gravity and recited his piece in the singsong of a schoolboy.

The cowboys were delighted. Their very hearts were warmed by this exhibition of impromptu brilliance, and they waited breathlessly. Destruction lay before the stranger, but certainly he was winning the battle of words, the cannonade before the shock of the countering charges.

The stranger had gone to the ovens again, and all men stared in wonder when they saw him heap up his plate more generously than before. It was an extra-large plate, and, even so, it was not nearly big enough to accommodate the vast appetite of this youth. Even Muldoon, famous as a trencherman, was outclassed utterly.

This gormandizing actually made the wagon boss stare until he was agape, and he could not help saying: "Where d'you put all that stuff, kid?"

"In cold storage," said the boy.

"Damn," said Muldoon as though he had stubbed his toe. "What's your name?"

"I got several," said the other. "The last one was The Medium Kid, or Kid Medium, anyway you want to put it."

"A great name," Muldoon said, throwing away all attempts at clever finesse. "Ain't you got another name?"

"They used to call me Lonesome . . . The Lonesome Kid."

"That's a fool name," said Muldoon. "Got no meaning to it, either."

"Hasn't it? I'll tell you what it means. It means that I was so far off in front that I was all by myself."

Muldoon tried to answer, failed of words, and merely gasped like a fish. Then he shouted: "Hold on! There was a Lonesome Kid over yonder in Nevada. I used to know a Lonesome Kid, over there."

"Did you?" answered the other. "Oh, I dunno. I got a way of forgetting faces, and I sure don't place you."

Muldoon exclaimed: "The Lonesome Kid! Why, you ain't any more like The Lonesome Kid than you are like . . . how d'you get that way?" He stood up, huge, irate, and took a step forward.

Said The Kid: "What do you want, Muldoon?"

"I'm gonna skin you," Muldoon said, "and see if the insides of you are more like the real Lonesome Kid than the outsides of you."

"Are you gonna use guns or fists?"

"I wouldn't waste bullets on calves."

"If you want a gun play," The Kid said, as imperturbably as ever, "get out your Colt and let it talk for you. If you want fists, or rough-and-tumble, or any game there is, I'll take you on in the morning, Muldoon, and I'll make you look like the county of Muldoon, and the town of Muldoon, and a back yard filled with tin cans in the street of the same. But just now I'm too full of steak and comfort to stand up."

The people of the West are poker players *par excellence,* and all the wiles and the ways of the bluffer are understood. Now, these students of cards, and cows, and humans, looked earnestly upon The Kid and saw him with new eyes and read, as it were, the list of unseen notches upon the handles of his guns. They saw in that flash, that The Kid was bad, and that he was very bad, and that he was worse than poison, to put it shortly.

Big Muldoon saw, also. He jerked his hand halfway to his holster, and there his hand paused. The Kid did not seem to look at him. Actually he was rolling a cigarette, and yet a moving point of ice wriggled down the spine of the wagon boss.

"You and me'll meet in the morning," he agreed.

And all the men of the camp looked down to the

ground, flushing a little. Brave and great-hearted as their chief was, they saw that he wanted none of the gun game of this stranger. He had to fall back upon his superior weight of shoulder and hand. However, the morning was something worth waiting for.

Chapter Five

That autumn night was both wet and cold; the wind blew hard, with frost in its breath and anger in its roar; it was trying to bring on a sweeping victory of winter all at one blow; it wanted to paint every mountain and every valley white, but it was too forehanded, and when the voice of the cook bellowed hoarse and distant as a fog horn through the darkness—"Come and get it, or I'll throw it out!"—the men wakened to find that the snow had not yet come. There were only flying edges of sleet, streaks and incrustations of ice, here and there. The tarpaulins were hardened to boards by this process and the hair of the sleepers had alternately been drenched and frozen into tangles.

They sat up from their damp blankets, shuddering, and clasped their sleepy bodies in their arms, wondering if they had the strength to rise, and wondering if rising were worthwhile. The next instant the wind had passed its fine sword blade through and through them and they abandoned all doubt. They began to drag on socks stiff with frost, and then the bitter pain of boots. They huddled into coats and hats, and only when both ends were clad did they rise from the huddling blankets, cinch up belts, clamber into clammy chaps. And then they galloped, like horses, toward the glare of the fire. It was as bright now as it had been the evening before. Morning appeared only on the clock, for it was dark as pitch.

They lived like sailors rounding Cape Stiff. Under such hardships, riding twelve to twenty hours a day, stiffened with cold and beaten with wind, men marching in an army for the salvation of their country would have collapsed and died like flies. But these cowpunchers were working for pay and foolishness, and, therefore, like the sailors of the clipper days, they survived miraculously. The exceeding bitterness of their lives made the mere absence of pain a cause for happiness. And this morning the rare aroma of the coffee that steamed from the nostrils of an enormous, fire-blackened pot gave them sudden hope, more than the rising of the sun. They were wedged into a ragged circle around the fire, looking ten years older than the night before, their shoulders humped, great tin cups of coffee clasped in their hands, sipping it while it was still as hot as fire, waiting for the warmth to come to their shaking knees, and waiting in vain. Sometimes the whole circle swayed under a fiercer blast of the wind, and at the same time the light of the fire cowered and seemed about to go out entirely.

Then they began to eat, staggering from one Dutch oven to another, groaning as they lifted the lids and stared at the familiar contents, for they ate three meals alike and every meal was as the other. Only at the first taste of the food they changed, as wolves change at the taste of flesh. Their shoulders began to straighten; they scowled into the eye of the wind; blood was beginning to run in their bodies.

It was at about this time that the last man from his blankets approached the fire, his slicker flashing and crackling about him in the wind and in the broken firelight. He did not come staggering in sleep and agony. He walked with an alert, light step, and, instead of crowding toward the core of the fire, he went straight to the ovens and began to pick out his breakfast.

"It's The Lonesome Kid," one man said. "He don't feel nothing of all this."

"It's Kid Medium," said another. "Say, Kid, do you carry your own wool?"

"He don't feel no cold. He's leather-lined . . . that's why!"

They laughed a little, and the laughter sounded like the snarling of dogs. Even if The Kid was immune to cold, something was going to happen to him this morning.

But he felt the cold, to be sure, though no one could guess it except those who looked closely enough to see the purple shadow in his cheek. He finished his breakfast in leisurely fashion, while the other cowpunchers were resignedly leaving the fire and making for the rope corral, struggling to fashion their Bull Durham cigarettes, while the wind snatched eagerly at the dry tobacco. They lit their smokes and began to unlimber their ropes.

Suddenly there were only three men at the fire—the cook, the wagon boss, and The Kid. The fire began to look less bright, and the mountains were rising in the horizon, and the valleys were opening to the bowels of the earth, as it seemed, all dim and dark. The wind howled still. Life seemed a pointless thing.

Said the boss: "They'll all be saddled before you, Kid."

"No, they won't," said The Kid.

"You better vamoose right along after the rest," said Muldoon. "Afterward, when we got light, you and me'll have a little talk. Now, go git on your horse, because maybe I'll leave you fit to ride, and ride you will, by gravy, if you have strength to sit in the saddle!"

The Kid hesitated. Then he nodded and said with wonderful calmness: "All right." And he left them.

"Look at that," Muldoon said loudly. "He don't feel so brisk in the morning. He ain't half so spooky as he was the night before. He's got half of the kinks ironed out of him already, but he's gonna be made as smooth as a starched shirt, before I get through with him!"

The cook was a man of many talents. He had been a sailor; the tattooing on his mighty arms was proof of it. He was minus one leg below the knee, though he was wonderfully agile on the wooden peg that he used as a substitute. Since he was past fifty and had only one leg, the cook dared to speak his mind to any man. Besides, the very fact that he was cook gave him a great importance in the cow camps. Therefore, he now said to Muldoon: "Muldoon, you gotta good full arm swing and you gotta good right smash for the body. I seen it break the heart of many a man, in my time, and of course you can down pretty near anybody when you get in at him and bring your weight to bear, but now I was thinking, suppose a gent had the footwork to keep away, he'd spear you with a straight left like I've speared salmon. He'd leave you all adrift, Muldoon."

"You talk like a fool," said Muldoon.

"I ain't a fool, and you know it," the cook said. "If you want to go ahead and get your face spoiled, go and do it. I'm just talkin' . . . supposin' that you might have sense enough to understand what I mean."

Muldoon did not answer. He went in his turn to get his horse from the corral.

It was a gloomy business, that roping. There was just enough light to deceive the eyes; one horse looked as much like another as twin brothers. The cowpunchers were here and there, bent over studying the silhouettes of heads and rumps and ragged tails against the gray dawn light in the east. Then a rope would be flung, lost to the eye of the dauber while still in mid-air, and the result of the cast hardly guessed at until the rope jerked taut in the hand. It was like casting nets for fish in the dark, except that here it would not do to catch another man's property. Many a man dragged his capture to the gate, only to turn it loose again with bitter curses, and again advance upon that milling, snorting, biting, fighting mass of horses, for they were frenzied with the cold.

Muldoon, shaking out his noose, observed these failures with contempt, for he was not the man to make mistakes, even in the false light of the dawn. And *then* he saw a tall man on his right, sauntering toward the mass of horses—and without a rope! It was The Kid. He paused, curious, to see what the next maneuver would be. He was not the only curious watcher, for yonder the men were frozen in their tracks with wonder.

They heard a thin, piercing whistle that came from the lips of the new man. It was not repeated. Then, out of the tangle of horseflesh a slender and proud form appeared. Even in that dusk, streaked across with flying snow and daubs of rain, the beauty of the mare was apparent, as though revealed by her own light. And she came straight up to her master. He turned, and she followed him, as a dog follows at the heel.

Muldoon, having watched, cursed with a soft violence, and his was not the only voice that was eloquent with wrath at that moment. Then they saw the mare stand like a statue, while saddle and bridle were slipped upon her. All around her, cowboys were working out their ponies, and every mustang of the lot was pitching with a savage vigor, getting the arch out of its back and supplying its frozen knees with educated bucking.

"What you got, cowboy?" asked one, in a pause of his torment, finding himself near the stranger. "Is that a picture or a real horse?"

"It's a picture," said The Kid. "They give away horses like these with every cut of chewing tobacco that you buy down yonder."

"Where's yonder?" the cowboy asked, but did not stay for the answer, his pony willing otherwise.

Then, suddenly, the sky was gray, pink-rimmed, and the whole scene rose up to meet the day.

"There's about light enough now," said Muldoon, "for you to make yourself useful. If you know anything about riding and working beef, you get down there with the boys. They'll show you which way we're drifting the weaners." He said this to The Kid, coming up behind him.

The Kid turned to him, carefully shielding the burning end of his cigarette, so that the wind might not blow the fire into his face in a shower of sparks. "I don't ride herd," he said. "You might notice that I don't carry any rope?"

"Hey!" Muldoon yelled, honestly amazed. And then, oddly enough he used the same expression that had recently been tossed toward The Kid. "Are you a cowboy, or just a picture of one?"

"I'm a model cowboy," said The Kid, "and models . . . they don't work. They just model."

Muldoon was silenced. He dismounted from his pony without a word. The wicked mustang jerked free and bolted. Muldoon let it go, unconcerned. "Boy," he said, "you've asked for what's a-coming to you, and you ain't asked only once. Are you ready?"

"I'm ready."

"By gravy," Muldoon said in a new note, "that's The Lonesome Kid's horse!" He pointed toward the mare.

"And I'm The Kid," said the other, unperturbed.

"You? Now, I'll tell you something. Unless you tell me how you got that horse from Lonesome, I'm gonna open you like an oyster."

The Kid was stripping off his coat, and at this tactically advantageous moment, Muldoon rushed.

Chapter Six

Every cowpuncher of the lot had been entirely occupied with his business. They had been drifting here and there, securing their horses, riding out the morning kinks, but when Muldoon rushed, even the cook was on hand. The farthest man was not twenty steps from the heart of the encounter.

It looked as though the fight would end before it began, since a man is fairly helpless when his coat is slipping down over both elbows, but The Kid stepped to one side, and carefully moved his head aside as Muldoon and his smashing fist hurtled past. He shook his coat, folded it, and laid it aside, then he side-stepped Muldoon's second plunge. The wagon boss was beginning to bellow like a bull.

"Why don't you stand still and fight, you yaller dog?" he asked.

"Yellow dogs don't stand," said The Kid, "but they fight."

Suddenly he leaped in and out. A streak of crimson appeared beneath the right eye of Muldoon.

"You . . . ," began Muldoon.

But the rest of his sentence was clipped short. The Kid had flashed in again, and again was out.

He had stepped just inside a ponderous, reaching right, and he hammered both fists into the body of the wagon boss. Those blows sounded like hollow thumps, as though they brought out an echo from the body of the big man. Then Muldoon, charging in, stifled with his fury, slipped in the mud and came to his knees.

"Have you got a left?" asked the cook in savage criticism and concern. "Have you got a left, or is your arm made of dough?"

In that pause Muldoon heard the good advice and recognized its worth. He knew much about the art of fisticuffs, and the time had been when he had known much more, but of late years art had not been necessary. Men were frozen to brittle statues by the terror of his name, and with one blow he struck them to the earth. Now he looked up at the alert, calm form of his opponent, whose hands were hanging at his sides. He knew that the man was a boxer and a good one, but he told himself that there never could be enough weight in that slender, sinewy arm to hurt him seriously. Yet the cook was right. He was being speared as men spear salmon. He was adrift and befogged by the attack of this youth.

He leaped up, driving a long left at The Kid. It was very low, but Muldoon never was worried about little technicalities. In a fight he struck where he could and let the chips fall where they would.

His long left failed. The Kid thrice bobbed the head of the wagon boss at the end of a long, straight arm. It seemed as though that head were attached to the fist by a rubber string, so that the blows could not be escaped.

Muldoon licked his torn lips. "I'm gonna kill you!" he promised, and worked in, for the first time business-like, his left foot preparing the way, his right foot jerking behind him, carrying his weight, leaving him poised with either fist, but chiefly prepared to hammer across his famous right hand. He felt himself now armored in his craft. He was tenfold confident, and he tasted the sweetest joy when he saw The Kid backing away, rubbing his knuckles on his hips, with a thought-ful face. Around him, he saw the faces of his men, baffled but not sorrowing, and his heart leaped with rage when he thought how they would rejoice to see him fall.

But he would not fall. At the worst, of course, there remained his invincible might at close quarters, but still all was not lost in honest fist fighting. Lodged in the back of his brain there was a master secret. His back and arms and knuckles tingled with the knowledge of it. It was his right that men began to notice after a fight started, and it had gone hurtling a few times like an iron bolt. But his left was as strong, though less favored. And he had practiced—for how many hours—a feint at the head with the left, and

47

as the light-footed enemy retreated, a forward gliding of the right foot, and a lightning shift that carried his whole weight with it, a dreadful and murderous blow. He had felt ribs crackle like dead wood under the weight of that shock. He told himself now that he would drive his fist clear through the lean flanks of this boy.

The wolf leaped at him again, slashed, and was out. Well, that would only serve as the touch of a spur to a willing horse. Never had he executed that well-memorized maneuver so neatly, with such crushing dispatch. The double kick of a mule was hardly faster than the double play of his left fist, while his right foot slipped forward, and all the weight, and all the might, and all the spite in his great iron frame pitched suddenly forward with that stroke. He saw the body of The Kid before him, saw the wind flutter the new silk of his shirt, and picked out the very cheek where his knuckles would bite home.

But there followed only a light brushing of cloth across the back of his hand as he hit with a jerk through the air. And, at the same instant, from the corner of his eye he saw The Kid glide forward, sway up on his toes, and settle again, and as he settled a trip hammer smote the base of Muldoon's jaw, and knocked him sidewise, and spun him around.

He fell on one knee and one hand. The yell of the cowpunchers was like the scream of an eagle, tearing his ears, and all the winds of the world seemed to be pouring their thunders through his brain. The crimson patch in the east was a broad stripe of fire that hurtled around and around the horizon.

Then his brain cleared a little. The men stopped swaying and seemed to stand still. The earth no longer heaved and staggered beneath him. Muldoon knew that he was a beaten man, but the greatness of his loss was too much for him to understand. A king at the crisis of the battle might have felt thus, seeing his kingdom poured like sand through his numb fingers.

"You're out of form, old-timer," The Kid said, stepping closer. "Suppose we lay off of this and shake?"

"Gimme a hand up," Muldoon said, and stretched forth his arm.

Instantly it was taken and he rose to his feet, and, rising, he felt that weakness was gone from his knees. Red fire within his blood and brain gave him a double strength, and he hurled himself on The Kid and gripped him in his great arms. He was regardless of the yell from the men at this foul play. He was merely occupied in pinioning both the arms of The Kid.

But that was like trying to pinion two strong serpents, one of which instantly was loosed, and a fist began to jerk up under the chin of Muldoon, tapping rapidly, a deadly sledge-hammering that flung across the brain of the wagon boss sheets of dark spray. He flung forward and they went to the earth together. But it was he whose back struck the mud. Somehow, he had been twisted about in mid-air. The Kid kneeled upon his chest, and that iron fist was poised.

"Am I Lonesome?" The Kid asked.

"You're Lonesome . . . and be hanged to you," said Muldoon.

"You never seen anybody but me on the back of that mare?"

"Maybe I never did," muttered Muldoon.

He was freed.

Slowly he climbed to his feet, and found all the men rapidly mounting and riding away to their work, where the rain-sleeked weanlings were drifting with the wind, their backs bowed, their hearts small with the misery of this world. Shame for the fall of their master was in the hearts of all those cowpunchers, and the wagon boss knew it. He knew, also, that the word would go out far and wide. The victories of fighting men often are not widely reported, but the fall of the great always is trumpeted far and wide.

It seemed to Muldoon, staring about him with wide eyes, that the black-faced mountains must be aware of what had happened. And yonder was the back of the new cowhand moving away from him. He felt a vast impulse to shout out, and when the other turned, to meet him with a leveled gun. But he hesitated, and in that moment of hesitation he knew that he would never have the courage to act as he willed. He had met a better man. The bitterness of gall was in the mouth of Muldoon, and passing down to the very roots of his tongue.

At the fire, the cook set out a basin of hot water. Muldoon washed his face. Then iodine was sluiced through his wounds, and he grinned at the fiery searching of it. Gladly he would have stood with one hand burning in the fire of real flame, if he could have undone this morning's work.

He looked at the face of the cook. That man was frowning, but not happy.

Someone cleared his throat and came closer. Muldoon did not turn. He knew that it was The Kid, and a loathing and horror of himself and of this man who had conquered him froze his blood.

"Muldoon," said the voice of The Kid.

Muldoon shrugged his great shoulders. Of what use was their greatness? Or the invincible length of his arm? Or the mighty hands that could break the neck of a steer?

"Will you listen?" The Kid asked. "I'm a four-flusher as a 'puncher. I can't handle a rope. I couldn't daub a rope on a post. I never handled a branding iron in my life. I don't know one end of a cow from the other. I ain't come up here to spoil your game for you, Muldoon. What's happened had to happen. Now I say this . . . the colonel sent me up here because he thought you could use me . . . but not to work the cows. If you want to use me, I'm your man. I won't back talk. I'll do the jobs that you point out to me. Does that sound to you? If it don't, I'm going back to town again and look for something simpler."

Muldoon looked across the iron mountains, and he heard the wind ringing, ringing in his ear. The burning of the iodine ended, but the ache of his hurts began. How had such a youngster delivered such stunning blows?

"Why not keep him and box with him?" asked the cook.

Why not? Muldoon thought. "Stay on and box with me?" he said.

"Sure," The Kid said.

"Good," said Muldoon. "Good, I'm gonna have a use for you." And he grinned a horrible, vast grin.

Who could tell—when he had put himself back in training?

Chapter Seven

Young cattle work slowly. With a foolish persistence, they mill at the slightest provocation or where there is no provocation at all except an idiotic thought in the most idiotic of all the herd. There is only one lesson which they have mastered, and that is that they must follow every bad example as soon as it is set for them.

The storm had favored the start of the day's drive, which should have been the last march to the main ranch house, for with its cold blasts and icy rattlings of rain and sleet, it whipped the weanlings in the correct direction. But before the drive was an hour old, and after the cook wagon had been dismissed to go careening and bumping and swaying on its way home, the wind changed its mind.

"It's acting up," declared Muldoon, "exactly like a weaver that don't know its own mind, because it ain't got any mind to know."

Sometimes it drove in from the sides; sometimes it leaped from the far horizon and smote the young cattle in the face. No matter from what direction it came, it quickly made them turn their rumps toward it and drift with its force, in spite of yelling cowpunchers who rode straight up and lashed at the heads of the stupid brutes. They even fired their guns under the noses of the leaders, but cold and wind and weariness had induced utter disregard of death.

"They ain't had their coffee," Muldoon said. "They're worse off even than us. Their coffee has been ice water, and their bunks these nights have been running wet. No wonder they're ornery."

Muldoon rode as the rearmost man, not from

indolence, but so that he could keep his eye upon the whole drift and progress of the herd, and, in case of need, he would dash in to render assistance. Beside him went The Kid, or Lonesome, or, as this camp was beginning to call him from his last name, The Lamb.

One might have called it a most surprising thing that Muldoon should select his conqueror as a riding companion. But since he kept to the rear for strategic and tactical purposes, and since The Lamb rode there to avoid possible labor, they began to come together. If The Lamb had been in the slightest degree superior or sneering, such consort would have been impossible, but, as a matter of fact, the youngster was polite and even a little deferential, and some of the edge had been filed from that sharp tongue of his, so that he gave the impression of one who would not willingly have risked an encounter in the future.

Such a battle, Muldoon vaguely promised himself. He would not set a date, but fiercely he told himself that one day he would even the score. This determination restored his self-respect. Moreover, he discovered that the other cowpunchers looked upon his gashed and still bleeding face with more awe and fear than ever before. So he consented to ride beside The Lamb. He even confided his problems to the latter.

"Here it is noon, and we're stuck. We ain't done half a mile in the last hour and the wind is settling ag'in' us. I got a good mind to try old Beacon Creek."

What was Beacon Creek? It was a deep and sheer-walled ravine that ran with a foam of currents in the spring, as the snows melted, and which was dry and dead the rest of the year. It formed a wide arc, cutting through the heart of the hills. And, best of all, while giving shelter from the wind and the driving force of the rain, it would conduct the herd almost to the door of the ranch house.

"Why not, then?" asked The Lamb.

"You dunno the lay of the land. That ravine has got doors in it, and all of those doors open out on the Montague side. Suppose that they was to be on hand, they'd pretty near cry with joy. They could just open one of them doors and shunt the whole dog-gone' half of the herd down their way. That'd please the colonel a good deal, I reckon."

"Maybe you could use me on that side of the herd?" said the boy modestly.

Muldoon looked earnestly at him. "You mean that you're willing to tackle that sort of a job for me, Kid?"

"I gotta earn my keep some way," The Lamb said.

Muldoon waited for no more, but he set out with a shout that was stifled and rammed down his throat by the hard fist of the wind. By gestures and arm swingings rather than speech, he told his herders what he wanted, and they turned the heads of the young cattle toward the ravine. When they came to the verge of it, they hesitated, and the leaders swung about and stood sidewise, wretchedly humping their backs against the weather.

For a great voice was pealing up and down through the ravine, and it boomed through hollow sides, and roared like the rushing of a thousand ocean waves, and sang in the deeps of the hollow until the ground trembled under the feet of the cattle, and the cowpuncher from the lofty verge looked down into that rain-made twilight beneath them. It was as dark as December in the Scottish Highlands, when the feet of the clouds trail through the bleak heather.

The wagon boss and two others, with a timely charge and an explosion of guns, finally startled the herd, and they tipped their leaders over the brim. Down the long, sharp slope they went, bellowing with fear, their legs braced, sitting down to the force of that toboggan. All in a moment, this trouble was ended, and the weanlings turned down the ravine in the proper direction.

The drive proceeded with trebled speed, for the whole weight of the wind was cut away by the grand rising of the ravine walls. The tumult that they had heard now seemed to range far over their heads. The mists boiled over the upper ledges, and wild, dark forms of shadow leaped out, and soared slowly across the street that was fenced along the sky. Those shoutings and apparitions, however, meant very little to men or to cattle, for all were weary. They cared nothing for spiritual dangers or spiritual beauties. All they wanted was a little comfort for the flesh, and down in the palm of the valley they had relief from the endless tugging of the wind, tied to them with inescapable ropes.

The cowboys worked in the rear of the herd. At the western side was The Lamb on his slender mare, working constantly between the flood of cattle and the rocks. Usually the herd was kept fairly well to the left, but now and again came to a place so narrow that the slow stream of tired animals covered the floor of the valley from side to side, like water. All the gaps in the valley wall, as Muldoon had pointed out, were to the west, and in crowded times, some of the herd was sure to be sucked down these narrow outlets, led by the invincible desire of a cow to go in the wrong direction. But these false starts were remedied without great difficulty.

"It's the bold move that works the best," Muldoon declared, exulting, for they had very little distance to go in order to reach the ranch, and there were only two breaks remaining in the western wall of the cañon.

And now, just as he exulted, he heard a weird,

small shouting that rang up the valley toward him, under the hood of the roaring of the upper storm, and he saw the whole head of the drive swirl into a western gate through the wall of the valley.

He thrust his horse wildly ahead with his spurs, but he knew that he was riding too late. So were the other cowpunchers, for they had a solid mass of beef between them and the danger point, where the rapid Montague horsemen had suddenly emerged and now flickered back and forth in front of the herd, turning it. Then he could hear the bellowing and sharp voices of the weanlings as they galloped forward, seeming to gain new strength from this new direction.

There was only Lonesome to stop the raid— lonely in very fact, now, against this flood of danger and great numbers. And the wagon boss looked toward his new hired man in an agony. He saw the rider of the slender mare gallop straight toward the break, and saw in the intense gloom the flash of the gun in his hand. Three riders were suddenly before that lone rider, firing in return. The saddle of one was empty, now, and a second dropped forward and embraced the neck of his mount, but the third dived straight ahead on a huge black horse, and The Lamb went down like a pasteboard man on a pasteboard steed before that charge.

Still, the weanlings were whirling into the open

mouth of that chute with terrible speed, but Muldoon himself was now driving up the flank, where The Lamb had been, cursing wildly, his rifle pumping in his hands, and good men struggling fiercely behind him to keep up.

They saw the clever riders of the Montagues split across the face of the young cattle, as though knowing that they had run off as many as they could safely handle. They had two thirds hurrying down their chute. One third remained to be driven home to the colonel.

Muldoon, sick with grief and hysterical with rage, turned into the western gate to follow and to avenge, but a pair of Winchesters were clanging in the heart of the gorge. A bullet clipped the brim of his sombrero, and another brought water to his eyes, jerking past his face. Wisely he reined his mustang around and came out onto the floor of Beacon Creek.

The weanlings hurried in the distance, switching their tails as though in guilty haste. The cowboys remained in a silent half circle, regardless of the young cattle that had been saved, as some lifted the dead body of the mare so that The Lamb could be drawn out from beneath.

He was not white, because it would have been impossible for his brown-leather cheeks to have assumed such a tint. But he was distinctly a pale yellow, and his eyes were closed.

They brought a hatful of water from a rivulet that streamed down the wall of the ravine and dashed it over his face. That instant he revived and stood up, staggering. His two hip holsters were empty, but out of the recesses of his clothes he mysteriously produced two more guns.

"Where are they?" gasped The Lamb.

"They're gone, and most of the herd with 'em," said one of the men.

"What happened?"

They pointed to the dead mare.

The Lamb put up his guns.

"Too bad," Muldoon said, "because I'd say that's about a thousand dollars' worth of gallop lying there."

The Lamb started to answer, but his lips merely twitched. He took off his hat like one who wants to find a thought that is difficult to come at, and the rain beat hard against his face, and the wind fluttered the mane of the dead mare, and streamed her tail along the ground.

Chapter Eight

They came home from that disastrous trail in silence, crushed in mind and in soul. The cowpunchers took in the dwindled body of young beeves. Behind them at a good round distance rode Muldoon and The Kid, or otherwise The

Lamb. The storm had abated as soon as the weanlings were lost, and the disaster completed. Now the darkness was fast coming down and Muldoon and The Kid—on a borrowed horse— trailed farther and farther behind in the black of the night. Since the wind had fallen, they could speak together with greater ease, but The Kid did not want to speak a great deal. Only, from time to time, wild words stormed up in his throat.

All the young cattle were under fence before the wagon boss and The Lamb came into the ranch house, carrying their saddles after putting up their mounts in the barn. The colonel himself was ready to meet them as they stamped into the long, low bunk room.

He shook hands with Muldoon and, cheerfully as though he had lost $50 at faro, said: "We can't always win, old man." Then he reached up and laid a hand on the shoulder of The Lamb. "I'll get you as fine a horse as the mare, son," he said.

The Lamb looked at him with eyes that burned like fire, then he struck aside the colonel's hand and walked on.

The colonel did not follow. He did not pay any attention to that utterly savage rejoinder, but he looked after the youth with a little pity and a little awe. So did they all. The boy was as straight and his step as light as ever, and there was no mark on his face of any hurt. All his wounds were inward. His face was white, his eyes were smudges of darkness, and if he tried to smile carelessly, he merely succeeded in pinching the corners of his mouth. Going to the bunk that was assigned to him, he flung his blankets on it, lay down, and began to smoke one cigarette after another. He did not go in to supper. He was not hungry, he said.

Muldoon's face was so black that, at the table, no one dared to open a conversation. Even the colonel, cheerful under such a stroke of bad fortune, would not speak, until at length Muldoon got up and took a great steaming tin of black coffee into the bunk room. The others looked knowingly at one another.

"He's gonna play nurse to him," said someone.

"What happened to Muldoon? Did a horse throw him and roll on him?" the colonel asked.

"The Lamb happened to him," said the cook, who had stubbed his way in with a freshly filled coffee pot. "Awful neat. Got a left like the slam of a double-barreled mule . . . got a right like the fall of a tree. A loopin' right . . . up and over . . . a regular letter home."

"And they're friends?" asked the colonel. "They're friends now?"

"Ain't you ever seen grizzly and elk go runnin' side by side, when the forest fire was makin' the trees smoke all around them?" asked Shorty.

Muldoon, returning, placed the tin cup on the table and stared at it with awful eyes. It was quite full. "He wouldn't have nothing," said

Muldoon. Suddenly he smashed his fist upon the table and bellowed: "Gimme some more of that tar bucket that you call coffee!"

The cook without a word swallowed that insult and refilled Muldoon's own cup. The colonel did not object to this language; neither did the ranch foreman at the farther end of the table. As for the cup that he had offered to The Lamb, and that was still untouched, Muldoon turned it thoughtfully about, like a mysterious vessel.

So deep a silence came upon the table that the men were all aware of the renewed shouting of the wind through the woods, and its shrill breathing through the cracks in the log walls. They became aware of uncomfortable things, like their own aches and pains, and the burden of winter, and the spider webs in the corners of the ceiling, and the grease hardening white upon the tin plates.

Muldoon burst out: "He says to me . . . 'Who done it?' I told him it was Jimmy Montague.

" 'I seemed to go down before him like nothing,' says The Lamb. 'Like I was a kid, and he was a grown-up man. I went over that easy. She's dead,' says The Kid. 'Her that never said no. She's dead.' "

"I shouldn't've offered him another horse," the colonel said. "I didn't know how close she was fitted to his saddle."

"You might've offered a man a new wife,"

Muldoon said bitterly. He pressed a handkerchief against a wound beneath one eye, and, removing the handkerchief, he looked at the red upon it. He shook his head. He seemed in a trance of grief. "He was took horrible hard on the way in," Muldoon said. "He wanted me and him to ride after all the Montagues. 'Two men and two guns can do something,' he said. I allowed that it was a good game idea, but that nothing much could come of it.

" 'No,' says The Lamb, 'he rode me down like a kid. He rode me down like I was only a picture of a man on a horse.' I told him that Jimmy Montague was the best man in the mountains, with all due respect to everybody. That seemed to please him a little. At least, he could breathe without strangling. But he's still pretty sick. Every minute a shudder runs through him, and he gets green around the gills. He looks like a gent down with fever."

"He will have a fever," the colonel said, "unless we can find something to do for him. I've never seen such fool pride, even in a six-year-old stallion that never had a strap on it before. What can we do for him?"

"I dunno," said Muldoon. "If we could give him a hope of meeting up with Jimmy Montague pretty soon, that would be a comfort."

"He could write out a challenge," the colonel said with a little glitter in his eye.

"Challenge?" Muldoon hooted. "What attention will an Apache like Jimmy Montague pay to a challenge?"

"Will The Kid know that?" asked the colonel.

Muldoon paused, choked with excitement, and then started up with a violence that made every dish on the table crash. He hurried into the bunk room, the floor shuddering beneath his heavy stride.

"He loves The Kid," the foreman said. "If you poisoned Muldoon or whanged him with a fourteen-pound double jack, maybe he'd clean go out of his head with affection for the gent that done it."

"I was over on the Little Muddy," said one cowpuncher, "and we had a pair of ornery dogs on the place. They was a cross between mastiffs and chained lightnin'. They ate the other dogs that was already there, and they spent the rest of their time tryin' to break their chains and get at each other. They'd pretty near go mad when they seen each other, y'understand. The only time there was any peace between 'em was when they was turned loose at a wolf. They was faster than a wolf, and they had better wind, except in the roughest kind of goin'. Most generally they'd come up to a wolf and take him at the same time. One would grab the flank of the wolf and the other would take him by the throat. Then they'd pull him apart in no time.

"But one day those two dogs met up with a hundred-and-twenty-pound double-action fool of a wolf, and it appeared like they was runnin' right into a whole wall of teeth that they couldn't climb and that they couldn't scratch their way under. We got up in time to drive the wolf off. Then we swept up the remains of them dogs and carried them home in gunny sacks. It took hours to fit 'em together, because they was like jigsaw puzzles . . . and it took more hours to sew 'em back in place. They would've died, except they was so full of meanness that it took the place of blood, y'understand? But while they lay there getting well, they took care of each other like a pair of brothers, and licked each other's wounds . . . and ever after that, if one laid down, the other would stand to keep the sun off him. And you could hardly feed 'em, because each one would want to hold off and let the other get his share first. You would've thought they was raised in France the way those fool dogs carried on."

"You didn't stretch that much, Pete?"

"There's no use shrinkin' cloth before sellin' to you gents," Pete said, "because you're that sharp."

"Shut up," said the foreman. "Here comes Muldoon ag'in."

Chapter Nine

It was well known that Muldoon would have risen higher in the employ of the colonel had it not been for one great defect. He was thoroughly honest, famous for courage, a bulldog in his persistent battling against difficulties, and, above all, familiar with every wrinkle of the cattle business. But, unfortunately, he could neither read nor write.

He brought the letter into the room with an important air, and he declared with a great deal of enthusiasm: "The Kid is a scholar, by gravy. He just laid back and wrote out that letter as slick as you please. He wants to give twenty bucks right out of his own pocket to the gent that'll take this here letter, this here night, right across the hills to the Montagues' place."

"I'll take the letter," Shorty volunteered, "but I'd certainly like to know what sort of poison is so carefully wrapped up inside of it."

"Colonel," said Muldoon, "you forgot to get me them reading glasses again?"

"I have, Muldoon," the colonel said.

"You keep me under a handicap continually," said Muldoon. "I wish that you'd remember them reading glasses the next time that you come out."

"I'll try to remember," the colonel said seriously.

Muldoon rolled his eyes about the table, but no one dared appear to doubt, therefore, he handed the letter over to the colonel, and the latter cleared his throat, and read it aloud impressively. It was addressed to James Montague, Esquire. And it ran:

Dear Jimmy Montague: The last time we met, you seemed to think more of my horse than you did of me. In the part of the country where I was raised, it was mostly thought that the rider came first, and that only skunks played for horses because horses made a bigger target.

These here ideas maybe don't sound to you. I'd like a chance to explain them to you in public where other gents could hear them, too. Suppose we meet up some day in town, any place you name, and any day. Right in front of the hotel would be a good idea, it seems to me.

A friend of mine is taking over this letter for me.

So long,
Alfred P. Lamb

This letter made a great impression upon everyone. The colonel himself was highly pleased with it. As he pointed out with admiration, it did not say what would happen when they met, and it did not promise to cut the throat of Mr. Montague, or to drill him full of holes of .45 caliber. But the meaning of the writer could not very well be missed by anyone who dwelt on the range and lived among the range ideas.

Shorty declared that it would be an honor to carry such an epistle. He knew the road to the Montague headquarters like a section out of a book, and he could ride it blindfolded through a worse wind than this.

The Montague house was ten miles away. It was now 8:00 p.m., and Shorty promised to be back with some sort of an answer by 10:00.

"Look lively," said one of his companions. "Suppose Jimmy Montague was to get riled by that letter, he might take it out on you, eh?"

Shorty grinned. "He might on the next gent, but I'm a foot below his size."

So Shorty departed, and the hoofs of his horse rang loudly upon the rocks, then were suddenly muffled as he passed over the rim of the high land and into the valley beyond. The others sat up for his return, though they were deadbeat by the work of the day.

The colonel and his foreman, sitting in a corner of the kitchen, put their heads together and talked earnestly, discreetly. No matter how cheerfully the colonel had borne with this loss, yet he was hard hit. More than once the Montagues had scored heavily over him, but never so heavily as this. And even if he were cheerful, his bankers were not apt to be. There were credits to arrange, and the prolonging of borrowed sums of money.

Such talk kept the poor colonel awake. While the men pried their eyes open by smoking many cigarettes, until they sat in dense pools of brown and silver, and played pedro and poker—for matches, since it was long past the first of the month.

When struck 10:00, and there was no Shorty, there was no worry because it well might be that it had required some time for the Montagues to decide what notice they should take of the epistle. It was even conceivable that Jimmy Montague would actually accept the challenge, though he was not the man to give away a trick.

Until 11:00 it was still conceivable that Shorty's horse had gone lame and thereby delayed his return—for the way was covered with just those small stones that are liable to cripple a horse. But, from this hour, general anxiety pervaded the ranch house. The colonel and the foreman came in from the kitchen.

At 11:30 the colonel conferred briefly with his foreman. Then he turned to the dark faces of the men and made a little speech. He said he feared that foul play had come the way of Shorty, and that he would wait until midnight, and at that hour, if the cowpuncher did not return, he and the foreman intended to saddle their horses, take their rifles, and descend upon the Montagues. All who wished were welcome to follow that example.

It did not seem necessary to return any answer to this, but straightway cards were put aside and every man betook himself to the examination of his arms. Rifles were cleaned, revolvers loaded, ammunition belts repaired, but even so the time went slowly and all hands were sitting grimly, like so many wolves on their haunches, waiting for the wounded moose to fall, when a weight lurched against the door.

The cook, with an odd look over his shoulder, unbarred the door, and pulled it wide. Then Shorty pitched into the room, tried vainly to steady himself, and lurched upon his face.

They carried him to a blanket, which was laid beside the stove. There they examined his hurts. He was naked to the waist and his hands were tied behind him. Across his shoulders and his back were great wales, swollen and turned purple by the cold through which he had walked, and in a dozen places the whip strokes had slashed through the skin. Blackened blood was caked and crusted around the edges of these wounds. They washed Shorty clean, but it was not until the liniment stung him that he opened his eyes, cursing in a feeble voice. The cook had prepared hot coffee in haste, and a long draft of that cure-all enabled the cowhand to speak, though brokenly, a phrase at a time.

He had gone straight down the road, meeting with no mishap, and had gone to the Montague house even more quickly than he had expected. He dismounted. Off in the distant woods he heard the bellowing of young cattle and saw the glimmering of fires. It was no puzzle for him to guess what was being done there, or from what source those beeves had come, or what brand was now being worked upon them. It had angered him a good deal. It also had made him wonder what would have been the effect if the advice of The Lamb had been followed, and the forces of the colonel had delivered a smashing counter-attack.

But he went up to the door of the big house—there was not a larger or more imposing house in the mountains than this one of the Montagues—and when he knocked and was told to come in, he found the two heads of the clan seated, side-by-side, before the great open fire on the hearth. Monty Montague, the father and grandfather of them all, was there smoking his long-stemmed Indian pipe. Opposite him was the bitter, handsome face of big Jimmy Montague, his tallest and his favorite grandson.

To Jimmy, Shorty offered the letter, but the young Montague had pointed to his grandfather. "All news comes to Monty first," he said.

So the letter went to Monty Montague, and that old and evil man opened the envelope and peered with his bright, wicked eyes at the contents. He folded it, crumpled it, cast it into the fire. Then he turned in his chair and looked at Shorty.

"That letter," he said, "was from the colonel's latest hired gunfighter . . . the young feller you rode down today, Jimmy. You said you'd flattened him for good, but it seems that you only flattened his horse. Instead of bein' grateful for his life, the rat asks you to come down and have it out with him in town. What about it?" This speech he delivered with his face turned steadily toward the messenger.

With his usual sneer, Jimmy answered that he saw no reason why he should give every fool and hired gunfighter a chance to shoot his head off, from around a corner or through a window.

"You're right," said his grandfather. "And what about this gent that comes in here bringin' this sort of message to us . . . while we're sittin' here and enjoyin' a little rest after a damn' long day of honest toil?"

They both laughed at this. An instant later Jimmy had brought out two Colts and covered Shorty. They secured him while he still was reaching for the ceiling in fear of his life. They stripped him to the waist, and with a blacksnake the younger man flogged him until Monty, in a fury, snatched the whip away and applied it with redoubled force. It was his shower of blows that had slashed the skin open. After that, they turned him out of doors, and he had struggled back toward the ranch house on foot, for Jimmy had led away the horse.

"Where's Lonesome?" Muldoon asked hoarsely. "Where's The Lamb? He'd oughta hear this."

They looked hastily about them. The Lamb was gone into the night.

Chapter Ten

There had been no sentimental outpouring from The Lonesome Kid, otherwise The Lamb, when he saw the condition of Shorty. Instead, he rose from his bunk, drew up his belt a few notches, and slipped from the house while the others were still milling about the injured man.

The wind, as he stepped through the door, cuffed him back flat against the wall, tore the hat from his head, and seared his eyes. Nevertheless, he let the hat go and started for the corral.

He was halfway to it, when he remembered that the mare was gone, and gone forever. He hesitated, paused, and then turned his face toward the trail with a grim resolve that he never would sit upon a horse again until he had satisfaction for the mare. He had started with the intention of getting to Jimmy Montague. But now he had another incentive. Big and formidable as Montague had loomed, it was the stallion he rode that had impressed The Lamb most. The powerful beast, sleek as a seal with the rain, had borne him down as though he were nothing, and the mare beneath him nothing. And though it might well be that the horsemanship of Jimmy Montague had something to do with the result, yet The Lamb had faith that the stallion was the conqueror. He had in his mind invincibly the ragged, flying forelock, and the head made ugly with ferocity. Having lost the mare, it was only a poetic and a human stroke of justice that he should first fit himself with one of the enemy's string, and, inspired by this hope, he leaned strongly against the wind and made rapid headway.

The trail was clear and open; it was not greatly broken with rocks, and, in fact, a buckboard could have been driven across it with no difficulty. He had a lantern hung before him, moreover. For the moon was up and washing through the tumbling, whirling clouds like a ship through a storm-tossed ocean. Sometimes the pale face of the moon glided through the branches of a pine tree, or sat like a signal fire on the top of an eastern pine, but always it gave him some guidance through the night.

He put that road behind him at six miles an hour, for he was not one of those workers of the range who cannot live out of the saddle, and who walk half a mile to catch a horse and ride half that distance. It was short of 2:00 a.m. when he came in sight of that ranch house of the Montagues. He had heard something about it before. It was as big as a castle for it had to house an entire clan. Old Monty Montague headed the outfit and gave law and order to it, and supplied wicked wisdom in all of its councils. Beneath him had gathered his sons, and their sons, and all their families. There had been no question of their moving away to find work, for old Monty Montague was always able to use every hand he could secure. Instead of letting them go, he built, entirely at his own expense, ponderous wings and additions to his original house, and then added stories on top, and dug out cellars beneath. Very few of the Montagues left him. The sons brought home their wives; the daughters brought home their husbands. There began, in this manner, to be a great mixture of names and blood, but the thought was always the same, and that was the thought of Monty Montague.

Even if he had never heard a description of the place, The Lamb felt that he would have known it by its confused outline and its bulk as for a moment it was solemnly crossed by the face of the rising moon. Then it was deeply gathered in shadows again, and all the forest seemed to be drawing together and closing up around it. The moonlight gleamed on the tenderer green of the tips of the pines as upon the surface of the sea, and in the black heart of that sea the house was sunk.

There was a sort of allegorical interest and significance in this thought that arrested the mind of the boy, but only for a moment. He was so entirely a man of action that he felt for his guns, and stepped on again.

Through the woods a creek rippled down the mountainside, and over the creek a moldering bridge had been built of massive, fallen trees, now half rotten. Upon the bridge he paused, listening to the whirl and roar of the water, for the larger voice of the wind was, for the moment, shut away to silence behind the rising woods. And he thought with what headlong folly he had approached up to this point. As though the Montagues would not be keeping watch and ward, no matter what the hour of the night.

He listened keenly. He probed the trees before him. Since he saw nothing, he went on across the bridge and paused again, close to a dripping pine. Behind him he heard a faint groaning. It was a wonderfully human sound, and, glancing back with a start, he was in time to see the bridge sagging out from the bank and turning. It came to a trembling pause. It had been forced out upon a central pivot and now pointed up and down the stream. Twenty broad feet of emptiness lay between the visitor and escape. He could not help wondering why, if he had been spotted, the watcher had not opened fire upon him instead of turning the bridge, but he realized that this was no light for accurate shooting.

He stepped aside through the trees, made a brief detour, and came back toward the road again. It opened up broad and straight, leading fairly for the house, and as he waited there, listening, intent and motionless, he saw a pair of shadows detach themselves from the gloom of the wood and pass slowly across the road behind him. Their heads were turned the other way. Perhaps they were fairly assured that they had penned him between them and the impassable banks of the creek.

At any rate, he could not pause for further deductions. He went straight on up the road, keeping constantly under the steep shadows at the side of it. His presence here was momently more and more hazardous, for though it was hardly likely that they could guess that he, The Lonesome Kid, The Lamb, was actually within their precincts, yet they were informed that an enemy had approached them, and their guns would hardly ask questions before they fired at the first suspicious figure.

This was bad enough even on a pitch-dark night, but the night no longer was pitch dark. The moon came out in stronger flares and for longer periods. The wind was as fierce as ever, as cold, as biting, and with it came strong flurries of sleet and rain that sometimes struck against the front of his slicker with the noise of an open hand striking his face. Sometimes he was like an ironclad warrior, half dissolving under a mist and shower of blows.

Then the house stood suddenly before him. He had passed the last tree. He looked out of the shadows and saw the stark, ugly, rambling pile, all glistening now with wet, its windows looking like squares of smoke. And from the corners of the eaves, a silver, steady stream of water was pouring down and crashing on the ground, and the spray from this small cataract, leaping up again, formed and clung in slender icicles.

Then a dark band of clouds passed across the moon, and the house was half lost, and pushed away, and banished under a thick penciling of rain. In the very midst of this rushing and crashing of noise, as the downpour burst upon him, The Lamb heard, as distinctly as though the air had been still as it always is before thunder, the uncertain, half-strangled breathing of a man immediately behind him. Then he knew that that breathing was indeed only inches from his back. He had been followed. Perhaps there were others behind him, too. They had drawn their net cleverly around him; they had mocked and laughed at him as he attempted to stalk their fortress.

The Lamb felt that this was his moment of death. But he determined to die with his teeth bared, at the least, and, slipping out a Colt with inconspicuous smoothness, he whirled about. He saw the loom of a big, dark form behind him, and the glint of a leveled gun. He heard the click of a hammer falling upon a cap. And then he jammed his Colt into the stomach of the Montague.

"Kind of wet for just one gun," suggested The Lamb. "Damp enough to spoil pretty near any powder and caps. Reach up for the first branch over your head, stranger, will you?"

The hands of the other rose. When they were the height of The Lamb's throat, they paused, but after a moment they resumed their rising. The revolver had fallen with a splash into the mud and the water at their feet.

"Who are you?" asked The Lamb.

"The unluckiest fool that ever stepped," the captive said.

"What name?"

"Dan Burns."

"Are you a Montague?"

"Sure. Ain't I here?"

"Who am I, then?"

"You're one of the Loring's outfit, of course."

"What one?"

"The new one. The Kid, I s'pose."

"What makes you bet on that?"

"None of the rest would've took such a fool chance as this."

"Why is it a fool chance?"

"Well, shouldn't you be dead in the mud,

there, where that gun of mine is now lyin'?"

"It's true. Did they expect me down here tonight?"

"Old Montague thought that you'd maybe come."

"Burns. . . ."

"Aye?"

"I don't want to be murdering you."

"I feel the same about it," Burns said, and, in spite of the gun that was jammed into the pit of his stomach, he seemed to chuckle.

"Could you play out this hand for the sake of a square deal?" asked The Lamb.

"I could, I s'pose. What cards do you want?"

"Only one. I want to draw a crack at Jimmy Montague."

"You want Jimmy?"

"Yes."

"Man, man, why for do you want to chuck yourself away?"

"That's my business. Can you take me to his room?"

"I s'pose I can."

"How many men are watching tonight?"

"Five."

"That leaves how many inside?"

"Fifteen, I think . . . besides the kids. You see what you're tackling?"

"Lead me on," The Lamb said. "I want to see the way in . . . the way out can take care of itself."

Chapter Eleven

Dan Burns appeared to be a philosopher.

He reasoned shortly and aloud: "If I take you in, you'll get your head blowed off . . . if I don't, you'll blow off mine. I like you a lot, but I like my own hide better. Come on, kid." He turned about, his hands still shoulder high, and led the way toward the house.

The Lamb said in his ear—for he walked closer than Burns's shadow behind him—"I hope that the wind don't stagger you into making no wrong step, brother. It's cold enough to make maple syrup, and if you make a bad pass, I'm gonna draw your sap."

Burns nodded, and as he did, the wind tore off his hat with a shriek and blew his long hair fluttering and snapping straight out behind him.

They came up to a small door, like a postern let into a wall, and here Burns fitted a key into the lock and opened it, the well-oiled bolt sliding softly in the wards. They passed inside. And closing the door, they shut out the roar of the wind, only its fierce whistling followed them indoors.

They stood unmoving for a time. The Lamb had pressed the muzzle of his Colt into the small of the back of Dan Burns, and the latter seemed to be pausing for thought. Their clothes dripped steadily, noisily to the floor—one stream spattered upon naked wood, and another sopped upon carpeting. The Lamb breathed short, for he was scenting the odors of cookery such as cling in a house when winter weather keeps the windows closed.

"Just slow and steady, Danny," he advised the other, "like your wife didn't know that you was out, and the stairs creaked a good deal."

With all the required caution, Dan Burns led the way through the hall and then up a flight of steps, a very narrow flight that angled once or twice from side to side. In spite of himself, The Lamb felt that the return trail was growing somewhat obscured in his memory.

Dan Burns suddenly stopped, and the gun was quickly jabbed deeply into his flesh. "You want a fair and square crack at Jim Montague, do you?" Dan asked.

"That's all I ask, son."

"Suppose I take you to his room, what you gonna do? Yell at him and start shootin'?"

"I'll give him a fair warning, by light or by dark," said The Lamb. "I never murdered, and I never will."

"You'll speak first before you start shootin'?"

"Why, man, I'm new in this part of the land. You dunno me, yet. I ain't a sneak. I don't . . . I don't . . . shoot horses instead of their riders." His voice had choked a little.

Dan Burns, deep in thought, now seemed to reach a conclusion. "All right," he said. "I'll do what I can for you."

"You've sworn that already, Danny. I ain't doubting you."

Danny said nothing, but led on at a brisker pace. Twice more they twisted from side to side in the hallway. Then they came to a door that, like most of the entrances in the house, was set in broad, and low, and solid. A man of a shade more than average height would have to stoop to pass through.

Here the guide paused.

"Is this it, Burns?" whispered The Lamb.

He heard Burns answer in shaking tones: "I'm a skunk. But what else could I do?"

"I had my gun on you," The Lamb said, swallowing his contempt for the traitor. "What else could you do?"

"They'll never think of that." Burns sighed.

"They'll never know of that . . . they'll never know what you've done."

"Monty? He knows everything. He's a clever one." Burns stooped, worked softly at the lock of the door, and gradually drew it wide. The air from the chamber wafted slowly out to The Lamb, and it seemed to him sweet and strange like the breath of the wind that has touched a meadow of spring flowers. Inside the room, there was a little dusk, light fit to make shadows only more shadowy.

Burns stood back. From the small flame of the lamp that burned inside the chamber there was only a single thin splinter of light, and this struck against the eyes of Burns, and they seemed to The Lamb as hard and as bright as the eyes of a bird. He sidled past his guide, shrinking a little low, with a ponderous Colt in either hand—the left hand for Burns, if the latter should attempt any treachery, and the right hand for whatever danger lay in the room before him.

Burns, however, attempted nothing, except softly to push the door shut behind the intruder. He closed it—but he did more, for a soft and heavy click now told The Lamb that Burns must have removed the key from the inside of the door. At any rate, he now had locked it from outside. The floor trembled with a deep, soft vibration; Burns apparently was running at full speed down the outer corridor.

But what matter that The Lamb was locked into the room with Jim Montague? Indeed, if he were to die, he never would have a chance to perish in battle by the hand of a more famous antagonist than this big man appeared to be. Besides, The Lamb was unable to think of the future or to weigh other dangers, for his mind was possessed by the picture of terrible Jim Montague as he had seen that monster riding through the storm on the great black horse, and the realization of the battle that now lay under his hand.

At the closing of the door and the changing of the draft of air, the flame in the lamp cowered down to a mere pin head of light that was really no light at all, but rather like a waning eye that observed but was not to be seen.

The Lamb leaned back against the wall and freshened his grip upon his guns. Then he remembered his promise to Burns; he remembered, too, his own sense of honor that was a cloth with many tattered places and with many holes in it, but nevertheless a cloth of gold.

Then he put up his guns so that he should have no advantage over his enemy. At the same time he heard a groaning voice that said: "I've done no good. You gotta do good to pay your way to a second chance. I've paid my way to punishment. I've paid my way to destruction."

There was such a sighing despair in this voice that The Lamb felt himself go chill. It was Jimmy Montague, then, his conscience speaking to him in the night. Something relented in The Lamb's iron heart.

Then he saw a white form pass across the dark of the room in silence. The form paused; the flame of the lamp rose with a flutter and a faint sound like the whisper of silks. By that light, The Lamb saw that a girl in a white robe was standing and leaning over the bed. He heard her murmur above the man, then she stepped back, and he saw, by the flare of the lamplight tossed lightly up and down by the pressure of the draft, a worn, haggard face, thin, pain-ridden, and by no means the face of Jim Montague.

The Lamb could remember it in another place that same day. One rider had swayed to one side and clutched at his horse to keep from falling as The Lamb rode in, delivering his charge. Here lay that rider. Then he heard the wounded man say: "Where are you, Miss Patten?"

"I'm here," she said.

"I dunno that I can see you," the wounded man said.

"Here's my hand, Sammy."

"Oh, where are you?" he said. "I can feel your hand, but I can't see you very good. You look like a ghost to me, Louise."

She sat down on the edge of the bed, and the watcher could see her face. She was very young, very pretty, and under the play of the rising and falling lamplight the sheen of her skin seemed to vary, until it appeared that a light was shining from within her. It was only a small thing to the eye, but the fancy entered deeply into the mind of The Lamb, and he thought of her as some translucent, unearthly thing.

"I'm not a ghost, Sammy. I'm sitting here on your bed, and watching out that any bad thing can't come near you."

She put her hand on his forehead. She talked to him as though to a helpless child, and the charm and the wonder of this half paralyzed the brain of The Lamb and made him forget that he had been betrayed into this chamber so easily by treacherous Dan Burns—made him forget that other consequences must follow upon this betrayal.

"You're not a ghost. No, no. I'm a lot more ghost than you, and I know that," cried the sick man.

"You're being foolish, Sammy. You're as good as well, if you'll sweep all the dust and the doubt into the corner of your mind and close a door on it."

"I got no trust in myself," Sammy groaned. "Hold hard onto my hand, Louise. There's no good in me, but there's enough good in you maybe to pull me through." He added in a rapid, trembling voice: "He come smashin' through the rain with his guns flashin'. When it hit me, it was like two hands of fire had took and broke me open . . . like you'd break a biscuit . . . and poured me full of fire, like you'd pour a biscuit full of honey. And I'm still broken, Louise. I'm shakin' and shakin'. . . ."

"Steady . . . steady," said her gentle voice. "It's mostly a bad dream, a lot worse than the facts."

"He's like something out of a nightmare. There's danger and death in him."

"Jimmy put him down," the girl said with a sudden ring in her voice.

"Aye, but it took Jimmy to put him down. What's that?"

"Nothing. Are you better?"

"Aye, a lot better. You gotta touch with you, Louise."

Chapter Twelve

The sick man relaxed. His hand fell suddenly from its grip upon the girl, and in one moment he was smiling sleepily upon her, and in the next he was lost in slumber.

There was another thing to take the attention of The Lamb, however, and that was an outbreak of voices far off in the house, at such a distance, in fact, that he hardly could tell in what direction they proceeded. There were footfalls, too, of heavy men moving at a run, but the sound of them was rather a vibration in the floor, and something on the table in the center of this room began to stir and tinkle lightly with the throb of the far-off running feet.

The girl rose from the bed, took the lamp from its stand, and, turning about, walked directly up to him. She raised the lamp, so that the light would fall more directly upon his face, and he had to pucker his brows into a heavy frown to endure the glare of the lamp so near to him. The same light slipped like water over the arm of the girl, from which the loose sleeve of her robe had fallen back, and gleamed upon the hair that ran like a twist of solid gold down in front of her shoulder.

She looked to The Lamb a delicately fragile thing. He grew a little dizzy as he stared at her, but her voice brought him back to his senses quickly enough.

"Who are you?"

"Me?" said The Lamb.

"Why are you here? Who are you?" she repeated.

He gaped at her, and knew that she had been aware for a long moment of his presence in the room. Perhaps even when he entered she had known, but she had gone to the sick man, first, and quieted him.

The wonder of The Lamb grew more intense. He felt as once he had felt before—a very small boy before a very tall teacher. And then the sense of his awe turned in him and made him laugh a little—that he, being what he was, should have ventured into the house of his enemies, being what they were, and that, having been betrayed into the most mortal peril of his life, he should stand now agape, helpless, overawed before a slender girl.

He said: "I'm Alfred Lamb."

"I thought so," she said. And she nodded at him, with a clear, placid brow.

He jerked a thumb toward the door. "A yellow coyote that I collared outside swore he'd show me the way to Jim Montague's room if I didn't blow his head off. He showed me here, instead."

"You wanted Jimmy?"

"I wanted him."

She stepped back a little, not in fear, but the better to survey that dripping, mud-splashed form.

He explained: "In my section of the country, they don't shoot down a man's horse when they want to get the man on it."

"They're coming," she said, and she put the lamp back on the table.

He could hear the heavy tramping of feet; a corner had been turned and they were swinging closer. He stepped to the one window in the chamber, and, looking out, while the wind cut at him like a knife, he saw a sheer drop of a hundred feet, down the west side of the house, and the face of the rock beneath, and to the boiling waters of the creek. It was plain why that careful cowpuncher, Dan Burns, had brought him to this room of all others in the house—there was no retreat.

He turned back, and the girl stood by the table, her hands behind her, her face tilted a little down in thought.

"They will surely murder you here," she said in the most matter-of-fact manner.

"They will," he agreed. "But though they have me sealed, they haven't yet got me delivered."

"Oh, yes," she agreed. "They'll have reason to remember this day." She hesitated. There was a roar of voices in the outer hallway, like the noise of water crammed into the narrow throat of a flume. Then she ran to a corner of the room and waved to The Lamb.

He followed her with eagerness, catching at hope before he saw what chance remained to him, or possibility of a chance. She flung back a rag rug and pointed to the floor.

"Can you lift that?" she asked.

An edge of boards projected a bit above the level of the flooring, and instantly he had his grip upon it. The tips of his fingers slipped, taking the skin. He tried again, in a sudden rush of terror, now that there was some hope before him, and the whole broad section of boards tipped easily up, and a gust of damp air rose into his face. He stood back and looked dubiously at the girl, and at the beginning of the steps.

"You'd better hurry," she said. "The man who brought you here thought that there was no way out for you. But the older men of the house will know better, and they'll be running to block your way."

It might be that she was actually giving him his

life. And it might be that she was inviting him deeper into the trap that already was closing upon him. He could not tell. Her face was as cold as stone, and she seemed to be almost as pale. Suddenly he caught her hand. Wild thoughts, wild words leaped into the brain of The Lamb, but all that he could say was: "Clean bred, by gravy." Then he sprang into the dark and the damp and ran down the steps.

Her voice followed him: "Straight ahead till you find a door. From that, turn left and . . ." Then her voice was drowned by a great crashing, and trampling, and shouting, and he made out, distinctly, a thundering tone that called: "Where is he?"

She would have something to do facing the rush and the questions of those angry men, but, for some reason, he did not fear for her. She who cured their wounded would have a right to stand up against them even on this occasion, perhaps.

He came in pitch darkness to the bottom of the flight, and stumbled heavily as he struck the flat. Almost at once his outstretched hand struck wood. Fumbling, he reached a latch, and the door, yielding instantly, was snatched outward and he with it by a sucking tentacle of the wind. He staggered against a wall of stonework, turned left, and went with difficulty up a flight of steps, more than half blinded, but aware that the moon was working somewhere behind stifling clouds, and that he was again under the open sky.

So he came to level ground and looked back. Only then he saw clearly what he had passed, for the moon broke out from the clouds at this instant, and sailing through only a creamy mist it showed to The Lamb a flight of steps hewn out of rock, uneven, slippery with rain and moss. At one time it had been a commodious stairway, no doubt, but now a fall of the cliff face had stripped away two-thirds of its necessary width and he had come up a slender ladder of steps not a foot and a half wide. The great god of good luck had stood with him during that passage.

Well for him, too, that the moon had not suddenly looked down upon him during that climb and shown him the dripping side of the cliff along which he was working. It was almost better that the girl had had no chance to warn him in any great detail. He thought of this as he gave that single backward glance, and then he turned and ran at full speed, with one naked gun in his hand. He turned the corner of the house, slipped on a flat-surfaced granite slab, and rolled headlong into a thicket of dead shrubs to which some straggling brown leaves adhered. The water from them soaked him instantly to the skin over every inch of his body, yet he lay as still as though he had fallen upon the warmest, driest lamb's wool, for voices rang about an angle of the house at that moment. By lifting his head, he was able to see through the branches five men, half dressed, and armed to the teeth, who ran furiously along, the water starting out in silver spray beneath their feet. And he who led them on was Jimmy Montague. He could not see the face of the man, but instantly he knew him, as one animal knows another—by the shock upon some extra sense. He felt that he should have known the man in the deepest darkness by the crawling of his flesh.

It was an easy shot, and afterward perhaps an easy escape through the brush, so that The Lamb was grimly tempted—he actually took his gun hand with his left and forced down the gun. Thus conscience mastered him with his own muscle, and he turned and writhed away through the bushes, constant showers dripping down upon him, soaking him over and over again. Then he stood up in the shelter of the trees. He threw off his slicker and his coat. He pulled off his boots, in which the water was sopping and squelching loudly. Draining the boots of water, he put them on again. Now he was free from encumbrance, light, half frozen, but ever ready to fight, if fight there were.

Behind him he heard a sudden fusillade of guns; he distinguished rifles and revolvers by the bark of the one and the longer, more metallic clangor of the other. Some sway of shadows beneath the wind perhaps had made them think they saw him. Perhaps one of their own number had been mistaken for him, and after the outburst he listened in cruel expectation. There was no cry of pain, however.

After this, he went on through the trees until the vague, dark loom of a building rose before him. The wind sifted through it, blowing toward him, and he recognized the half-sweet, half-musty odor of hay. It was the barn, and no place in the world is more welcome, more suggestive of warm comfort to a cold and tired man than a barn, with its mow into which a refugee can burrow deep. He hurried to the side of it just as the clouds shut the moon away and the heavens opened in a torrent of rain. He was sheltered a little by the overhang of the roof, but, listening to the steady thunder of the rain that sounded like the crashing of a dozen mighty rivers, he felt his way along the wall until he came to the gap of a window, and behind the window he heard human voices in the dark.

Chapter Thirteen

Nothing that he ever had known appeared to The Lamb so eternally comfortable, secure, and peaceful as the sound of those voices drifting lazily out of the warm darkness of the barn. Outside, the cold lanced him through and through, and the wind catching a drift of rain beat it through the clothing of The Lamb to his already drenched skin. He shuddered, but he remained at the window, unmoving, for the first words he distinguished were enough to stiffen him in his place.

"Why doesn't the boss stir up a mite more action, then?"

"This is all what he's gotta watch," said the other. "When you've landed a horse in the corral, why you gonna bother except to see the gate is barred? And this is the gate, ain't it? He sent me out here."

"How you make this out the gate?"

"Listen, cowboy, the brain you got wasn't made to ride on or to rope with . . . but it was made to think with. How's he gonna get out of here, unless he breaks his neck down the rocks?"

"Have they swung the bridge?"

"Sure. What else would they've done first? And the only way he could break out would be to slam down the drive and try to jump the creek."

"That ain't possible," said the other.

"Did I say that it was? I didn't. I said the only way . . . I didn't say the possible way."

"What else would that be meaning, then? Damn me if you don't talk like a scholar."

"Do I?"

"You do."

"Son, we gotta little job on our hands tonight,

97

but when the mornin' comes, I'll give you my whole argument, if you're man enough to stand up and take it."

"You poor dried-up bundle of weed," said the other, "I'd meet you day or night."

The Lamb went rapidly back along the stable wall until he reached the next window, and through this he wriggled like a snake through a hole. He paused close to the wall to listen, but high debate went on before him.

A long line of stalls ran down the side of the big building. The aisle turned a corner, and here a dull glimmer of light was showing. The Lamb slipped about that angle and found a lantern hanging from a peg on the wall, blinking slowly as the draft sucked down the flame or let it rise again. That light let him see the pinched rumps of the mustangs lined up on either side of the aisle, and now and then the squarer quarters of an animal of better breeding. As a learned man walks hastily down a bookshelf, dismissing one title after another, so The Lamb went hurriedly past these horses and could not find the one for which he was eagerly seeking.

He carried the lantern with him to the farther corner of the barn and there the open stalls ended and the box stalls began. There were only half a dozen of them. Two were unoccupied. In the remaining four he looked in on a chestnut mare with all the signs of a thoroughbred, a big gray gelding of the Irish hunter type with a head worthy of a draught animal and enough bone to carry even the weight of Jimmy Montague, a slender bay colt that was not past its second year, beautiful as a stag, and then a black head and wild eyes and flaring forelock were thrust out an open door. It was the big black that had trampled down the mare that day.

Straight into his stall went The Lamb. The big fellow heaved himself up on his haunches until he looked like a winged horse about to take flight or, more than this, a monster swooping out of the air to crush The Lamb. But the latter looked up unafraid. He was beginning to grow tense with hate for this great brute, and with admiration of him.

Down pitched the black with driving forehoofs that cut the air scant inches from the head of the boy. Yet in striking the floor those pile-driving hoofs were muffled in the fall as though striking wet sawdust. He spun about with his tail lashing like the tail of a black leopard, and struck out, but his heels shot harmlessly over the shoulders of the man. Then the stallion twitched about and stood in a corner, his ears pricked, looking with a great deal of interest at this calm stranger. For whether a horse is wise or foolish, there is one thing he instantly understands—courage or the lack of it. He was now sufficiently intrigued to let the stranger step closer and pat his neck—it was like fingering a mold of hard rubber, covered with silk. He made no protest, either, when the bridle was offered to him, but accepted the bit, and then the saddle and blanket that were tossed over him.

The Lamb measured the withers of the stallion against his nose. This giant was seventeen hands if he was an inch, and, in stooping to gather up the cinches, The Lamb took note of such a girth as he never had seen in a blooded horse. From the points of his shoulders to behind the cinches he was like a plow horse, and behind that he was cut away like the fine run of the lines of a clipper hull. His flanks were as hard as tough leather, sheathed in loose silk, but the quarters behind them were as square as a carpenter's rule could have made them. Here was the mechanism of power for running. The Lamb looked to the long and tapering neck, and to the long and powerful legs, with knees and hocks and all below naked of flesh and feeling like well-worked iron. Seen close up, felt and handled, the stallion seemed too huge for action at great speed, but rather might he have served as a charger for a knight of those old days when a fighting man was always over-weighted with rattling ironware. But, seen on a distant hill, The Lamb knew that this fellow would look all the part of an English racer.

He went out hastily from the stall and replaced the lantern on the peg, and as he did so, he heard a rumbling and scraping sound such as a heavy door makes when it is pushed back on a slide. He slipped to the corner, and, looking up the aisle, he was met by the cut of the night wind, which blew in through the open entrance with the wet of the rain-spray hanging in it. Two lanterns and four men were coming. One paused and began hastily saddling while another fell in at a different stall.

"There ain't gonna be any riding," he heard one of them say, "but we gotta get things ready. Get out the black for Jimmy, Dan. If there's to be a chase, he'll want nothing else."

The Lamb fled back to the box stall, thrust the door wide, and whipped into the saddle. The reins slid through his fingers as the black felt for the bit, and he rode out into the narrow aisle between the stalls.

"Where's Jimmy's saddle?" he heard a voice call in the distance. And then a shouted answer, which he could not distinguish, only the ripple of the usual oath.

A hurrying cowpuncher rounded the corner, and The Lamb opened fire. He shot not at the coming man, but at the lantern. There was a crash of glass, and in the darkness that followed The Lamb went by at a trot, with the excited yell of the greatly dismayed cowboy in his ear.

A gun coughed behind The Lamb. A bullet thudded against the heavy log wall, and then the stallion turned the corner. Before him, up the aisle, The Lamb could see two horses being backed out from their stalls by swearing cow-boys, and very small the mustangs looked to one mounted on the black stallion, or compared with the lofty height of the beams above them. None-theless, they and their riders would be hornets in his flesh, he knew.

The men were jerking their horses around with one hand, and dragging at their guns with the other, and shouting furiously in excitement and anger. The Lamb tickled the stallion's flank with his spurs, and the result was a forward lurch that brought them into full speed at a single bound. The head of The Lamb went back, and out of his throat welled up a wild cry that sounded like the yell of a wolf at the kill, and the sob of a puma far off in the night. The war cry of a red Cheyenne was the shout of a child compared to that weird note, the mourning of the owl was in it, and an edge like the eagle's shrill scream.

He was shooting while his throat still swelled with his cry. Through the humid air of the barn the two lanterns hanging from the tall posts shone like two broad, soft, golden moons. These were his targets rather than the armed men before him, for he well knew that had he twice his speed in action and twice his accuracy with a revolver, he never could shoot down those hardy fellows while they had light by which to see him. Yonder in a stall mouth, for instance, was one dropping to his knee, and throwing his Colt into the bend of his left arm to get a perfect rest for it. Such a man would shoot like a rifle expert at short range.

So The Lamb sent a .45-caliber slug through the first lantern. It was not dislodged from the nail, but the flame was dashed out and the wick and wick holder with it were snatched away. Glass tinkled. Two guns roared vainly beside The Lamb, and he fired at the second light, and missed.

He fired again and again, thumbing back the hammer and shooting by instinct rather than by careful aim, for who can aim in any settled fashion from the back of a running horse? With the last bullet in that gun he smashed the second lantern, and the tinkling of the glass was music in his ears. But now he was riding in almost utter darkness except that he could see before him the door of the barn where, behind the slanted shadows of the rain, the moon kept a ghost of light.

The stallion sprawled on the wet floor, recovered, plunged on, but the dim square of the door was half blotted out by the silhouette of a horse that had backed squarely into the way. There was no room to swerve past it on either side, and The Lamb, despairing, drew back on the reins. He might as well have drawn against a leaping avalanche. The stallion gathered himself, reared, and The Lamb, clinging instinctively, was carried across the obstacle, his head sweeping close to the rafters above.

He heard, behind him and beneath, a yell of wonder. The crack of a gun seemed a small sound, without meaning, and then he was through the open door of the barn and dashing into the million cold threads of the rain. Wild shouting rose from the barn, beaten down and blanketed by the steady roar of the storm. The curves of the road-way leaped past beneath him like a swaying snake. A yell rang before him, the black gap of the creek was there, and the bridge across the chasm. They soared again. He saw beneath him the white face of the creek made narrow by the speed of their flight, and then the ponderous hoofs struck the bridge. It reeled with the shock upon its pivot, and reeled again as the great horse sprang on. The farther bank shot up before them, impossibly high, but, striking it solidly, the stallion scrambled like a cat, tipped over the brim, and, behold, they were free, and the flooded road was now rapidly shooting back beneath them.

Chapter Fourteen

Ten strides of that mighty creature down the road dropped all The Lamb's past behind him, as a sailor's past is dropped below the horizon when he sets sail in the ship of ships. But all that he had done and all that he had been seemed to The Lamb nothing, and his life began here. For the first time he breathed, and his heart beat with the rhythm of a song, and to him it was as though he was riding a wave that pitched forever forward with a sway more magic than the beat of the wings of a bird.

What men had he known then, or what women, in all his days? For never had there been man or woman worthy to sit the back of this flying giant. What horse had he known, also? The good mare was forgotten, her grace, her beauty, her gentle, wise ways, and her speed that had floated him so many a time out of peril of his life. He had ridden out of his boyhood on her back. Upon her he had grown old while she was still young. But what was she compared to this monster, blasting a hole through the wind?

He looked up. The lowest tufts and streamers of mist reached at his head, and were jerked behind him by the speed of that gallop. He looked to the side, and the dark trees were blurred into solid night. He looked down, and the tarnished silver of the flooded roadway was dashed into milky spray, so that it seemed to the half-dizzy mind of The Lamb that he was galloping through the heart of the sky, with the snowy breasts of the clouds smitten by the hoofs of his horse.

He was a thing of ice. His soul was frosted through and through. In his knees and hands there still was a sense of riding, but the rest of him was gone numb. It did not exist. The wind of the gallop blew utterly through him, and for that very reason he rejoiced.

He told himself that this ride would kill him. No, he did not care for that, but only to see whether or not he could gather the strength of the pride of this animal into his hand. One other man had ridden the black and made him his own, and if he were worthy of calling himself the peer of Jimmy Montague, he must do as much. He freshened his grip. He wrenched and tugged at the reins. He might as well have tugged at a stone wall. He tried again, and pricked the flank of the stallion with his spurs.

That brought a result, but not what he had hoped. As though scorning to run longer upon the mundane roadway, the stallion flung himself up as if to climb the sky. The heart of The Lamb rose and knocked mightily against his teeth. Then the stallion dropped dizzily down the height, and landed upon one foreleg, rigid and strong as a bar of iron. The chin of The Lamb struck his cold breast and bruised the flesh to the bone, and a cloud of bursting red sparks flew up and exploded before his eyes.

That red shower had hardly dissolved when the black hurled himself backward, and The Lamb barely had time to throw his numbed body from the saddle. He came to his feet with a lurch, as the black, raising himself, snapped tigerishly and nearly caught the man by the shoulder. But when the big horse was up again, The Lamb was in the saddle, getting both stirrups as the black lurched upward.

They began to fence with one another. The stallion used the dizzy heights of the air, and the hard face of the earth. He wove and fence-rowed and sun-fished. He lunged like a flung stone upward, shook himself, and swooped down again to the earth with head dropped between his front legs, and his back humped so that man and saddle were perched upon a narrow and lofty pinnacle. There was no let-up in the fury of this attack, no slowing of exhaustion, but always the whiplash cracking and the smiting of the hoofs upon the roadway. And against this furious assault the rider matched wit, and craft, and old experience —the experience of the born fighter, the experience of the rider of hundreds of cunning, bucking mustangs. The great stallion seemed to shed his bulk. There was no weight to him. He was light as a spirit rising, and plunging then like a plummet downward.

So dreadful were those shocks that The Lamb, in spite of all his experience, never had known such a thing before. As a rock breaks when dashed down, so he expected the stallion to break, but his bones seemed of finest steel, and of iron from his heart. If his strength decreased in the slightest degree, it was not apparent to The Lamb, whose head was beginning to spin, and darkness floated in vague clouds before his eyes.

The changing wind now smote the clouds and tore them apart, and the white flood of moonlight rushed through, but that light could not reach to the darkness that was besetting the brain of The Lamb. Only, in flashes, the white radiance flowed in upon him, and the dimness followed, like a bright landscape over which cloud shadows are trailing. So that sometimes, in a dream, he was detached, and far away looked down upon himself dueling, struggling eternally with the horse, and, again in the clear moonshine, he knew he was committed, body and soul, to that strife.

Again the black was down, flinging purposely back and then rolling cat-like to regain his legs. Back into the saddle struggled The Lamb, and kicked away the muzzle of the stallion as he reached around to seize the leg of his rider. But the man knew that he was far gone, and that there was only one sensible thing to do—to draw his Colt and shoot the great brute, for, otherwise, he would be flung and trampled and stamped to death while he lay on the rocks of the roadway.

Twice he reached for the handle of his Colt, and twice he snatched his hand away, and, gripping leather, strove to keep his place in the saddle. Blood trickled from his nose and mouth. It trickled from his ears. He had been battered into warmth and comfort; he had been battered into another sort of numbness again. Now the stallion, which had striven in all other ways to dislodge the man, used that last and most fatal of all the tricks known to a pitching demon of a bronco. He began to buck and whirl at the same time until, having gained momentum, a buck-jump punctu-ated the spin, and he revolved with equal speed in the opposite direction.

At that reversal of direction, The Lamb lost a stirrup and spilled out to the left. He fought with all his might to drag himself back into the saddle. If he had had his original strength he could have done so in an instant, but now instinct could not take the place of muscles weary to agony and dead.

He spilled farther from the saddle, all balance was gone. For another moment he clung as a runner clings to his race after all sense has gone from his pounding legs, and in that moment The Lamb saw the moon flash in a solid circle around the sky, and saw the white foam flying from the gaping mouth of the stallion. Then he was cast violently through the air and crashed into a thick bush.

The stinging cold of the shower of drops that fell upon him restored some of his wits, shocked back some clearness to his mind, though it left his body inert, and in that strange brightness of thought he knew that he had been beaten, utterly and sadly defeated for the first time in his life.

And the victor came at him like a tiger with flattened ears and gaping mouth. Dimly The Lamb wondered how his death would come— whether from the crunch of those great jaws, or the pile-driving strokes of the forehoofs, smashing in the frame of his body utterly.

The stallion, at that instant, skidded on the iced face of a broad, flat rock and fell headlong, and the sight of him was blotted from the eyes of the man.

That fall raised The Lamb to such a strength that he was able to break from the entangling brush and stagger weakly forward. The stallion, sprawling desperately upon the icy surface, twice again fought to rise. The third time he won to his feet, but only with The Lamb once more clinging to the saddle—but how feebly, now, with sagging head, with nerveless knees, and with hands that seemed broken at the wrists.

He was no longer himself. He was a limp rag of humanity cast into the saddle, and the stallion sprang up as lightly, as powerfully as ever, with the quiver of strength working beneath the saddle, and with his head high and dangerous.

Yet the black was changed. It was as though he had felt the intervening of a magic hand that had cast him down to the earth at the very moment of his victory. Suddenly the man knew that the horse was afraid, and was waiting.

Then the Lamb laughed, a foolish, droning

laughter, and drove his spurs cruelly deep into the flanks of the horse. The stallion sprang forward in no fiercely fighting lunge, but with a light, rhythmic gallop, like the forward flinging of a wave, and as he galloped, his rider swayed drunkenly in the saddle, and laughed, and his laughter was half a sob and half a groan.

Suddenly he saw before him great trees, whose limbs glistened with white streaks of rime, the moonlight full upon them. Beneath the trees there stretched a long, low house of logs, and above the house rose a chimney from which smoke twisted up slowly into the air, for the wind had died away, there were no clouds in heaven, and only the silent burden of the frost settled upon the face of the earth.

The Lamb wanted to ride on, and yet the horse had stopped, as though he felt that this should be the end of the journey, and when his rider made no move, the stallion walked straight up to the nearest door and smote against it with his forehoof.

The Lamb suddenly understood and remembered. It was the ranch house of Colonel Loring.

The door opened and the face of the cook appeared. "Jimmy Montague!" he shouted. Then he heard the foolish, droning laughter of the boy, and he looked up again. "Love o' Mike!" cried the cook, and, in spite of his stump of a leg, he pulled The Lamb out of the saddle and half dragged, half carried him into the house. There he placed him in a chair and bellowed. In answer to his shout, men flooded in from the bunk room. The colonel and the superintendent came in haste from their bedrooms. The cook pointed to the figure of The Lamb seated before the stove, his clothes rent to tatters, naked and streaked with blood to the waist, torn by brambles, sagging in his place like a drunken man, and foolishly, feebly laughing. At this strange picture the cook pointed, and then turned around and indicated, through the open door, the great front of the black stallion.

First there were shouts, and then there were murmurs of wonder so soft that the voice of Shorty could be heard calling plaintively from the bunk room: "Lemme see! Boys, help me out to see! If it's true, it'll make me a well man *pronto!*"

Chapter Fifteen

The colonel brought out a new man. He had driven out through the heaped white snows of the mid-winter, with the horses knocking the dry drifts to powder as they trotted gingerly forward. When he reached the log house, which looked more than half buried in the white heaps around it, he merely said: "Cook, here's a new man for you. His name is Ray Milligan. I hope that you can please him better than you've pleased some of the others."

He marched on across the kitchen and disappeared into his own quarters at the rear of the building, while the cook, with lowered head, scowled bitterly after his employer. But the words would not come to him until the door was actually closing behind the fat colonel.

Then the man of the kitchen shouted: "Hey! Wait, will you? Hey, Colonel! If you don't like the way that I throw up the chuck to the boys, I'll tell you what you can go and do! If you're a man, come back and talk to me."

Plainly they could hear the steps of the colonel departing deeper into his sanctum, but he did not reappear at the door.

Even while pouring forth these violent challenges, however, the one-legged cook was picking up a tin cup of great dimensions and filling it from the huge coffee pot that, night and day, often having the weak grounds bailed out and fresh dippers of coffee poured in, simmered upon the back of the stove. It was not really coffee. Or what coffee appeared in the flavor was drowned in the quantities of cheap chicory and other adulterants, but, nevertheless, this was the drink most favored upon the range, and the purest Java, or the rarest mocha from Arabia, prepared by a master, would have been snorted at by any cowboy. This dreadful black potion the cook ladled into the cup, filled it automatically, and, without glancing at it, passed it to the new man.

Milligan accepted it. He took it with a hand that went all around the cup, and disdaining the handle, as though to prove the asbestos-like toughness of his skin, he drained half the coffee at the first swallow. He paused, put down the cup, and rolled a cigarette.

The cook was still talking to the closed door. He luridly described a man for whom, he said, he slaved by day and slaved by night. In the whole length and breadth of the great range, let another cook be found who set forth such prime feed as he, and yet the colonel had nothing but harsh words for him, and he was through.

"Are you gonna pull out for town?" asked Milligan.

The cook turned suddenly toward him again. "He knows that I won't quit in the middle of the scrap."

"What scrap?" asked Milligan.

The cook opened his eyes. "You don't know?"

"Why should I?"

"How long was you in town before the colonel signed you on?"

"Why, a couple of hours."

"You never heard of the Montagues, or Jimmy Montague, or nothin'?"

"I heard of Jimmy Montague. Everybody's

heard of him. He's the one that had the black horse that was stole."

The cook smiled. "And this is the outfit that stole the black horse."

Milligan hastily took refuge behind his coffee cup. He set it down, empty, and inquired if it were not a shade on the side of irregularity for an outfit to replenish its strings of horses by—borrowing?

"Borrowin'?" the cook said, his yellow teeth showing almost white against the thick, dark stubble of his beard. "Borrowin'? Sure. You dunno how things is worked in this part of the range. Folks don't care so long as you got friendly intentions. You take the Montagues. Suppose they get hard up for some young cows. What do they do? Go to town and buy some stuff? No, they just up and cut out fifteen hundred head of weaners that the boys are drivin' home from the range for Colonel Loring to get 'em under fence and feed. They borrow fifteen hundred head, as you might say, you see? Well, along comes one of our boys and says, if the Montagues are so dog-gone' liberal, he'll sure go over and borrow a new horse for himself, him havin' lost the best you ever seen in the fight in the cañon. So over he goes, and he borrows Jimmy Montague's black."

Milligan whistled. "The sheriff must be a pretty old man in these parts," he suggested.

"The sheriff is all fair and square, but the Montagues don't go botherin' him none. If he rode out this way, he might get too interested in seein' the funny-lookin' new brands that some of the Montague beef is wearin' . . . run all over their sides from their shoulders back to their hips. And the colonel ain't askin' the sheriff in, because he don't figger that he has enough money to take this kind of a talk into court. He ain't half as rich as the Montagues. He ain't had as many hands ready for . . . borrowin'. He never took to it so quick and nacheral, as you might say. He wants to settle this little job right up here in the mountains, the same way that it was started . . . without botherin' no judges and no juries. Maybe just a coroner's inquest would be heard, now and then, when the spring had thawed out the winter snows and turned up some of the winter graves. Outside of that, he don't want to bother no law. The colonel, kid, is a white man." He paused in the act of slicing bacon, and poised his great, sharp knife aloft to emphasize his point.

"A white man." Milligan nodded knowingly. "He pays a white man's wages, right enough."

"He's gotta pay high. He's gotta pay through the nose. I'll tell you why. It's because the breed of 'punchers that they got on the range these days ain't a breed of men, mostly, but a breed of ornery coyotes. He brings out one man, and two men quits him. And them that stay, they loll around

116

and look at the floor and wisht they was back in town. I'm gonna buy me a cork foot and go out and ride the range, and show 'em that half a man with a whole heart is better than a whole man that's got no nerve."

Milligan nodded again. He was a big man with sharp little eyes that wrinkled up and almost disappeared in mirth every little while, though his lips were hardly more than touched at the corners by these smiles. And this trick of expression gave him the very look of a fox, seeing far into others and revealing nothing of himself.

He received another cup of coffee from the cook. "I don't aim to be so high, wide, and handsome, when it comes to sashaying around with a gun," he declared. "But maybe I could stand my watch out. I wouldn't mind seeing the black horse, though."

"You'll see it when The Lamb comes in."

"How come they call him The Lamb?"

"Because he ain't," the cook said shortly. "You peel your eye out over the hills and you'll see him come driftin' along, maybe, along about the time that the day gets dirty. Even him has gotta ride range for this outfit."

"Even him?" Milligan echoed with interest. "Is he too good to ride range, speaking ordinary?"

The cook paused in his work and smiled faintly upon the other. "After you've been here a while, you'll begin to understand. You'll have a chance to see The Lamb, but you ain't gonna see him the way that *we've* seen him."

"What I'd like to know," demanded Milligan, "is what a man could be doing here if he didn't ride to work?"

"I'll tell you what he could be out here," said the cook. "He could be the margin around the page that keeps the print from gettin' rubbed out and the page tattered. He could be the gun handle by which you hold the gun. He could be the lock on the door and the key that's in it. He could be the dog that runs the sheep and the iron point on the shepherd's stick. He could be the edge of the knife and the fire of the match. Maybe that gives you a kind of an idea?"

"You need his guns," translated the other shortly.

"We need his guns, and the eye behind his guns," the cook affirmed. "And, by gravy, I say, would you have hands like his cramped up with the cold, and fingers like his thickened and stiffened with the rope work and the tailin' up of water-logged steers? Hands like his that might one day be fishin' to keep our lives out of the current, when it's runnin' downhill?"

Milligan drained his second cup and stood up. "I follow that drift," he said, and went outside.

It was the hour that the cook had recommended for seeing the return of The Lamb. It was the dirty time of the day. One would have thought that a train had just passed around the wide rim of the western horizon, sweeping with an equal speed up shaggy mountains, down vertical cliffs, and leaving behind it a dissolving cloud of smoke that stained the pure white of the snow like a thin smudge of soot on the purest of white paper. The winter night was coming quickly down. Already the lamplight through the kitchen window was turning yellow and holding out a dim promise of the warmth and content within, and the half-buried walls of the house seemed a haven of profoundest refuge.

Milligan walked up to the top of the first knoll, and, looking down the valley, he saw a tall rider on a tall black horse come up the rise straight toward him. He dropped his left hand to his hip. He raised his right hand above his head.

"Look here," Milligan said as the rider came up, "is your name Lamb?"

"That's my name."

He spoke, and the horse halted. Dexterously, in one blue and ungloved hand, he rolled a cigarette, as skillfully brought out a box of matches, sifted one out, lit it and the cigarette, and ever with his right hand hanging free.

Milligan, fox-like and observant, saw, and admired, and understood. "I'm Milligan," he said.

"We never told our lies at the same camp," said the other positively.

"I come from the Montagues," Milligan said.

The Lamb looked mildly down upon him. His

face was blue and red with the cold, however, and his mildest expression could not soften his features greatly.

"They've sent over a stand-up gunfighter to get me at last, have they?" he said.

"I've come to get you," said Milligan, "but I ain't come to get you with a gun."

Chapter Sixteen

In reply to this mysteriously significant speech, The Lamb looked into the bright fox-eyes of the other and finally said: "You ain't smoking?"

"No," said Milligan, "I'm talking."

"I speak Spanish," The Lamb said, "and I speak a sort of an English lingo . . . but I dunno that I talk your language, partner."

"Everybody talks it," answered Milligan.

Suddenly he began to laugh softly. In the excess of his confidence and his swelling surety, he stretched out his hand as though to stroke the neck of the stallion, and the teeth of the black clacked together on the nap of his sleeve. The big horse, disappointed, stretched his head straight forth, like the head of a snake, and his evil eyes burned at Milligan, who stepped back and shook his head.

"Nothing but wickedness in that horse," he commented, his jaw thrusting out a little.

"Somebody had oughta put that beast out of his pain, because living is a pain to him."

"Maybe," the rider said, and touched the firm ridge of the stallion's neck. At this, the head of the big horse rose, his ears slowly pricked, and he turned his head a little, as a horse does when it wishes to look straight back, and his eyes softened. "Maybe," said the rider. "You should come along, if you want to talk. The big boy is due for a feed and a rubdown."

He rode into the barn, drew off saddle and blankets, and then, having tethered his horse to the filled manger, he fell to work with a pair of stiff brushes. The black stood motionlessly, regardless of the good sweet hay, his eyes half closed. Even the grain in the feed box could not tempt him, so utterly was he given up to the sensuous pleasure of that grooming.

"You slicking him up for the Derby, maybe?" asked Milligan, who lounged outside the stall, safely beyond the range of those long hind legs. "Or does your best girl come out on Sundays and take a ride on him?"

The Lamb did not reply to this. He went on vigorously with his work, until he had finished the horse down to the fetlocks. On the tender skin above the hoof, he carefully worked with a bit of chamois.

One by one, the stallion lifted his black hoofs, hard as iron, and offered them for this care, and when his new master came to the forelegs, the horse lowered and turned his great head and sniffed and nibbled at the shoulder of the rider.

"What in hell have you done to the black brute?" asked Milligan. "Last time I seen him groomed, there was four men to hold him and an extra hand behind, to swing a blacksnake."

"Because Jimmy Montague didn't hanker to work on his own horse?" suggested The Lamb.

"Him? There was only one place that the black would have him, and that was in the saddle. He never dared to wear spurs on this one, either."

The Lamb, finishing his work, leaned against the burnished flank of the horse and began to brisk the two brushes together to free the bristles from dust and dirt. He looked upon Milligan with kindly eyes, half dreaming, so that the emissary could see that he had touched a soft spot, at last, in this armored youth.

"Him and me have agreed," he explained simply, and as he walked from the stall, the stallion turned his head and looked after him.

"He's off his feed, though," Milligan suggested rather anxiously.

"He'll eat later," The Lamb said, and walked on down the dark aisle of the barn, with the chilly whistling of the wind about them, and the small, cold hands of it reaching at them through the crevices. Behind them, the stallion whinnied. "You ol' fool," said The Lamb, "shut yer face, will you?" The whinny softened to a nicker, and then they distinctly heard a rumbling grinding. "He's said good night," The Lamb said. "Now he's trying to bust his way right through the bottom of that feed box. You were talking about a lingo that everybody understands?" he resumed.

"This here." The hand of Ray Milligan dipped into his pocket and presently made a soft chuckling of coins, one against the other.

"You'll talk to me with that, eh?"

"Well?"

"Aw, I dunno," The Lamb said. "I'm human, maybe."

"Yeah, maybe," Milligan laughed, and he had a fierce sort of triumph in his voice. Then he added an aside—as though, his goal being assured, he could speak of other things—"I used to know a gent about your cut. By name of Dunstan . . . him that Jimmy Montague done in."

"I never heard tell of him," said The Lamb.

"Well, coming back to facts and figures. What would you want?"

"Wait a minute till I catch up," The Lamb said. "Where we've been going?"

"Well, toward a big stake for you. You know yourself, kid. What's your price?"

"From the Montagues?"

"That's it, I suppose."

"They got plenty of kale?"

"Why, I dunno. 'Punchers think that everybody that's got a barn and a cow is rich. But what you want?"

"That depends on the hours and the job."

"There's two things you can do. One is to leave the Loring gang. There's a price for that. The other is to hook up with the Montagues. There's a price for that, too."

"You mean to double-cross the Loring tribe?"

"It ain't double-crossing for a gent to quit his job, is it?"

"Well, I could use a couple of thousand."

Milligan gipped the arm of the other—and instinctively let the tips of his fingers wander and pry a little among the stringy muscles. He said: "A couple of thousand?"

"Yes. To get away from even numbers, I could use twenty-five hundred for leaving the colonel."

Milligan choked, then laughed, and the laughter sounded like the cackle of an old woman. "That's pretty good," he said. "We'll have a laugh out of that. Twenty-five hundred dollars? Why, you're crazy!"

In his quick, smooth way, The Lamb made another cigarette and lit it. When the match flared, he was looking through the glow, not at the tip of his smoke, but at the tempter. "Well, cowboy," The Lamb said, "you can't catch this dogie without spreading your loop a bit. You can't daub a short rope on me, son, because it couldn't fit on over my horns."

"Twenty-five hundred dollars! You got a bit of a nerve, kid. I'll say that for you. I'll publish it for you."

"Go home to Monty Montague and tell him to send a grown-up man to talk to me, the next time. I can't do business with messenger boys," The Lamb said.

Milligan gasped, with a snarl at the end of the sound, like the flash of teeth behind the growl of a wolf. Then he said: "Twenty-five hundred for quitting . . . it ain't reasonable, and you know it."

"It *is* reasonable," said The Lamb. "Since I came here, you've run off one big gang of weaners. But we've snaked in several hundred dogies off your range. Since I've got going, your boys ain't been showing much on our side. They keep out of rifle range . . . even long range at that. Why? We ain't got a decent number to do the work here . . . the riding and feeding . . . but Montague and all his crowd don't dare to bother us. I ask you why, old-timer. Can you tell me?"

"You mean it's you?"

"Aw, I'm modest," The Lamb said. "I got my good name that I'm selling."

"That weighs like lead, I guess," said Milligan.

"Or gold," said The Lamb. "You've heard my little story, Milligan. How do you like it?"

"For busting away and joining the Montagues, then? How much more for that?" demanded Milligan.

"Does Jimmy Montague want the horse as bad as all that?"

"I ain't talking about the horse. I'm talking about you."

"I hear you talking. I'm wondering about your meaning . . . but suppose for twenty-five hundred more I should come down to the Montagues?"

The other exclaimed: "You oughta be selling mining stock! Take the way you add up a list and put in the items, dog-gone' me if you don't beat the expense account of a traveling salesman."

"The way that you bargain, you oughta be a pawnbroker," suggested The Lamb. "I'll tell you what I'll do. Lump the two things together, and I'll quit the colonel and join the Montagues for four thousand. Does that suit you?"

"That gives me gray hair and'll turn the rest of the boys clean white."

"I'm worth it," The Lamb insisted. "Besides, this'll give Jimmy Montague another chance to get back his horse." He laughed a little. "Take this bargain or leave it, because it's a cut price and dead cheap."

"You're a mind-reader," sighed Milligan. "You've hit my outside price on the nail. You must've had some inside dope on what I was to give as a limit. What do you want for cash down?"

"One half. That's two thousand, I suppose."

"Light a match, will you?"

The Lamb held the match, and Milligan counted twenty $100 bills out of his wallet. He counted them again into the hand of The Lamb. The last two he delayed over. "No commission?" he asked.

"Commission?" The Lamb declared vacantly. Then he added in haste: "Sure. Take it down." He put away his bribe money into his coat. His head was bent thoughtfully. "I gotta go in and face the old colonel and the rest of the boys," he said.

"The first dip is the one that gives you the chill," suggested Milligan. "C'mon along."

They passed from the barn into the open. It was the very end of the day. There was a sheen of purple upon the snow. The smoke from the horizon had climbed to the vault of the sky, and two or three pale stars were looking through. Before them, the snow rose in a sudden whirl of wind, like a pool of dust in a street.

"A hard life!" exclaimed Milligan. "It takes hard men to live through it!"

And he laughed again, richly contented.

Chapter Seventeen

Good Colonel Loring was worn with many months of anxiety. There was a streak of red in the yellow whites of his eyes, but still the smile upon his thick, wide lips remained as beaming, as rich, as fervent as ever, and his eyes, as ever, melted quite out of sight under its full influence or, at least, left only two narrow slots from which he looked out upon the world. So he looked upon The Lamb when, after dinner, that youth stood before him in his private room.

"You want to talk, kid," said the colonel. "You get choked with snow dust, the sort of lingo that's passed around up here on my farm!"

"Why no, sir," The Lamb said, "dust ain't a thing that ever I could get tired of, after this winter's ice cakes, and sleet, and frost in your pocket, and icicles hanging onto your nose."

"Sure," the homely colonel said, "it's a rough life up here in the hills."

"It is," said The Lamb. "You could sandpaper this here sort of life a good deal just to rough off the outside bumps."

"Have a smoke," the colonel offered, his smile relaxing several degrees from anxiety.

The Lamb accepted the bowl of tobacco that was poured toward him and rolled his own with his usual one-handed dexterity. As he did, he said: "I gotta cut this short. I been asked to sit in at a new game, and this here is the first hand that was offered me, without the draw. What do you think?"

He took the money from his pocket. Like a poker hand, he fanned it out and laid it upon the edge of the table.

The colonel leaned over and scanned it with an intimate curiosity. "It's a big hand," he said, without looking up.

"It's pretty high," The Lamb agreed.

"As far as I'm concerned," said the colonel, "it's a straight flush, and I ain't gonna call you . . . I can't afford to." He smiled at The Lamb.

"You're pinched, I'd say," The Lamb said.

"Pinched ain't the word for it," said the colonel. "I owe for the chuck that I carted out to the camp last week, and I'm gonna owe for the next bunch that I bring out, too . . . if I got the luck to bring out any at all."

"You're sort of deep for wages, too, I suppose," said The Lamb.

"I don't wear laces in my boots," said the colonel. "If I did, I wouldn't be able to afford 'em."

The Lamb, as though this speech made him at home, though thoughtful, slumped into a chair. "You've been a considerable burden to me, Colonel," he said.

"I have," said the colonel. "I've been a load to myself, for months and months. Maybe I can last to the spring roundup. I dunno."

"If you had to sell out now," The Lamb opined, "you wouldn't get ten cents a dollar on most of your stuff."

"I wouldn't," the colonel agreed. "I'd get nothing on a pack of it. There ain't any market

129

that I could drive to in this sort of weather, except down the hill to Montague."

"You'd drive quicker down the hill to destruction," The Lamb suggested, and he raised his brows.

"I would," said the colonel. "I would just that, and maybe a little bit more. But as for you, kid, you've done me proud, you've given the Montagues the lash for me while you lasted, and now that they've offered you a chair in a better game, I gotta admit that I can't play in that company. I wasn't fixed to pay off, this trip, but out of regard for the way you've kept my range cleaned of the Montagues, and out of the way you've raided 'em for me, I ain't going to offer you any compensation . . . I'll only ask you to take a little memento from me." He drew from his vest pocket a fine old gold watch and passed it across his table.

The Lamb took it, and turned it in his hand with an impersonal admiration. "I'll take it," he said, and dropped it into his own pocket without a word of thanks or of comment. The colonel did not seem hurt, however, but leaned back in his chair and smiled again at the boy.

"While you were with me," the colonel said gently, "you've done a proper good job for me. I wish you luck with anybody that you go to, even to the Montagues, and most of all, I wish that you get a square deal from them."

"They've started by handing me a pretty high hand," young Alfred Lamb said.

"They have," said the colonel, "but where there's Colts in the deck, there's always a higher hand than a royal straight."

"There is," agreed the boy. Then he took from his money a single bill. The rest he pushed across the table.

"What's this?" asked the colonel. In the middle of his cheeks, a gray spot gradually had been growing.

"I want to leave my savings with you," The Lamb said.

"You're sitting in at a game," said the colonel, and he straightened again, and looked at the boy with a new hope in his eyes.

"I'll take my chance, chucking this hand into the discard," The Lamb said. "I'll take my chance on a new draw."

"You want me to keep this for you?" the colonel queried.

"This'll fill up the chuck wagon for you a few times, and pay off some of the suckers that've had enough," The Lamb explained.

The lips of the colonel twitched. Suddenly his eternal smile had gone. He stared. He looked all at once like a white-faced owl. "You want to sort of make a donation with this?" the colonel said, looking down.

"You'll play banker for me," said The Lamb.

"I'll put this in a safety deposit vault for you, lad," the colonel said uneasily.

"I'd rather you dropped it into the business," said The Lamb. "Because I'd like six percent at the end of the season."

The colonel stared again. He drew his hand across his big, loose-lipped mouth. "I don't understand," he murmured, his voice quite robbed of its usual richness. "You're making me a loan, kid."

"I'm going to play another game," The Lamb said. "I don't need that." Still the colonel stared. "I'm only going to seem on the other side of the fence," The Lamb explained at last.

At this, the colonel rose, as though lifted from his chair, and he stood with drooped head, and braced feet, clutching the edge of the desk and looking wildly toward The Lamb. "You're gonna double up on 'em?" he asked.

"Oh, damn it all!" exclaimed The Lamb, but then controlled himself. "It ain't only your side that I play, when I play against 'em," he declared.

"Hold on. You mean to say," the colonel said, "that you come out here of your own accord to fight the Montagues?"

"Do you think," The Lamb said with bitter pride, "that I ain't hot enough to've melted away through the hands that grabbed me in that one-horse dive of a town?"

The colonel moistened his lips, which were still gray.

"That night I came into the sheriff's office, I saw you both as I opened the door. The sheriff's lantern was ajar, a mite. However, that was what I wanted. I couldn't come to your place at all, unless I came with some kind of a reputation, and there was the quickest place to get one, I suppose."

By degrees, the wonder of the colonel diminished, and he began to smile again, all his features losing their strangeness and returning to their usual expression of content with life.

"You had me bluffed, son," he said. "What drove you the way I was going?"

"You'll know when my job is finished," the boy said rather gloomily. "There's no good talking now."

"I thought you were so bad"—the colonel smiled—"that you couldn't get anyone bad enough to travel with you. I thought you were so hot that you could be trailed by your own smoke."

"I ain't on ice," The Lamb said dryly. "Anyway, that's on the side. The main job, and the only real job, is how can we get at their hearts? The dogs have sent money to buy me. Well, I'm gonna be bought. And when I'm on their side, I'm gonna squeeze myself right into the top circle and learn all of their plans. You savvy?"

"Aye . . . if you could do that."

"Not many times. But once I'm there, I could arrange with you for one grand bust. That's pretty simple, I guess. I could slope all the Montague gunmen right into your hands, and you could close the top of the bag with a bit of string and drop it on the fire. All that I want would be to hear the sizzling."

The colonel looked far off. He wiped his brow. "When you first came in, kid," he said, "I thought that you meant what you said. I thought that they really had bought you, except that you wanted to see if I'd overbid."

"Why wouldn't you think that?" Alfred Lamb said. "But how would we get in touch with each other?"

"That's up to you. There's smoke by day and there's fire by night, for instance."

"There is," The Lamb said, "and there's Montagues spread all over the face of the range, with brains like the brains of a wild Indian. But I'll tell you. You can see the shoulder of Patient Mountain from here, and it's turned away from the Montague house. Two smokes side-by-side on Patient Mountain, or two fires side-by-side by night, mean that I want to see you. Would you come?"

"I'd come to the bottom of the sea, kid."

"Suppose it was a double-cross?" suggested The Lamb.

"I know, I know. I ain't a judge of men, and you're a hard nut, but, by hickory, I can't help trusting to you, kid."

The Lamb stretched forth his hand, which was briskly taken. The colonel walked slowly to the door of the room, gripping the arm of his new confederate.

"Suppose they're baiting you, kid? Suppose they simply want the black horse back? And think of how the boys here will hate you when they suppose that you've double-crossed us all. And I'll have to cuss you as loud as the rest . . . it's a pretty damn' tangled way you're gonna jog, kid. That's what I'm thinking."

"I got two horses to ride," The Lamb said grimly, "and there's six steps in each one of 'em."

Chapter Eighteen

Through the bunkhouse that night there was one predominant sound, and that was the groaning snore of the great Muldoon. That big man, who had labored like ten all the day in the driving of exhausted dogies toward the fences and the feeders, now lay with both his arms cast wide and the blanket pushed back from his chest. All the other sleepers in that bunkhouse were restless, but none gave such nasal and guttural voice to it as Muldoon. Like a giant he had labored, and like a giant now he rested, and to listen to him was almost to feel the departing of the pangs of numbness from his great limbs.

Beside him, The Lamb paused, and even leaned a little, so as to stare deeper into the face that was clouded over with unshaven whiskers. Then he straightened and went on again to the door, and, unbarring it with the greatest care and softness, he stepped out into the snow, with Milligan behind him.

The air was wonderfully gentle and warm. It had softened the brittle upper crust of the snow so that their boots sank deeply into it with a squashing sound like the fall of a snow shower dislodged from the bent bough of a pine.

It was deepest night, without a moon. But there was starlight to show the loom of the big, dark evergreens up and down the hillsides, and there was the loom of the big barn before them.

They walked on without a sound, side-by-side, Milligan crouching a little as he stepped, until his companion said: "Stand up, Milligan. The wind ain't hard enough to blow down the tall trees tonight."

Milligan, ashamed, stood up again. He muttered: "I dunno how we get past the guards at the barn, do you?"

"No," The Lamb answered.

"You don't," gasped Milligan. "Then we'd better stop and think it out, hadn't we?"

"If we stopped to think out every little thing like that," The Lamb said, "we'd never get any place in this here world. Leastwise, we wouldn't make the Montague house tonight."

"But, what will we do?"

"I'll think of something when the time comes. I always do. It's only the big jobs that need the big think."

Ray Milligan hesitated, turning his head toward his companion, but then, suddenly admitting the superiority of the other, he walked on at his side, and they came to the big sliding door of the barn, which swayed ever so gently back and forth in the pressure and the release of the wind. The Lamb thrust the door back with a great loud rattling that froze Milligan in his tracks. Out of the dark of the interior a long rifle barrel gleamed at them like a moonbeam.

"Who's that?"

"It's me, Shorty," The Lamb responded.

"What's the matter with you?"

The Lamb burst forth in a great rage. "What d'you think is the matter with me, you sawed-off runt?" he said. "Am I up at this time of the night for fun, d'you reckon? I never heard such a fool question in my life! Why am I up? Because I got dirty work to do, and that's the reason. And I got a green hand to take along, that don't know one side of the place from the next!"

"Runt?" Shorty said. "Did I hear you say runt?"

The other raged on: "Why am I up? Because I couldn't sleep. I don't seem to get tired enough in this here dude ranch to get no proper sleep at night. So I come out to sashay around through the lovely white snow and breathe the beautiful air. Is that a good enough answer for you?"

"Runt," Shorty repeated. "Did you call me *runt?*"

"Aw, shut up!" The Lamb hissed, and strode past him, followed by Milligan.

They found their horses, and led them out.

Shorty stepped before them. "Runt, you called me," he said. "You're takin' something on yourself to call me that. I'm gonna give you some information that ain't been asked. The average height of a man is five feet six and a half. I got pretty near a whole half inch over that. You called me a runt. I say there's some that needs education. By gosh, all I can do is to pity the kind of ignorance that you show, kid."

"Get out of my way," The Lamb declared.

"I won't get out of your way," said Shorty.

"You little chump!"

Shorty threw his rifle to one side. It sank from sight in the snow. "Am I little? Then you're a big chump to think that you can call me a little one and get away with it. I'm here tellin' you . . . and you listen to me . . . you can't get away with nothin' from me."

The Lamb looked distantly down upon him.

"The bigger they are, the harder they fall!" Shorty raged. "You can take that and swaller it, if you got a big enough gullet. You hear me? You couldn't push nothin' over on me, nohow, because I ain't made that way!"

"You want me to bust down and cry and beg your pardon?" The Lamb asked dryly. "I didn't mean to call you a runt, Shorty. I take it back, if that pleases you more. You'd better pick your gun out of the snow."

Shorty fairly groaned with relief. "I thought I'd have to soak you one," he admitted, "and then the beating up I would've got would've made me look like a poster painted in red. I'm sure sorry that you gotta ride out tonight, kid. But the Chinook is blowin' for fair, ain't it?"

"Aye," said The Lamb, "and there'll be a lot of beef down before morning. We'll have to be tailing 'em up again, Shorty, there's that to look forward to."

"Ah," sighed Shorty, "this is the life for a cowboy. I dunno what I done with my wages last summer. So long, boys. You ain't ridin' the black ag'in tonight, after havin' him out today, are you, Lamb?"

But The Lamb returned no reply other than a wave of the hand, and, with Milligan beside him, he rode across the brow of the hill.

They were no sooner out of sight than Milligan breathed: "That was drawing it pretty fine. The little wildcat . . . I thought that he'd go at your throat, any minute."

"He would," The Lamb confirmed. "He's all

skin and bone and gristle, is Shorty." He looked back. The top edge of the roof of the colonel's house, and the chimney above it, showed in a black wedge against the sky. It looked like the silhouette of a broad-shouldered man wearing a top hat. The Lamb began to whistle and waved his hand to this sinking picture.

"It ain't hard for you to leave?" Milligan asked.

"Well, why should it be?" asked The Lamb. "I never seen a harder worked camp than that. Besides, no matter what sort of coffee they hand out at the Montague dump, I know that I'm gonna have enough sugar to stir into it. I've had my hand filled with the sugar, first."

Milligan looked away to conceal his sneer of disgust, but he added: "Some of those boys are pals of yours?"

"Pals? Oh, sure. You know how it is. In a camp like that, you gotta talk. But a cowboy's a fool that wastes time picking up friends. Them that you make in the fall, you gotta chuck in the spring. I take things the way I find 'em, and my neighbors . . . they can keep the change. But there most generally ain't much left over."

Milligan cleared his throat. Then he said quietly, tentatively: "I was just wondering. Suppose this was all framed on you just to get the black horse away from you?"

"What good would it do 'em?" The Lamb asked with a loud laugh. "Nobody on the range'll ever

140

ride the black ag'in but me. I got two thousand dollars that says that nobody on the range can sit this horse for ten minutes, and that includes Jimmy Montague."

"I dunno what you mean," Milligan said in wonder.

"Why," murmured The Lamb, "it oughta be easy to work out. Look at it this way . . . that was an educated pitching horse from the start. But he picked up his ideas all by himself. Now he's got some of mine, and a man's ideas are apt to be neater than a horse's."

They worked around the shoulder of the hill until starting off in a direction opposite to that in which they had ridden from the barn. They headed on to the snow-covered trail to the Montague house.

The Chinook breathed against their faces, carrying with it the humidity of the melting snow, and bearing also the fragrance of the pines, from whose branches it was stripping the loads of white and thawing all the small resinous twigs. And there was other life abroad than the life of the wind, for out of the south they heard a wolf cry, and the bay of a lobo answered from the north.

"They'll have what they want before long," commented Milligan. "They've gone for a good long time with their bellies sticking against their backbones, but now they'll have enough to make 'em fat, all right."

"They'll pick up a lot of beef that's laid down to sleep," answered The Lamb.

"Damn 'em," Milligan said with an honest indignation. "I'd like to camp on the trail of those brutes. I've never seen why the ranchers didn't put a trigger bounty on wolves. You take what they eat . . . why, it's beef. And what's the price of beef? That's the way to figure out a decent bounty that'd make a cowboy want to rustle all winter, collecting the scalps."

Up from the dark of the valley just beside them a wolf howled with sudden violence, as though to answer and defy those human words, and Milligan shrugged his shoulders. "Sounds like he'd almost heard me," he said, uneasy in spite of himself.

"Maybe he has," The Lamb commented. "They've eaten better stuff than beef, before this."

At this sharp speech, Milligan jerked his head about. Next, with a start, he sent his horse into a gallop. That rapid pace was not followed by The Lamb, who lingered in the rear, laughing and making not another sound.

Chapter Nineteen

They came to the bridge, at last, which had so nearly been the entrapping of The Lamb before. He could not help checking the great black horse at the edge of it, and looking critically down the dark avenue of trees beyond.

"I know," chuckled Milligan. "You had your scare before. And this looks like putting your head in the lion's mouth, I suppose?"

"Why not?" The Lamb argued aloud. "They've paid over two thousand, and for that price they get back the horse, and they get me."

However, with a shake of his head, like one resigned to his fortune, whatever it might be, he suddenly gave the black the rein, and the stallion bounded across to the farther side. Milligan had no sooner joined him than the bridge they had just left creaked, and their end of it swung away with a lurch. The Lamb turned the stallion about with a touch, but though the bridge was half removed, it now swung slowly back and once more made a perfect roadway out of the Montague house. The Lamb sighed. There had been a murderous suddenness about that first lurch of the bridge. There was a hesitating change of mind apparently represented by the next movement. That change of mind might have been caused by the reflection that this rider and this horse already had vaulted that chasm.

But The Lamb, looking down into the shadowy heart of the creek, astir with the lines of white water, realized that only the sweeping rush down the driveway that night, only the desperation that he had felt, and the hum of the bullets that so narrowly had missed him, had given him the courage to attempt that leap with the stallion. Yet now he faced the entering drive, and went slowly down it.

"You've got sense," Milligan said with an air of relief.

The Lamb could understand why. For if Milligan had spent the $2,000 and returned without his fish, he most assuredly would have had some trouble explaining the size of his bill for bait.

At the stable, they found one man. He was a dark-browed and forbidding fellow with a beard long unshaven, so that his features were hardly distinguishable. Only his mouth seemed a white gap, the mustache having been brushed back on the upper lip.

He stood gravely aside, a double-barreled gun upon his arm. His manner was not as forbidding as that of Shorty, but there was something about him that made The Lamb understand that this sentinel would shoot him down without hesitation, as one shoots at an animal. The very air of the Montague establishment differed from that of the colonel's outfit, where there were plenty of rough characters spoiling for a fight, but only wishing to fight fairly and squarely in the open.

The sentinel wore a bandage about his head, and this bandage suddenly took on significance, when Milligan said: "Here's your friend, Al Lamb, come to stay with us, Jack."

The sentinel instinctively touched the bandage that surrounded his head.

"This is Jack McGuire, kid," went on Milligan.

"Glad to know you," said The Lamb, and extended his hand.

The other stepped back a little. "You think that I'd set and take it!" he snarled. "Which I won't do it. You're gonna have another idea about me, young feller, before we're quit."

The Lamb paid no heed, but shrugged his shoulders and went on into the barn. As he finished putting the black into its big box stall, Milligan rejoined him.

"He's bad medicine?" The Lamb suggested as he rubbed the nose of the big horse.

Milligan looked on at this performance with narrowed eyes of wonder. "That horse loves you," he said understandingly.

"He does," The Lamb agreed quietly.

"He'd've ate a man quicker than a quart of barley, when he was here before," said Milligan.

"Him and me, we talked things out together,

and neither side should've won," said The Lamb. "But I had the luck." He sighed a little, and then he turned his back with a jerk upon the stallion, for he felt that he was leaving the only friendly presence that he was likely to find in this place. "That McGuire," he said. "What's wrong between him and me?"

Milligan touched his forehead. "It sort of riles him to think that he was dropped by you."

"By me?"

"Two weeks ago, when you sashayed over the hills and rounded up a bunch of the Montague dogies. You and Muldoon and the other pair, I mean. McGuire was with the gents that tried to cut you off, and when you stopped the party by dropping one with a fifteen-hundred-yard shot . . . it was him that fell. Luck, you understand, on your part, and bad luck on his. But he don't see it that way. He figures that you saw him and wanted special to down him. Low-down and ignorant, that's the kind McGuire is."

With this sort of talk, he passed the time until they reached the house. At the rear door, The Lamb paused for a moment. Perspiration stood out on him.

Then he said to Milligan: "I figure that probably I've been a chump, letting myself be delivered like this. But I gotta say that I'm full of guns and meanness, and watching for the wrong step on the part of anybody."

"Don't talk that way, son," urged Milligan gently. "You go ahead in. There's the door wide open. It never was wider for anybody than it is for you right this minute. I'll bet you that old Monty and young Jimmy never seen any man come through their door that they was so glad to see."

"I bet they didn't," sneered The Lamb. "That's the way the wolf feels when he sees the sheep stray out of the flock. But go ahead. And you walk first, Milligan, and I'll be close behind you, with a gun held steady in my hand. That's the way that we'll go inside."

Milligan flashed one glance at his companion, and it seemed to The Lamb that this look was filled with hate and fear, and that the face of the man changed color a little. But Milligan did not argue. He walked straight ahead down the bleak, dark hallway. The Lamb kicked the door shut, and as it slammed and sent a mournful, profound echo through the old house, he stepped on after his guide.

Behind him, he thought he heard the subtle closing of another door, and then he appeared to pass a stir of voices, soft as the rustling of silk. Of this he was not sure, or he would have stopped his guide and paused to investigate, but he refused to allow himself to become panic stricken.

The house was amazingly large. Twice they

had turned corners. Always the halls seemed the same—narrow, dark, damp. Then Milligan paused at a door and knocked. "Here it is," he said. A voice called out in a deep note. Milligan opened the door and stepped inside.

"You're back damned quick for a quitter and a failure," said the harsh, bass voice within.

Then The Lamb entered slowly behind Milligan and saw before him a very comfortable and spacious apartment with a big fire burning upon a wide hearth, and in front of this fire, in shirt sleeves and carpet slippers, there was a very old man, with a beard long, and white, and pointed, that touched the middle of his body. But that beard was no denser than a mist, and like pale smoke, the hair of the ancient man curled around his wicked face. The Lamb knew that he was standing in the very same room where Shorty had stood before him, and he knew that this was Montmorency Montague, whose nickname was so famous through all the range. The old fellow was now twisted about in his chair, his thin neck seamed with wrinkles.

"By gravy," he said, "and there he is. Ray, here he is. The Lamb has come into the fold."

Another door was cast open, and Jimmy Montague leaped into the room. Then, at the sight of The Lamb, he paused and slowly an expression of the most savage content spread over his face. His eyes filled with a soft fire.

"Ha," murmured Jimmy Montague, and his voice was as deep as that of his grandfather, but to The Lamb it sounded softer, like the purring note of a great cat. "You got the man, Milligan. Tell me, did you get the horse, too?"

"I got the horse, too," Milligan confirmed.

What joy there was in Jimmy as he spoke, so that he could not keep the bubble of pleasure out of the sound. The Lamb took note. He had stepped carefully back into a corner. He had a Colt in each of his loose, big coat pockets, and a hand was dropped upon each. Under this thin cover, he kept an instinctive aim upon Monty Montague, and Jimmy, his grandson.

"Go try the horse, Jimmy," said The Lamb with firmness, "while I stay back here and have a little talk with the old man, will you?"

"What've you done to him?" Jimmy asked. "Look here, young feller, I flattened you once, but I was too hasty and went before finishin' up the job good and steady. I ain't gonna be in any such a hurry now. There's time . . . there's time."

"You sound like a fairy story," said The Lamb. "You're smelling blood and bones and you want to chew and champ on 'em, right away. All right, old son. But first, you go out and find how useful the black will be to you, or to any other gent in the world. Then you come back inside and talk to me."

At this, Jimmy Montague leaned forward a little, as though he needed a lesser distance to examine the stranger and to look into his mind. "By Jiminy," he whispered, "I dunno . . . I sort of think . . ."

"Go do what he tells you," barked the deep, harsh voice of Monty. "I wanna have a little talk with this here youngster. Get yourself out of the way, will you?"

Silently the giant slunk from the room. Only at the door he hesitated for an instant to glare at the new arrival. Then he went on, with Milligan crowding at his heels.

The Lamb turned back to the old man, and found him leaning to warm his hands at the blaze. Then, beyond the door that opened at one side of his corner, he heard the knock and the light metallic clang of a rifle butt being grounded, and he knew that armed men were gathered at that possible point of exit.

Chapter Twenty

"Just you take your time and look around you," said the old man. His voice was so extremely grating that it sounded more like the croaking of a prodigious bullfrog. It made the throat of The Lamb contract with sympathy, so sore and broken did the vocal chords appear to be. "There's nothin' like rubbin' the moss off a new place. When you turn a colt into a new corral, you wanna give him time to make himself to home."

"They don't take such trouble with a steer in the butcher shop," declared The Lamb.

"Tut, tut, tut," chuckled Monty Montague. "You just look around, and then come over and sit down here beside me."

The Lamb willingly availed himself of the chance to look around. The big room was quite bare. On the mantel there were a few books, and on a table in a corner some yellowed newspapers and newsprint magazines. Two scraps of rag rug, worn by heel and spurs, inadequately covered the floor, or rather spotted it. There were four or five chairs. All of them were comfortable in appearance; all of them were homemade. There was much of interest, but the chief objects were not visible. He knew that they undoubtedly were posted behind the door at his back, and behind each of the other two doors that opened into this room.

He considered the windows. There were two, each small and set inconveniently high in the wall, and across each of these windows several strong iron bars were stretched. Now that he was in the lion's den, it was plain that the lion had him irretrievably under his paw. He shrugged his shoulders and settled himself to his fate, whatever it might be.

Monty Montague was filling his pipe. When he had packed the deep porcelain bowl with black plug tobacco, tamping it hard and compact, then he picked from the hearth a large coal, oozing little yellow flames. This he expertly shifted from his fingertips to the palm of his hand, and from his palm slipped it onto the tobacco. He puffed strongly, and clouds of smoke gushed from the bowl, from the mouth and nose of the ancient. These wreaths of smoke were as thick and as real as the misty hair and beard of the old man.

"And here you are," said Monty Montague. "And here you are, my son." The rattling voice gave an indescribable irony to the last words. He turned in his chair. "Sit down and rest your feet by the fire. It's kind of chilly out, even with the Chinook blowin'."

"I'll rest better standing," said The Lamb. "Standing . . . and walking." He moved restlessly up and down, close to the wall, his eyes alert.

"I've been hearin' a good deal about you," went on Monty Montague, not attempting to press his invitation. "A good deal from the boys on the place, for one thing. You've been turnin' up under their noses pretty frequent."

"They've been keeping their noses where they hadn't ought to've been," said The Lamb.

"One man shot down and pretty dog-gone' sick in bed for weeks and weeks. And another three gents have tasted lead out of your gun."

"Which was the reason," said The Lamb, "that

you wanted to have me on your side of the fence, I s'pose?"

To this, the other did not answer immediately, for he went on: "Then I've heard a good many other things. I hear that you've been a bad one."

"I dunno that I've been," The Lamb said. "I've never been turned down yet, wherever I tried to pass myself."

"Maybe you ain't," said Monty Montague. "A bad coin will go around until the brass begins to show through the silver."

The Lamb, coming to the door by which he had entered the room, tried the handle with a swift touch, and he was not surprised to find that it was locked. This, and the manner of the old man's speech, convinced him that he was trapped, and trapped for a sinister purpose. But he allowed no signs of this to appear, except from his restless pacing back and forth through the room.

"I've been hearin'," rumbled on his host, "about your start, and everything important that you've done. You started young. They called you The Kid, when you was fifteen. Is that right?"

"Where'd you hear that?" The Lamb said, impressed.

"I hear everything," said the other harshly. "I know pretty near everything about everybody that I want to know about. You started bein' called The Kid. Not the Boise City Kid, or the Slim Kid, or Al, the Kid, but just *The* Kid.

Because they thought that starting that young, with one man knifed and one man shot, you'd pretty well be known apart from all the others that was called Kid. Is that supposition right?"

The Lamb paused in a corner and performed his skillful trick of manufacturing a cigarette with one hand, and lighting it. He snapped the match across the room in the direction of the hearth.

"Keeping the right hand free for a gun," Montague said, and smiled. "That's a good idea. You've been keeping your right hand free for a gun for a good many years, haven't you? You've been hating to sit down at a table where your back would be turned to any window, or to any doorway. That's right, too?"

The Lamb did not answer. He smoked leisurely, was evidently thinking very hard.

"You went to Texas, and comin' out of the north with your northern saddle and your northern horse, and your long rope, they called you Montana. Just plain Montana. Him that downs three and kills two of 'em in a barroom, he's got a right to be known as Montana . . . not Montana Al, or anything. Just Montana. Is that right?"

Receiving no answer, he went on: "Texas didn't seem big enough to you. It sort of peeved you to find that you were bumping into the borders of a little old state like Texas, all the time. You wanted a chance to just sort of spread out your elbows. And so you drifted up to Nevada. There

154

was more sand in Nevada, and sand doesn't keep tracks preserved for very long. That pleased you, too, I dunno why."

He laughed a little. It was a terrible hoarse, painful laughter, the smoke pouring out of mouth and nose the while. He had gathered himself into the dim heart of a cloud, out of which he rumbled: "Up in Nevada you began a different tune. There were quite a few *hombres* on your trail, and listenin' for news of you with both ears peeled, by this time. And so along about this date, when you met up with a bad-actin' two-gun gent by name of The Lonesome Kid, you stopped and admired him a good deal. You saw that he was about your size, about your cut, and not much older. He was called The Lonesome Kid because mostly he stayed out by himself . . . the sheriff in a dozen counties not givin' him any encourage-ment to sit still any length of time. Well, you let The Lonesome Kid have words with you. He was pretty damn' well-known, and he was a fine hand with a gun, but you beat him fair and square, and you killed him. And then you did a pretty smart thing. You started off with your mare and called yourself The Lonesome Kid, and wherever any-body knew The Lonesome Kid pretty well and said that you wasn't him, you poked the muzzle of a gun down his throat and made him change his mind. But, after a while, it got so that you was gettin' a little too well-

155

known as The Lonesome Kid. Living off card games and fights, you felt that you'd better duck and run ag'in. And it seemed like it was better to run from one name into another name than it was just simply to run a long distance in miles."

He paused in his speech and nodded, and the smoke broke before his face and allowed his eyes to be seen. They were covered with a furling of very loose eyelids, but the eyes themselves were needle points of exceedingly brilliant power.

"There was a gent by name of The Doctor, over Denver way," continued the old man, "and you heard about him, and saw that he was about your general cut. You laid for The Doctor, and him and you had it out plenty, I reckon."

At this, The Lamb suddenly chuckled. "I reckon we did," he said. "That was a grand fight. Believe me, I'll never forget that." He touched the scar that disappeared from his throat beneath the band of his shirt. "That was an all-night fight," said The Lamb.

"You left The Doctor lyin' under the leaves, in spite of his fine operating work with his knife." Montague grinned. "You rode off, callin' yourself by his name, and that name was so damn' well-known that you had a little trouble wearin' it, but still you stuck to it pretty well for about six months, and your old trail was fairly well covered up, and everything was beginning to go along pretty smooth for you. And you picked up a pretty good job, and you were allowed to pick up a few cows for yourself, and you got some of the weakest weaners, and started 'em on the way to make good husky dogies. And you had a patch of farm land given to you by the old codger that needed your guns to keep him free from the rustlers. Is that right?"

The Lamb frowned for the first time.

"Aye," said Montague, gasping out the words with a great deal of vicious pleasure, "you don't mind a bit when I tell you all about the crooked and the mean and the fightin' things that you've done in your born days. But it sort of riles you when you see that I've worked your trail right down to your home nest, eh? That touches you under the skin, and touches you with salt and pepper, eh?" He laughed, his toothless lower jaw falling widely agape. There was something demoniacal and altogether inhuman in the delight of this bad old man.

"You don't mind nothin' that I've found out about you but that," insisted Montague. "But how you hate that. How you'd hate to have me send up word that the fine, upstandin' law-abidin' youngster that has done so damn' well, is really a trouble-raisin' gunfighter with eleven notches filed into the handles of his guns!" He laughed in the same hideous cackle. Then he paused and through the smoke shook his hand at the

157

youngster. "But mainly what I'd like to know from you, friend," he said, "is why you pulled up stakes from that there ranch where they was all eatin' out of your hand, and why you barged off here, and why you started raisin' hell so hard? Open up and tell me that."

Chapter Twenty-One

The Lamb, listening to this indictment, and to this quick questioning, continued to frown. Only gradually his frown faded and a grin took its place.

"These here deep thinkers," The Lamb began, "pretty near always are walking around corners when all they gotta do is to march straight ahead. I remember a mighty smart dog that I had once. One day, he had a fight on the street and he got licked bad. He ran away, but the next day the other dog died of the cuts he'd got in that fight. Now, my dog didn't know the other was dead. I couldn't tell him. And every day after that, because he was a smart dog and had done a lot of thinking, he never would go down that street, but would always run three blocks out of the way. Here you are, dodging around corners and trying to get the right idea about me. It ain't so hard to find. You don't have to run three blocks out of the way to find out about me."

"Go on, then," the old man said curiously. "I wanna know."

"I don't mind telling you," said The Lamb. "You're right that I was pretty well fixed up yonder, and that I'd got a herd started, and that I'd got some land of my own handed to me, and that I'd had the making of a real start. Well, you wonder why I barged off and started getting into trouble?"

"I wonder considerable."

"I had a horse once," The Lamb continued, "that was raised out on the Staked Plains, where grass grew fewer than hairs on a bald head. That horse was all ribs and shoulder blades and withers, when I got him. His neck looked like the neck of a sheep. He was gaunted up till he looked like a bow. I fetched him north and put him on good grass, and he got sleeked up till he *was* a horse to look at, but his heart was different. Down there on the Staked Plains, when he was thin as a rail, he always had a fire burning inside of him. He always would give you a snaky ride in the morning. And when you climbed off of him at night, he'd try to eat your leg off. Up north, he just went to sleep. He didn't have no heart. He couldn't run as fast as a cow. I happened to go back south with him ag'in, and the first day that he saw the sand and the sun baking and burning over it, and the cactus sticking up like tombstones here and there, he let out a snort, and frisked his tail, and pitched me right over his head, taking me that much by surprise." He paused to fashion another cigarette in his own peculiar way.

"You mean that livin' peaceful was like meat without salt?" said the old man.

"That's what I mean," The Lamb agreed.

"You had to ramble out and get on a rampage?"

"What for else?"

"I dunno, I dunno," said Montague. He closed his eyes and suddenly looked a very old and tired man. His lips parted, his face sagged. "Why pick out the colonel's place?" he asked.

"There's always more action on the losing side."

Montague shook his head. "What sort of action on the winning side?" he asked. "Because that's the side where you are now."

"Four thousand dollars hard cash is action enough for me," said the boy. "I've worked two years to get me a start that ain't worth that much in cash." He laughed and made a little gesture with his right hand, as though with it enclosing something from the empty air. "You understand, Montague? Four thousand dollars maybe isn't so much to you that has got plenty more. But four thousand sounds to me. I don't sink it in any bank. But I wait for the time when the big drives go by, and the lame dogies begin to drop out, all skin and bones. Then I pick 'em up for ten dollars a head, maybe. I fatten 'em up. In a year they're

160

hard cash for every pound that they weigh, and they weigh plenty of pounds. Is that business? I think it is. But how can you play that sort of a game unless you've got working capital? It can't be done. I don't want to crawl all my life. I want to run. If there's a ladder, I want to start and run all the way to the top of it."

He said this with a certain amount of fire, his eyes shining, and his head back. The old man, his chin resting on his breast, his pipe forgotten and going out in his hand, watched, and listened, and pondered. Silence fell between them, so deep a silence that The Lamb could hear the flutter of the flames on the hearth as they snapped off and sailed toward the black mouth of the chimney.

"You've said your piece. You've talked right out," the old man said slowly, his words grating out so that they were almost indistinguishable.

"I seen where I had to talk turkey or eat mud," said the boy. "That's why I didn't try to lie."

Monty Montague shrugged his ancient, thin shoulders. "What urged you on, kid?"

"The gunmen that you got behind all these three doors . . . and the keys that you've got twisted in the locks on the far side."

At this the ancient grinned suddenly, his eyes lighting. "I take to you a good deal, kid," he said. "I take to you a pile, I gotta say. I cotton to you, in fact." Then he puffed hard at his pipe, and the almost dead spark was rekindled and grew and spread in a red flush across the bowl, and the clouds of smoke issued forth once more and drifted up to join the mist that formed across the ceiling and made a soft silver gloom there. "It's the balancin' of the scale," he finally continued. "If you aim to double-cross me, you might bust me wide open. But . . . nobody ever has double-crossed me before. Nobody ever has had the grit to dare to do it." His eyes flared at the boy. "You're tough stuff. You're clean hickory. But even you, I don't think would have the nerve. And if I got you on my side, as soon as the freeze comes, I'm gonna crumple up the colonel and his gents like sand. And throw the sand into the wind, and to hell with it!"

His big mouth writhed into a knot at one corner, like one who tastes something sour, and enjoys the sourness. "Suppose I chance you, son?"

"Suppose you do."

"You'd have to chuck the black horse in the first place."

"No, I wouldn't."

"You wouldn't? And you'd expect to stay livin' on the same place with Jimmy Montague?"

"He'll tell you that he doesn't want to try the stallion any more," The Lamb said, and smiled evilly.

They studied one another gravely, that old man and that young one.

"You'd be good for cuttin' teeth," declared old Montague. "Tigers could cut their teeth on you, kid." He laughed, enjoying the thought. Then he said: "We'll wait and see."

They waited. The long minutes stole away, without a word said. Beyond the windows, the steady Chinook sighed, and the flames wagged upon the hearth and from a corner of the room a tall hall clock tick-tocked with ridiculous indifference and gravity. The brain of The Lamb, turning back the scene that he had just enacted, weighed and tested all the words that he had spoken. And he told himself that he had lied well, and that perhaps he had lied well enough.

Then the voice of the old man said: "You reminded me of somebody. I don't know. Relation or something."

He raised his head a little, and as he did so, The Lamb heard a footfall coming up the hallway. A key then turned noisily in the lock and the door was cast open. They had sight of Jimmy Montague, filling that doorway from side to side, and his head bowed a little, while he stared into the chamber. There was blood upon his face. A sleeve was ripped from his coat. He strode into the room with a limp, and all the time he stared with white face at The Lamb. His fury was so great that he could not speak, though his throat worked.

"Well?" said the grandfather, leaning forward in

his chair a little. "What's happened? You look at The Lamb as though he'd done it? But it couldn't've been more than his ghost, eh?"

"His ghost . . . aye . . . still on the back of the horse," said Jimmy, and he leaned his great shoulders against the mantel. His head strained back, with closed eyes. So he suffered, wrung with hatred and with pride.

The grandfather began to nod. "There's brains," he declared. "That's why we could use him, too. Brains have shot more men than guns. Brains have a longer range and shoot harder and straighter. That's why we could use him."

"For dog feed!" Jimmy shouted. "That's all. You old chump, are you changin' your mind about him?" Then he said rapidly, quietly: "He's stolen the horse from me. You understand that? He's stolen the horse from me, and I think that no man'll ever be able to sit the black again."

"A damn' shame to waste that kind of a horse, then," said Montague.

"I'll waste him!" cried Jimmy. "I'll turn him into dog feed . . . and throw him out with this . . . in the morning!"

He pointed to The Lamb, and The Lamb looked earnestly back at him and said not a word. He had a feeling that the old man would fight his battle better than his wits and guns could fight it.

"Open your eyes and look at The Lamb," said

the old man. The grandson obeyed. "Does he remind you of anything?"

"Aye . . . of poison . . . and the taste of brass. . . ."

"No other man, I mean."

"No. He's by himself."

"That's all, then" said Montague. "You can leave me alone with him, now."

"And?"

"And keep your hands off of the black. It belongs to The Lamb, and The Lamb rides for us."

Chapter Twenty-Two

By Monty Montague himself, this new recruit was ushered to a room. It was a small chamber in the second story, with deeply projecting eaves sheltering its window from the snow and the wind. Its smallness made it appear snug in spite of its barrenness. There were in it merely a wooden cot and a chair. As for washing, bathing, shaving, there was a room in the basement of the house that looked like a laundry, and there The Lamb for the first time met the rest of the household.

They were as rough as bears. Razors were not often used in the establishment, for the good reason that there was little warm water available to work up a lather, and by the time that a stiff beard had been properly prepared for shaving, the soap was apt to be frozen to the skin in rigorous weather. The result was that almost all the men wore natural beards that, being of equal length all over, inclined to make their faces round and owlish. Only here and there, as in the case of Jimmy Montague, was found a man to whom the beard gave an air of nobility.

They greeted The Lamb with a surly sort of respect, as though they knew that he was different from them, and that, nevertheless, he was a useful fellow to have about. The majority of these men were actual members of the clan, and the others, without exception, hoped to gain a place in the family by marriage, or perhaps by being formally included among the Montagues. This was done after a well-established precedent, the lucky claimant receiving for his share a certain number of cows to start his herd, together with a proportionate number of weanlings, and a bull. Upon these animals he was allowed to put his own mark, above the marks of the Montagues. All increase in his own herd was returned to him. He could sell, or he could let the animals run. The property was large enough to accommodate several such herds, but it was the ambition of Monty Montague, the controlling genius of the family, to crush Colonel Peter Loring and drive him from the range, not so much for the sake of appropriating the property of the colonel as to give greater room to the aspirations of the

Montagues and their protégés. This family was a solid unit of a patriarchal mold.

They retained a patriarchal simplicity in their manners, too. They ate at one long table, which was loaded down with food, to be sure, but the food was nearly all meat. Vegetables were reserved for invalids and children. Grown people were supposed to consume meat alone, and thrive on it, and the hard labor they performed enabled them to do this and keep fairly healthy. They all rode out early in the day. They worked until late. Each, being a part owner or aspiring to be one, was tireless and alert. It was a silent house, for each man was considering his own task; or, returning from it, they were mute from the fatigue of a hard day's work.

They took their orders, when orders were necessary, from Monty, or from his son Jimmy. These orders were terse and to the point. There was never any necessity of threatening a man because of laziness or neglect. Instead of that, in some extreme case the old man himself would call the delinquent into his own room and there he would quietly mention the faults that had been observed, and point out that they must cease, or else there was no place for the man in the clan. That always was enough, with one exception, for there had been but a single case of expulsion in the whole history of the clan. As for the others, men who came remained forever, with the exception of a scattering that had been hired in times of great need and discharged immediately afterward.

There were a score of children about the place. Old Monty interested himself in them a great deal. He saw to it that every boy and girl had a pony to ride as soon as it was able to straddle a bare back. In summer he saw to it that the youngsters scattered across the range and lived as much like wild Indians as they chose. In the winter months, such as this season, he insisted that they should have instruction, and for that purpose a big room was selected, and there Louise Patten held her school.

Her pupils ranged from six to sixteen, though no boy was kept at books after he was fourteen. At that time he was declared a man, able to take his place as a scout or as a Montague warrior. The day he definitely left the school, he was considered to have ended his novitiate.

Such a system of Arcadian simplicity caused the household and the clan to have much strength, and also many weaknesses. But the lack of law, and of submission to the law of the land, was replaced by the rules of the clan itself, and perfect obedience to them. These rules advanced the pleasant thought that nothing really was of importance except the welfare of the community. A theft or a crime on the outside, so long as it redounded to the strength or in some manner to the credit of the tribe, was admirable rather than reprehensible.

The Lamb, a careful observer of all things, took note of his surroundings for several days.

During the time, hardly more than a monosyllable was spoken to him by the other people in the house who were at the age of discretion. Only some of the boys, who knew that he was a famous fighter, could not overcome their intense curiosity and admiration. They, when occasion served and no older person was observing, would slip up beside him and shyly enter into conversation, trying to draw out the hero and learn, as it were, some of the secrets of Achilles's might. They found The Lamb perfectly amiable. It was to his advantage to create as much good feeling as possible. Perhaps from one of these children he would learn enough to make his errand profitable to Colonel Loring.

But he felt that his progress was very slow. It never was suggested that he should join the other men in their work. It was accepted that he was a drone, valuable in his case for his sting in battle, but that the sooner the battle and the end of his usefulness, the better. Then they would throw him out.

The longer he lived here not only did he come to doubt his own usefulness, but also he began to wonder more and more what there might be in this naked life that attracted men to live it. He determined that he would have to talk with Louise Patten, when he could. He saw her from time to time, her pale face silent at the long table, or passing from one room to another, always deftly avoiding his eye.

He could guess that she despised him because he had become an adherent or paid retainer of the Montagues, but he was willing to endure her scorn, face to face, if he could gain her information. She herself had never a companion except some of the older girls she was teaching. The young men, married or unmarried, never so much as glanced at her. All her friendship was given to a sleek, white bull terrier that followed her day and night. It was at her heels on the day when he accosted her in the grounds of the house.

He had made it a point, from his first coming, to stroll about the house and the land constantly so as to give himself a clear picture of every inch of the establishment since that might be the sort of knowledge that would be the most useful. After all, he was in the fortress of the enemy. Luckily the arrangement was not so complicated that he had to put it down in drawing. He could trust his memory, but he wanted that memory to be accurate for use by day or night.

The house had been built on a naturally impregnable post. On three sides, there was a sharp descent of rock that never could be scaled without ropes or ladders. No matter how often

The Lamb eyed the sheer walls, he could not find a path by which even a dog could climb or descend. On the fourth side, the neck of the promontory was cut by the ravine of the creek. Here the rock walls were not much more than fifty or sixty feet in height, but the creek itself was a formidable barrier. The water was neither very shallow nor very deep, but it came with the speed of volleyed arrows, rushing to white spray and foam upon the rocks. On the steep and narrow banks, here and there, was barely footing for a man, but no chance for him to run and leap. Therefore, the crossing of the creek was sure to be extremely precarious. It was the most natural precaution in the world that had caused Monty Montague to build the bridge, of the most simple type, strong and secure, but working on a great pivot so that it could be swung out or in, and locked in either position. Then the house was as secure as a ship at sea with a strong wind blowing.

Even these precautions were not enough to suit the Montagues, since the open wars with Colonel Loring began. And every night one or two men were moving constantly about as guards. Sometimes half a dozen were put on watch, if danger seemed imminent.

As for plans of attacking the Montagues, The Lamb could not find one. He would have to wait until they revealed their plans to him. For that he hoped, if once he could win their trust.

He was rounding a thicket of brush, the ice-rimmed branches glistening in the sunless air, when he saw Louise Patten come briskly out from the trees, with the white terrier streaking before her, here and there. At the sight of The Lamb, the dog paused, and came to a challenging position before him. The Lamb took off his hat to the girl, but she gave him the slightest of nods and passed by, her eyes fixed straight before her.

The Lamb, nothing daunted, fell in at her side.

"There's a good view of Old Mount Chandler beyond the firs, there," he suggested cheerfully. "The whole south side is plastered with white this morning."

She did not answer. They passed through the firs, and here he paused and stretched out his arm so that he blocked the narrow path as he pointed.

"You see?" he said.

The bull terrier growled softly, and looked up to his mistress for directions. She in turn regarded The Lamb with the calmest of eyes.

"I want to go on," she said.

"Even the dog can understand that," admitted The Lamb. "But I want to talk to you." She was silent, eyeing him without dread. "There's reasons why you and me should open up and talk freely," suggested The Lamb.

"I don't see them," she said. As he started to explain, she interrupted: "I don't want to talk to you. I want to go on."

"Sure you do," The Lamb said calmly. "But I want you to stay here. I'm busting with curiosity about you."

"I'm not curious about you," she declared.

He nodded. "Sure," he said. "I'm Benedict Arnold, or something like that, except that I ain't been made a general, yet. Maybe that'll come later. But I want to talk about you, not myself."

She hesitated. Then she nodded. "I've been rude enough," she said. "And I'm sorry for it. What can I tell you?"

Chapter Twenty-Three

The Lamb sighed with relief.

"This is a good deal easier than I thought it would be," he admitted. "When I saw you going by with a frosty eye, I thought I'd be up against trouble, talking to you. But here you are, pretty good-natured. I've noticed that before," breezed The Lamb. "When a person has done a good turn for another, it's hard for him to get hard-hearted. Him that does the favor is the one that's bound by doing it, the same as you seem to be now."

"What favor have I done for you?" she asked.

"Only showing me the way out, to the saving of my neck."

She nodded. "I suppose you can call that a favor," she said.

"Even a thing like me can't afford to chuck himself away, ma'am," he said.

At this, a slight flush appeared in her cheek. "Are you proud of leaving your friends?" she asked.

"What friends? Loring's lot?"

"Yes."

"What friends were they of mine? They hired me for pretty good pay. Along comes some other folks and offer me a raise. What's wrong with taking it?"

"Is that the way you reason?" she asked, and her eyes wandered upon his face, like one who reads a strange book.

"I'm on the make," declared The Lamb. "I need cash and I intend to get it."

"You came here to find Jimmy and kill him," she said. "Now you're here to take his orders."

"Between the evening I came to find him and tonight, there's the difference between a dead mare and a living horse. And there's four thousand dollars to boot thrown in."

"Did you come here for Jimmy because he'd killed your horse?"

"I wanted trouble," he admitted. "But I suppose that we've talked enough about me. Everybody knows that I'm a hired man. But why are you here?"

"For board and lodging," she said. "And so many dollars a month. I like my work, too."

"Teaching?"

"Teaching, yes."

"You can't teach 'em nothing but reading and writing," he said. "And what's that worth?"

Here she looked up at him suddenly with a brightness in all her face. "I think I know what you mean," she said.

"Of course you do. But what nails me to the mast more than anything else is why nobody pays any attention to you, here."

"Who?"

"The young gents. Even these here Comanches want squaws. But they don't seem to bother you none."

She seemed a little angered, at first, by this excessive frankness, but suddenly she laughed. And The Lamb smiled in his turn.

"Well, that clears the air," she said. "They don't pay any attention to me because they don't want me, of course."

"Does a trout rise to flies?" asked The Lamb. "Sure, except when the shadow of the rod is floating on the surface. Does a horse try to stand on his nose in his feed box? Sure, except when he smells a snake in the oats. But why don't these gents make a rush for you? I dunno. They walk by like they were blind in the eye that was next to you."

She looked earnestly at The Lamb. "There's no way to answer you," she said. "Of course, you see that."

"Isn't there? I don't see," The Lamb said. "Here I am, miles outside of you and clean different. I'm a hired man. I'm just a pair of hired guns, as you might say. Couldn't you talk to a pair of guns?"

She smiled a little. "You're talking yourself down," she said. "But I may as well tell you that it isn't pleasant for people who pay attention to me here. I should warn you . . . unless you've already heard . . . Jimmy doesn't like to have me noticed."

"He's the shadow of the rod on the water, and the snake in the feed box, eh?" murmured The Lamb. "I should've guessed that. But why do you stay here to be bullied by them? You were raised pretty good, or else you've had a lot of attention showed to you."

"Why do you say that?"

"By the language you daub," he said. "You can tell a cowboy by his boots and a girl by the way she talks. Besides, you've got an emerald there that wasn't picked up at any counter sale."

The jewel was at her breast; it was the ornament in a golden pin, dark sea-green, with the sea's shadow of blue in it. She covered it hastily with her hand and stared at The Lamb. His keen, bright eyes searched her very soul, and in between them pressed the terrier with a growl, as though he guessed at a crisis of some sort.

The girl quieted the dog with a word.

"What's his name?" asked The Lamb.

"His Lordship."

"Sure," said The Lamb. "By the way of his walking and talking, a man could guess that. Here, old son. Here's my hand."

The dog bared his teeth.

"Be careful!" cried the girl. "His Lordship is an ugly noble when his temper comes up."

"I never knew a dog to refuse my hand, ma'am," The Lamb said. "Look at His Lordship, now. He doesn't see anything wrong in my hand."

The dog growled, presently sniffed the hand, and now came a little closer to the stranger, his tail wagging in a small circle, as though it worked upon a spring.

"I've never seen him act that way before," admitted the girl.

"He'll act that way again, though." The Lamb smiled. "He's made friends with me. You take a fighting dog and he doesn't change. It's the same with a fighting man, ma'am. When he's made up his mind to be a friend, it's worth having him. Would you say no?"

She hesitated, filled with an odd anxiety, and The Lamb went on: "Look at you! I speak about an emerald that you're wearing, and you begin to get red and white in turns. Look here. That's a fighting dog, and he's our friend. I'm a fighting man, and I'm your friend. You live here like a wolf among dogs, or a dog among wolves. Why not talk out, ma'am?"

"Did you ever see this pin before?" she asked him suddenly.

"Jewels don't wear faces, for me, ma'am," he answered.

She watched him with a sudden hunger of curiosity. "Did you ever know Will Dunstan?" she asked.

The wind leaped across the valley and smote them, so that The Lamb bowed his head against it and clutched his hat. And yet the wind appeared to have caught him so much off balance that he staggered into it a little. It released him.

"That was a puff enough to sink a ship," he said. "I didn't catch what name you said."

"Will Dunstan," she said. "Did you know him?"

"Dunstan? Dunstan?" he repeated. "I knew a gent by name of Dunbar. He was a half-breed and . . ."

"No, no! There never was a trace of Indian blood in this man!"

"Dunstan?" murmured The Lamb. "I don't seem to quite place any name like that. But what did he look like, because gents have a way of changing their names, when they go wandering around the range from place to place. That's because a name that might fit in pretty good in one place wouldn't be so very good in another, y'understand?"

178

She raised her head a little, and said in her quiet voice: "Will Dunstan was not that sort of man. Wherever he went, he couldn't have carried more than one name. His own name was the right name for him. He had no other, ever."

"Ah, yes," The Lamb said. "He was a gent that you knew pretty well, eh? When you've seen a horse all the way from foal to saddle, you can pretty well know what he's like."

"I knew him less than a month," she told him.

"Hello!" said The Lamb cheerfully. "Less than a month? I dunno that even a teacher can learn a man that quick."

"I must go on," she said hastily.

"The emerald had something to do with this here Dunstan, did it?"

"He gave it to me."

The Lamb watched her with his keen eyes. "Excuse me," he said, "if I've been making myself too much at home. This Dunstan is sort of on your mind, it seems."

"He gave me this," she said. "He was working here for the Montagues and . . ."

"Ah, then he was one of 'em, was he?"

"Will Dunstan?" She paused to let the emotion pass from her. "He was no Montague," she said. "He gave me this. And the next day, he fell from the trail around the mountain, there, and they picked him up, dead."

"It's a long time since?" The Lamb asked gently.

"It was last fall. The leaves were dropping, and it was just before the first snow fell," she answered. Then hastily: "I have to finish my walk. I'll talk to you some other time, whenever you wish." She brushed past him and hurried down the path, swinging immediately out of sight.

The Lamb made as if to follow her, but changed his mind and sat down abruptly upon a stump of a felled tree. There he remained for a long time, looking before him with a blank face, as though he were struggling with a thought too great for utterance, too great for conception. At last his lips stirred to a faint muttering. He got up, then, and looked around with a glance both dark and guilty, as though he feared that other eyes might have looked upon him.

Then he turned down the path that rimmed the plateau, walking in a direction opposite to that which the girl had taken. He was, in fact, watched from the brush, for he hardly had started away before the brush parted and the dark face of Jack McGuire looked out, with the soiled bandage drawn about his head.

Chapter Twenty-Four

Five minutes later, McGuire stepped before him and glowered.

"Old son," said The Lamb, "you always look at me like I'd stole your calf. What's the matter?"

McGuire merely hooked his thumb over his shoulder. "The chief wants you inside."

"Thanks," The Lamb said, and started on back to the house beside the other, shortening his step when McGuire showed signs of purposely falling behind.

"If you were a cook," The Lamb said, "the boys would sure turn out *pronto* when they heard you holler in the morning, and them that come late would look for poison in their beans the next time they fed. What's on your mind, Handsome? Because I nicked you with that slug? Why, I was just shooting at Montagues in general. I didn't pick out your face. I'd never had the fun of seeing it."

McGuire, with an ugly twitch of his lip, said: "You and me don't come of the same breed and we don't run on the same trails. Leave me be. You'd best."

To this The Lamb replied with a shrug of the shoulders, and then walked lightly on, with Jack McGuire bringing up the rear. In that position they appeared in the room of Monty Montague, and found Jimmy with his grandfather.

"Here I come," The Lamb said, "with the sheep dog behind me." He sat down uninvited upon the arm of a chair and looked cheerfully upon the others.

"All right, Jack," said the younger Montague, and McGuire withdrew reluctantly, as though he expected dour proceedings and wished to be present at them.

"He's going to bite, one of these days," The Lamb declared. "He's been getting his teeth ready for a long time to eat me up."

Monty Montague dismissed that subject with a gesture. Then he passed his fingers smoothly through his fluff of a beard, and he nodded knowingly at The Lamb. "You ain't had a bad time here, son?" he began.

"I been resting," said The Lamb, "and waiting for the trouble to start."

"It's started now," Jimmy said.

The Lamb waited.

"You ain't camped on one homestead all your days?" suggested old Montague.

"No, I've sashayed up and down the range a good deal."

"You've met up with a few rough ones?"

"Sure. I've met some that wore the leather side out."

"And what was the roughest?"

"One that shot my horse, and rode her and me down afterward," The Lamb stated. He did not look at Jimmy, but his smile was most unpleasant.

Jimmy smiled, also, openly, and with great satisfaction.

Of these two smiles, Monty Montague was aware, though he appeared to be looking at the floor as he declared: "That's forgot! You two are friends, now, and going to stay put that way. Outside of my boy, here, you've met up with other rough ones?"

"There was Dutch Binderloss in El Paso. He was as good with his left hand as he was with his right. I shot him through the right shoulder, and with his left hand he caught his gun while it was falling and put me in the hospital for a month."

"What did you do to him?"

"Just that slug through the shoulder. I missed him with my second and my third."

"Bad luck," Jimmy hissed with an evil sneer.

At this, The Lamb shrugged his shoulders. "I ain't a fellow who's always won. I ain't that kind of a fairy tale."

"You've had your ups and downs, eh?"

The Lamb laughed, and, in laughing, his boyishness appeared in the backward tilt of his head as he sat like a boy on the arm of the chair, carelessly, his back humped, his attitude most ungraceful. "I've had my ups and downs. I've just batted over five hundred, that's all. They ain't put me on the bench yet. But outside of the books, where are the pitchers that always win by shut outs?"

Jimmy Montague's nostrils flared and his eyes glittered. But the grandfather smiled with a genial understanding.

"You gotta hammer iron before it makes good steel," he said. "You've had the hammering, son, is that it?"

"I've had it, plenty," said the boy. He closed his eyes and groaned softly. "Ran into an Irish lad when I was a kid at school. He was smaller than me . . . and I wasn't as big as I thought. He pretty near tore me in two. I wore the marks of that licking for years."

"Ever fight him again?"

"No, I never had the chance. He moved out of town while both my eyes were still closed. Fargo got him finally, from what I heard."

"Fargo?"

"Sure. The great Fargo . . . him that they talk about so much. Lefty Fargo."

"I've heard of him," said Jimmy. "He's got a record behind him."

"Nobody has a longer one. But it's part talk, of course."

"How d'you mean?"

"Aw," The Lamb said with a shrug of his eloquent shoulders, "all of these yarns about the dead-eye Dicks are part made up. This here

Fargo . . . they tell how he takes a gun in each hand and smashes a couple of dimes at twenty yards with snap shots, one from each hand . . . bang, bang." He laughed.

"You don't believe it?" asked the old man.

"Sure I don't. I've been in too many gunfights, and I've seen too many. I was on hand when Harry Corson, and Jack Peters, and Lew Marquis, and Jemmy Bone all met up in Tombstone and shot it out."

"Aye, that was a great fight."

"Was it? Corson got killed and Bone got shot through the hip. That was all. And those four dead-eye Dicks were all in one room together for pretty near ten minutes. They must've planted a hundred pounds of lead in the walls, and the ceilings, and the floors. They busted all the windows. The floor was flooded and smelled like a big mixed drink, because they'd potted most of the bottles behind the bar. After they got through, it looked like a bunch of Comanches had gone for that barroom with hatchets . . . but they hadn't. It was only four dead shots, so called, that had been firing off their guns. One killed . . . one wounded. The lead they fired off, they could've embalmed Corson in it."

"Folks exaggerate. There ain't any doubt of that," said the elder Montague. "But Fargo is a pretty fair man, I'd say."

"Why, sure he is."

"Have you met him?"

"Two years back."

"Friends?"

"Pretty fair. He put me under the table, that time."

"Drink?"

"A half-inch chunk of lead straight through the middle of me," The Lamb said. "Fargo, he ducked his head under the table and grinned at me. 'I'll see you later, kid,' he said. Meaning in Hades, someday, you understand? But I lived through it." He laid his hand on his breast and made a wry face, as though the agony of the wound, and the long hospital weeks of weariness, were rushing back upon his mind at that instant. Then he said: "But what's up?"

"We've got a letter from a gent that Colonel Loring has hired. Professional gunfighter."

"Does he tell you to hop right off of the range?" asked The Lamb.

"He wants to meet Jimmy, here, in the middle of the floor of Beacon Creek."

"If you went there, he'd never show his face, most likely," The Lamb said. "Unless he's a kid."

"What you mean by that?" put in the heavy bass of Jimmy.

"You take 'em young . . . fifteen up to eighteen or nineteen . . . and a kid'll do any fool thing to get himself famous. He *likes* to fight. He ain't got any sore places to start aching on him. You take me," continued this veteran of one-and-twenty, "and when a cold wind hits me, it goes right through fifty channels. I feel like the side of an old barn . . . full of holes and cracks, where bullets and knives have punched through me. I feel like a transfer ticket that's been punched ten times, and folded and punched over again."

"This is no crazy kid," Montague insisted. "But he's the kind that will live up to his word. What's the matter up there at the colonel's shack, sendin' out challenges, this way? Do they think that the old story-book days of knights have come back, where gents fight for the sake of fighting? There was you, before."

"I wanted to get Jimmy," The Lamb said. "I wanted him bad." He laughed with perfect good nature. "You going down to clean up this gent?" he asked.

"I'm not," said Jimmy. "I'm gonna accept. I've sent back my acceptance already. He's gonna be in the creekbed in an hour or so. But I don't expect to do the shooting for my side."

"Who will, then?"

"Why not you, kid?"

The Lamb rose from the arm of the chair. "I've got all kinds of fondness for you, Jimmy," he said. "I've got reason for having it. But you want me to go down there and play dummy for you? Thanks!"

Jimmy said: "You lie around here and sleep

soft and eat fat. What d'you do for yourself and us? Have you lifted your hand? For all we know, you might be a spy for Loring, right now, snoopin' around into our affairs."

"Shut up!" commanded old Montague. "You gotta talk like a bull. You always gotta roar and paw around and raise such a dust that nobody can see what we're talkin' about. But listen to me, Al Lamb. You got a personal interest in that other man, because his name ain't nothing but Fargo."

"Lefty Fargo!" exclaimed the boy.

"It's Lefty, right enough. Loring has got so low that he has started in hirin' professional gun-fighters to drive me off the range. He's got that killer, Fargo."

The Lamb drew in his breath with a hiss.

"I'm gonna chuck a saddle on the black," he said, and left the room in haste.

Chapter Twenty-Five

The Lamb went to his own room first, and there he looked to his guns with the most loving care. He saw to it that his rifle was in perfect condition, that the cylinders of his revolvers spun like tops at a flick of the finger, and that the weight of the hammer was exactly right, so that it could be flipped back by the thumb easily, and yet retain sufficient force to explode the cap of the cartridge when it fell. For this purpose, hardly a day went by that he did not adjust the spring a little and perhaps sharpen the point. The fingering of the pianist is a delicate matter, for it deals with the souls of many notes to make them strong or small, but the fingering of a pair of Colts is infinitely more delicate, and it had to do with the preservation or the perishing of the life of men.

For an entire half hour, The Lamb worked intently. It was cold in his room, and into the damp chill of the apartment a finger or two of icy wind penetrated from without. Yet he was dripping wet with the intensity of his application. This was only the first of his preparations.

The slightest tremor might upset his aim. Therefore, he set about arming himself against the cold. He stripped to the waist and redressed, putting on two flannel shirts, then a closely knit sweater, and over this apparel he donned a coat lined with rabbit skin, loose and warm and last of all he wore a slicker. His hands were sheathed in two pairs of bulky woolen mittens, and he looked like a fat man when he left his room and went down to the stable.

There the news had gone before him. When he came to the stall of the black, he found Louise Patten and His Lordship lingering outside the door. The girl said nothing while the saddling went on, but the terrier ventured inside the stall and almost had his skull shattered by a crashing stroke of the stallion's forehoof. He leaped back with a growl and stood in the aisle, bristling, and making low thunder. Then his mistress said to The Lamb: "Why are you riding out to fight?"

He pulled up the last cinch without answering. Not that he wished to be rude, but the question startled him a little. He turned his head to her.

She continued: "Is it for the money that the Montagues pay, or for the fun, or because you hate this Lefty Fargo?"

"The cash will do me," he answered, and led the big stallion into the aisle, as Jimmy Montague walked up to get his own horse. He passed them without a word, and with two separate looks—a keen one for the girl, a dark one for The Lamb.

The latter went out to the front of the barn and Louise Patten followed him.

"You'd better go back," he said. "Jimmy will be pretty cross if you waste any time on me."

She answered: "I'm trying to make up my mind. The money hasn't anything to do with it. It's only the game that counts with you."

"You mean the hard job?" he answered.

"Yes."

"I could have stayed with Loring if I'd wanted that. There were enough on this side of the fence to keep me pretty busy, wouldn't you say?"

She frowned in deep perplexity, and, stepping back from him, she shook her head a little.

"Even the head of the clan is going," she said, and pointed to Monty Montague, coming down the drive bent into the wind, with his beard whipping over one shoulder. "I'm going along, too!"

She went back into the barn as Montague came up.

"You can go along out into the road," he said. "You'll find a couple of the boys waiting for you there. Me and Jimmy will be along behind you."

The Lamb pointed with his thumb. "The girl says that she's coming, too."

At this, the old man blinked a little. But he made no answer other than a nod, and went by The Lamb with an odd glint in his eyes, while the talker swung into the saddle. It was like mounting to the back of a rock, to swing up on the black horse. There was no sway and give to him; he stood solid and massive as black basalt. And there were angles from which he looked fit more for the plow than for the saddle. The huge girth of him, for one thing, pried the knees wide. But the instant that he stepped out, all sense of ponderous bulk disappeared.

He jogged lightly as a pony down the driveway. When the full blast of the wind struck him as he drew out from the lee of the stable, he lowered and shook his head for an instant, then bounded into the air and flirted his heels like a colt, as though in defiance.

The Lamb laughed suddenly, and sent the big

fellow bounding down the drive. The bridge shook and gave out hollow thunder as they rounded onto the roadway. Three huddled, wind-blown forms waited for him there; three wretched mustangs shook their heads and slowly turned in at his side. Then he saw the sour face of Jack McGuire leading the party.

"We gotta walk on!" yelled Jack into the teeth of the wind. "We're gonna have some more company."

The Lamb rode his horse closer to the dark-faced fellow. "You're here with the boys to be the cotton batting, Jack. Is that it? The old man wouldn't ship a high-priced machine like me without packing it pretty safe. And Jack is my life insurance." He had pitched his voice so that it cut easily into the wind.

McGuire replied with a sudden roar of rage. "Keep off of me!" he yelled. "I'm gonna do you a harm, one of these days, I tell ye!"

He sent his horse ahead with a start, but The Lamb laughed, and remained in line with the other two. They were the true range type—lean, thin-cheeked, supple as whalebone and as unbreakable by labor or by weather. They looked curiously back at him with the wide, clear eyes that knew no fear. They were not like McGuire. They never had pretended to be great gunmen and therefore they had no great fall to lament. They were like ten thousand other staunch cattlemen—not at all on the hunt for trouble, but willing to meet all that came their way with capable hands. For his own part, The Lamb would rather have fought with a practiced bully than cross one of these unpretending bulldogs who only knew how to bite, and not how to let go.

The wind fell as they came under the shoulder of a hill. Behind them they heard the crackling sound of hoofs upon the frozen road, and, looking back, he saw that Jimmy was in his rear, and old Monty of the white beard beside him, looking wonderfully small and youthful in spite of his white hair. They came up fast, but never quite joined, keeping a hundred or more yards to the rear.

"This is like a funeral," The Lamb said to one of his two immediate companions, "and I dunno whether I'm the corpse or the chief mourner."

They looked at him with steady curiosity, because he could jest at such a time, and then the nearest one smiled faintly.

"They's apt to be *one* funeral today," he said, and nodded, and then laughed aloud with his thin lips held close, as one accustomed to ride against the wind.

That wind fell with unusual suddenness as they began to stretch across the range.

When The Lamb spoke of this change, one of the cowpunchers chuckled. "The black horse scared the wind away," he said.

For the stallion went into it with his ears flattened, and his head looking snaky and dangerous. The black clouds above them began to break, and though the sun could not get through, at least it turned some tumbling masses into nebulous puffs and whirls of shining white, so that it looked as though cannon were pouring out white blasts of smoke in heaven.

It was midafternoon as they came to the edge of Beacon Creek. The appointed meeting place had a low bank upon either side; the bottom was flat as the floor of a room, and covered with large, round pebbles. And above the other bank, they saw the men of Colonel Loring, and the colonel himself among them.

When they were sighted, two riders started out down the slope of the farther side. One, by the bulk of him, was Muldoon. The other was a much smaller and rounder form—Lefty Fargo, beyond a doubt. And The Lamb raised his head like a dog that scents danger in the wind.

Old Montague came up to the youngster and beckoned him forward. "We gotta go down and chatter with them for a minute," he said. "They'll want to hear why you're substitutin'."

"Suppose they take a mind to finish you off, now that you're close up to them?" The Lamb asked.

"The big gent is Muldoon. He's an honest fool," said Montague. "Besides, I ain't the kind of a bone that'll be worth picking. It'll be plumb starvation before anybody risks breaking teeth to crack me for the marrow inside. Come along."

They went down into the draw and met the other pair. Muldoon looked huger than ever. He was made almost on the scale of big Jimmy Montague. And when he saw The Lamb he roared with anger. He wanted to know what double-crossing trick this could be. And old Montague gave him a proper answer.

"You came up with the best scrapper on the range," he said, "and you want me to stack my closest heir ag'in' him. That ain't right or nacheral. You bring me up a hired man. Here's The Lamb to meet up with him. Ain't that fair enough to suit you?"

"I've seen rats, and I've seen snakes," said Muldoon, "but I never seen nothing as low as him. Him that bunked in with us, that ate our chuck, that seen the dirty Montague game played . . . him to double-cross us. What's your price, you skunk?" asked Muldoon.

He shook his fist at The Lamb, and the latter shrugged his eloquent shoulders.

"You better keep your talk for a colder day to warm you up," he said. "I've got conversation with the other gent just now."

Muldoon glowered. "You was a better man than me when you played straight, kid," he said. "Everybody saw it, I admit it myself. But now that you've turned crooked, you've turned yellow. I'd eat you up myself, except that here's a surer hand."

He gestured, and Lefty Fargo came forward.

Fargo wore no slicker. He was dressed in a light coat, and his shirt was open at the throat. For Lefty Fargo, like a whale, was lined with fat against the temperature of cold seas. And he was fairly rounded and plumped out with what was beneath his skin. He had pale red hair, and hazel eyes with a touch of red in them, also. He now let his horse drift forward.

"It's The Doctor, after all!" he exclaimed.

"It's the finish for you," said The Lamb with equal geniality. "You've eaten your last steak and topped off your last coffee, old son."

"Fine," said the gunman, and he laughed in an absurdly high, shrilling voice. It was like the shrill bark of a bull terrier. "When do we start?" he asked.

Chapter Twenty-Six

The famous Lefty Fargo always had a parboiled look, as though his skin was as delicate as a baby's, and as though the sun recently had peeled off the epidermis. It was painful to think of what that nose must feel when a finger touched it, or a towel, say. Even his pale eyebrows appeared to be sunburned and painful. But his eyes were always cheerfully bright and his smile was continually happy. The Lamb looked upon him with a hungry grimness, but Lefty Fargo's amiable nature was not at all perturbed by this. His smile continued, and his eyes remained as bright as ever.

"We start now," said The Lamb.

"How d'you want to begin?" Fargo asked.

"Partner," The Lamb said amiably, "it doesn't make any particular difference. I'm ready for you on horse or foot, and with knife, or gun, or plain bare hands, Lefty."

The fat man smiled and nodded. In fact, he could not help laughing in great pleasure, and his shrill laughter rang and pulsed in the air. It ceased to have a human meaning, and began to stab the mind like the cry of an animal.

"I remember the last time that we met up, son," he said. "I said then that we'd meet ag'in. But I thought it'd be even lower down than this."

"We met the last time. You stretched me out," said The Lamb thoughtfully. "But those days I was in school. You were my last teacher, old-timer."

"Was that a diploma that I gave you?" asked the fat man.

"I dunno," The Lamb said. "But since then, I've never been scratched by knife or gun, Lefty. And I've never been downed by hand or fist."

"For a gent that stirs around, that says a

considerable lot," admitted Lefty Fargo. "But things bein' so long distant, I sort of forget what I was teachin' when I was your professor."

"I'll tell you," The Lamb said. "The thing that you were teaching to me that day was accuracy. I'd been working to burn up the world with my speed. I'd been flashing my gun so dog-gone' fast that it pretty near blinded even me. I used to get it out with such a hop that I didn't know where it was gonna go myself. Maybe you disremember that I got in two shots, before you planted me. But your third was better than my two."

"Sometimes it turns out that way," Lefty said. "I take a likin' to you, kid. I took it to you that first time that we met. I was sorry, then, that we had to have words."

"Matter of fact," said The Lamb, "it's a dog-gone' bad failing of mine that I get pretty excited when any gent pulls five aces out of one pack. I dunno how it is, but it always makes me see red. I ain't changed, either."

They smiled at each other with a grim understanding.

"We're gonna have a good chance today," said Fargo, "to find out if you really graduated. We're gonna find out how fast and straight you are."

"We are," answered the boy. "I'm gonna write the answer on you, Lefty. Lord help your big heart . . . it's gonna stop thumping before night."

Lefty frowned. "I been interested in you, sort of," he said with gravity and disapproval. "But the fact is, that I'm turnin' out disappointed before ever you pull a gun out of leather. You talk too much before the job starts. And you blow off a lot of hot air. I'm sorry, kid. But I gotta salt you down. We'll start right now."

"Oh, man," Muldoon said, "I hope that you blow the inside out of the double-crossin' yellow hound."

"His whole insides is what I mean to get," Lefty Fargo said, and he laughed again, that horribly high, shrill laughter. "What suits you, kid?" he demanded.

"I've left the naming to you," said The Lamb. "I've got a rifle, a Colt, and a knife. Or . . . bare hands. You hear me? Bare hands, Lefty."

"I'm an old-fashioned worker," said Lefty. "A six-shooter always has been good enough for the range, and I dunno that it'll be out of place here."

"Lefty," The Lamb said, "nothing could please me more. It was with a Colt that you give me my last lesson."

"A Smith and Wesson," answered Lefty Fargo. "And that's what I pack today."

"The same one, I hope."

"The same one. It'll wear two notches for one man, it looks like."

"How d'you want the party served up?"

"Supposin'," Fargo said, "that we ride these horses off fifty steps, and, at a given word, we whirl 'em around and go for each other, with the guns talkin' on the way? How would that do?"

The Lamb blinked. "Shootin' off the back of a horse with a Colt," he said, "is pretty dog-gone' inaccurate, Lefty, and you know it. I dunno that I want to spoil the black horse, here."

Fargo's lips curled in high disdain. "If that don't suit you," he said, "you name the way."

"Anything suits me," The Lamb responded. "You . . . Muldoon! You stand off and holler when we're to stop the horses. Montague, suppose you holler when we're to begin?"

He jerked the stallion about. The big fellow spun as on a spring, and Lefty Fargo, who had been counting upon the superior agility of his own mustang, bit his lip. Then he turned in order.

They jogged their horses until the shout of Muldoon stopped them. To one side, Monty Montague sat his horse in a lump as the wind parted his mist of beard. His old eyes flamed with a wild fire.

And The Lamb looked to him as he stripped off the mittens from his hands. With the pressure of his knees and with a murmured word, he brought the stallion to a high tension beneath him, ready to whirl in a flash. Then, looking instinctively before him, The Lamb saw a steer on the rim of the high ground, hunch-backed from the cold, head hanging. It had given up the attempt to paw through the encrustation of snow and now it stood waiting for death to weaken its knees. The Lamb understood, and he set his teeth hard. If death came to him, he prayed that it would come suddenly.

Like the howl of a wolf, old Monty Montague yelled: "Shoot, you cowboys!"

The stallion whirled like a dodging cat, and, with guns ready, the big horse controlled only by his knees and the sway of his body, The Lamb found himself brought into line with his target at exactly the same instant that Lefty Fargo turned about to fire. At the speaking of their guns, the hat leaped from the head of The Lamb; he knew that his own first fire was wide, and then the horses lunged forward. Their galloping, as he had expected, made accurate shooting impossible. Two hornet sounds buzzed at his ear, and those quick deaths went by, while he noted with a mute admiration that Lefty Fargo was shooting for the head. For himself, the body would do.

But when he sent in his fourth shot, as the horses neared, the mustang of Lefty heaved itself into the air with striking forehoofs. He saw Lefty himself pitched far back in the saddle, with a yell of fear and surprise, while his own gun was poised, ready to drive the fatal ball home. But the breadth of that helpless beast disarmed him. He dropped the long barrel of his gun across the head of Lefty, instead, and shot by.

Looking back, he saw Lefty sluice like water from the saddle, then strike the ground, and tumble over and over upon it. He was back and dismounted beside him, instantly. It seemed to him that this whole affair was very largely a joke, a horrible jest. There was not the high seriousness that should be about a struggle in which men fight for their lives. They had fired and missed, two experts as they were, and then one of them had been beaten out of the saddle by a bludgeon stroke.

But the fat man looked a serious enough spectacle. His face was patched with white and purple. His teeth were fixed in his lower lip so deep that the blood flowed in a steady stream, and his eyes glared fixedly up to the clouds of the sky.

Old Monty Montague rode up and looked down at the fallen man without dismounting. "That's a fractured skull," he said, "and maybe the end of Lefty. Go back to Loring," he added to Muldoon, "and tell him that this is what will happen to all his hired gunmen, before the finish. This is the biggest scalp that we've took, and it's the begin-ning of the finish."

Muldoon, on his knees beside the prostrate form, returned no answer to the old man, but he glowered sullenly up at The Lamb. "You, and Lefty, and me," he said, "could've gone through 'em like a hot knife through butter. And there you are on the far side of the fence. Go back to your own kind, then, and heaven forgive you."

Loring and two more were coming down to the succor of their fallen champion. Therefore, The Lamb swung into the saddle on the black once more, and with old Montague, he returned up the steep slope to the waiting party on the bank. Then, looking to the side, he saw Louise Patten on her pony, on the crest of a small hill from which she could command an excellent view of the creekbed. She had seen the whole battle, and suddenly The Lamb turned cold with shame.

The proceeding seemed most unheroic. He had gone out like a hired murderer, and tried to take life at the bidding of his employer. He looked deep into his own soul, at that moment, and what he saw made his heart fail.

He was indifferent to the praise that he met all around him. There was Milligan, looking more like a fox than ever as he grinned and nodded.

"That maverick had to take the brand, after all," Milligan said to him.

And old Monty Montague stuck close to his side, and struck his champion on the shoulder with the flat of his hand.

"That's the last chance that they had, and they've used it up for nothin'," he said. "Their boys were pretty down-hearted before. They'll be a sick lot of critters now. The time has come to shake the fruit off of the branch, kid, and you're the sun that's ripened it and got it ready to fall."

Chapter Twenty-Seven

They went straight back to the house and the procession grew on the way. It became a sort of flaunting triumph—there were a dozen men in that group—and then Louise Patten joined them, with His Lordship skipping over the snow crust, through which the horses broke.

She steered through the group and came up beside The Lamb, smiling. "That was a mighty fine thing," she said to The Lamb. "I don't think any other man could have done just that."

Jimmy Montague said without enthusiasm: "I didn't know that you liked the knock down and drag out as much as this, Lou."

"Shut up, Jimmy!" commanded his grandfather. He laughed, and his laughter was like his speaking voice, indescribably harsh and grating. "This here is the way to multiply a hero by two . . . giving him a chance to see a pretty girl smile."

But Louise answered the young Montague gravely: "It wasn't the beating of Fargo, Jimmy. But he could have shot that man and he didn't."

"Shot him?" growled Jimmy. "His gun jammed on him, I suppose. So he beaned him with the barrel of it."

"He changed his mind," the girl said firmly. "I saw!"

Jimmy was silent, looking with a curious interest from the girl to The Lamb, and back at her again, as though he were drawing a most potent deduction.

"Could you tell at that distance?" The Lamb asked.

"I thought I could," she said.

Old Montague threw a clenched fist above his head. He laughed again. "When you think how that flat face, that Loring, is gonna feel!" he broke out. "That's what's milk and honey to me. Boys, it's the damn' end of this here trouble. Inside of a week we'll have 'em swept off the range. We'll have elbow room. They've lost their Lamb . . . they've lost their Lefty Fargo that cost 'em so much money. And old Loring has his back ag'in' the wall. He's got no more money. He's flat. Jimmy, this is where we start our war council."

But The Lamb looked aside in spite of this flattery and met the eyes of the girl, and she smiled back frankly at him. It seemed to him that he was enlarged and ennobled by that glance of hers. He looked at her no more, but inward on his own soul, and upon his own life, where he began to be aware of blemishes that never had troubled him before. All the scars, the brutality, a certain shiftiness at cards, a certain cruel cunning, he was aware of now, and he knew that others were aware, also. What things the world could tell this girl about him, if it chose to gossip.

Blind to the ground before him, he let the stallion carry him on, and all the time he registered and named, one by one, the list of his ill doings. It seemed to him that his crimes were a sort of Tower of Babel, broad-based, and tapering to the top. For he could remember the beginning, when simply to be known as a very dangerous boy had been a delight to him, and when he had rejoiced in the whisper that ever trailed behind him when he walked among his fellows. He had grown up to a more narrow worship of violence. His creed had improved a little; it had lost some of its brutal scope, but growing smaller in field, it had been more burning, it had cut deeper.

These things would come to her ears about him—and she would never know that in this last adventure, at least, there had been a great purpose driving him on, something more than the mere blood lust. So it would be reported to her, and so it would appear—merely the passion for fight, which had drawn him away from his home and brought him into the midst of this feud.

Suddenly they were at the house. He unsaddled the black horse in the stable, and found Jimmy Montague waiting for him outside. The sky was a solid gray again. Thin snow was flying down, blown almost horizontal with the ground. It was far colder than the air through which it fell. It was so cold that it stung the skin like little flakes of fire where it touched. Jimmy walked beside him to the house, silent, head lowered a little in gloomy thought.

Only when he came to the rear door of the house, he paused, and words came out of his bull throat. "Look here, kid."

"Well?" said the Lamb.

"You got your start here, now. You've done pretty fine. The old man is for you. So am I. You gotta chance to have everything that you want. We'll fix you up. You can have what you want out of us. Land. Cows to stock it. Hard cash to start on the side. I don't mean by that, that you can have the whole world with a fence around it."

"What are you ruling out?" asked The Lamb. He looked up into the dark face and the contorted brows of the big fellow and for almost the first time in his life, fear colder than the snow passed into the heart of The Lamb. Not that he doubted his ability to meet this man with weapons, but he felt in Jimmy a dark sea of malevolence that would be capable of producing many marvels of sinister form.

"You can guess what I mean," Jimmy said. "She don't like me none too much. If I win the game with her, it'll only be because I keep the other aces out of the pack. You're an ace with her. I saw that today. So did you." He paused.

The Lamb, strive as he would, could not keep the color from mounting in his face. He wanted to turn his eyes away, but the grim regard of Montague held him.

"Mind you," Jimmy said. "You've done fine so far. You've had the horse out of me. You've got yourself talked about pretty famous. And that's all right. I don't mind that. Only, she's out, y'understand?"

He waited a little. And they stared at one another. It was to The Lamb as though he were facing drawn guns.

"Now," said Montague, "I'm gonna give you some time to think it over. It won't be worthwhile. Turn it back and forth and you'll see that I'm right."

They went up the stairs together, in silence, through the big, dark house, with the stale smell of cookery in the air. In Monty's room they found the head of the clan in person, seated alone, filling his pipe and tamping down the tobacco extra hard.

He smiled at them. His toothless grin was like a horrible scar across his face. His eyes were absent, plotting mischief. He seemed to have the impish spirit of a child, united with the ancient experience of a long and evil life. He finished his task as the two younger men sat down. He dusted the tobacco crumbs from his hands and lit the pipe with care, saying in gasps, through the smoke:

"You two young fools. You look like poison at each other. You got woman on the brain. Like dogs that are dreamin' about a bone. Well, a dog can crack a bone and get at the marrow. There ain't any marrow in a woman. And there ain't anything to her. She's a face. And faces get old and wrinkled. But you take a young girl, there's a freshness about her, and a milky look to the eyes, and a sweet breath like a cow. And the young gents, they figger that she's a saint. I talk to you . . . I know. It ain't the woman that a man loves . . . it's his idea of her. Marriage is the noose with which a woman snags a man, and ties him, and puts her brand on him. And here are you two wantin' to cut each other's throat about that girl. Why, if there's gonna be trouble about her, I'll send her out of here. I'll give her a ticket to Chicago."

"You leave your hands off of her," Jimmy said.

His grandfather glanced aside at him. There was a little pause, and then the old man said: "We want some ideas about how we're gonna handle this here job with Loring. You got any, Jimmy?"

And The Lamb wondered. His esteem for the formidable nature of Jimmy rose, for he saw that the grandfather respected this giant as a physical force, and also as a brain.

"You got the first speech," Jimmy said. "Lemme hear what you got to say. You're the oldest head here. Does he sit in on this deal?" He turned a keen eye upon The Lamb, and the latter could see that jealousy was, for the moment, banished from the mind of the young Montague. He was simply a crafty fox, striving to work out a hard problem.

"What do you think . . . after today?" asked the patriarch. "If he's straight . . . sure . . . we need his head as bad as we need his guns. Go on. He's a part of us, now. He's burned his bridges behind him, today." And he rubbed his hands together. Those hands were eternally blue with cold. Even the summer sun could not warm them. After that, the old man continued: "It seems to me like a pretty easy thing. Any night, now, we can start up the hills and put a net around the house. In a couple of days we'll have it."

Jimmy grunted: "Is that your idea?"

"It's simple," said the grandfather. "But that don't mean that it's bad."

"It *is* bad," Jimmy said.

"You young gents," said Montague, "are always after something fancy."

"You're gettin' old," Jimmy said brutally. "I never seen how old, before this minute."

"You gotta prove that," Montague said angrily.

"Easy," answered the grandson.

Chapter Twenty-Eight

All other things young Al Lamb forgot in his intense interest in this struggle of two generations. They looked at each other, old and young, with the penetrating, cruel eyes of duelists. The Lamb almost forgot that he had at last a priceless opportunity to learn what he had come to this house for—information about the plans of the enemy.

"You think that your idea is worth something," sneered Jimmy. "I'm gonna show you what it's worth."

"You got a fancy idea," repeated the veteran. "You think that you'll play Napoleon. Lemme tell you . . . if you knew the facts, you'd find out that Napoleon was simple, too."

"But not a fool, I guess."

"Am I a fool, young man?"

"You're old," Jimmy said. "You're too darn' old!" Then he went on: "Suppose we scatter out around the house of Loring, what'll happen the next day?"

"Why, most of the yellow-hearted dogs would come right over to us," said old Montague.

"Half of 'em would. But the other half would be enough for us," countered Jimmy.

"We'd range rifle bullets through them log walls, and through and through 'em!"

"Would you? They got them walls sand-bagged," Jimmy said brusquely.

"Ha!" grunted the old man, and was gloomily silent, admitting this point against his plan.

"Behind them sandbags, they could lie snug and blow the life out of us if we tried to rush 'em."

"We'd have the Loring cows!"

"You can't get the Loring cows that way," said Jimmy. "You got an idea that there still ain't any law in this here country. There is."

"A lot of law," sneered Montague. "Law is on the side of the gent with the most cows."

"Law ain't on the side of the gent that's got *all* the cows," Jimmy said. "Right now we got a lot of Loring stuff run into our herd. We got weaners, and all. It wouldn't take no expert to see where a lot of those brands have been changed."

"I had experts run the irons on them calves," said the old man.

"A fine hand can put the irons one by one on a hundred calves, maybe," Jimmy said, "and no court of law could swear to what it had used to be. But a thousand is different . . . and two thousand is a lot more different. There's pretty sure to be a mistake, and one mistake would show up big."

The old man nodded. "You got brains in that big ugly head of yours," he said.

"Leave the ugliness of my head alone, will you?"

"Aw, she wouldn't be stopped by that," said old Montague. "It ain't your homely phiz that would stop the girl, Jimmy."

"Leave her out, too!" boomed the young giant. "I'm talkin' business, now."

"Go ahead, then."

"We gotta be pretty smart. We gotta be foxes. You make a murder party out of this, and it's one thing. You make a cow raid out of it, and they'll have us in prison."

Monty Montague grinned broadly and without much mirth. "This here law . . . it prizes murder more'n cattle lifting?"

"Sure," Jimmy said. "It always has when you take it on a big scale. I mean . . . you shoot one man and you get tried for murder. You take a gang and meet a gang . . . that's a cattle war . . . that's a battle. There ain't any murder about it . . . unless there's a lot of cow liftin' alongside of it. Raid the house, and it's murder. Raid the range, and it's just another cattle war. Then the newspapers gotta chance to talk a lot. Everybody is a hero that ain't dead. Everybody says that something has gotta be done to put down this here sort of business. And there you are. Nothing is done at all."

"You've been free and large, criticizin'," Monty Montague said. "Now lemme hear you step out and talk for yourself some. You can blame me, maybe, but that don't put you in heaven, nor halfway there, even."

Big Jimmy kneeled by the hearth. He took a stick, one end of which was burned, and began to make a sketch upon the floor. The paint fumed and boiled under the burning wood, and the stick point itself crumbled away, but old Montague made no protest. He leaned to the side in his chair and studied the map with a frown, and nursed the big bowl of his pipe in both his ancient hands.

"This here is the Loring house," Jimmy explained. "Now, you look down here. This here is where the three hill ranges branch out. Is that right?"

"Sure. That's right."

"Where they meet makes two valleys."

"Of course. You don't have to tell me what that country is like. Loring has hogged the best part of the range and with no right to have it."

"A man has a right to what he can get . . . and keep," Jimmy advised his grandfather, with the superiority of a more brutal attitude. "Look here. This is the Black Hills, nearest to you. There's the valley head between the end of 'em and the Capper Hills."

"I remember old Capper like yesterday," said the old man. "Him and me used to trout fish, over in them same hills. He loved 'em. He swore that someday he'd strike gold rich in there. There

214

was an old strike of porphyry that stuck its head up above the rest of the rock, and old Capper, he used to say that . . ."

"What has that got to do with what I'm talkin' about?" Jimmy demanded.

The old man rambled on, nevertheless: "He used to swear that that streak of hills would make him rich. Well, he got rich there, well enough, if dyin' and gettin' to the golden Kingdom Come is to get rich. Go on, Jimmy. You talk like you got some sense, today. Woman is all that's the matter with you. Get that girl pried out of your head, and you'd be fair-to-middlin' intelligent."

Jimmy straightened up on his knee and looked with a dark forbearance upon his grandfather. Then he went on slowly. "If you've finished your chatter, this is what comes next. Between the Capper Hills and the line of Mount Solomon, there's another valley head, ain't there?"

"There is, boy."

"Where does the Loring range lie?" persisted Jimmy.

"Why, he claims . . ."

"Damn what he claims. What has he got? Where does he run his cows?"

"Why, between the Capper Hills and the Black Hills on the one side, and Solomon Mountain on the other side."

"He won't run 'em much longer if I have my way," the boy assured him.

215

"Aye? That's good. I like to hear you talk that way, Jimmy. I like the whole way that you talk. I sort of like the attitude that you got about this here thing!" exclaimed old Montague with feeling.

Big Jimmy laughed fiercely and softly. "I know what you like. Fightin'! You could live by it. Well, you're gonna have that, too. You're gonna have everything that you want, out of this here job. What've you been doin' all this time that you and Loring's been growlin' and snappin'?"

"Runnin' cattle off from each other, most of the time," said old Montague.

"What good was that?"

"No good. That's why I wanted to hit right from the heart of the business. Go after his house. And why not? No more trimmin's. But the meat nearest to the heart. That's what I want to do."

"I've showed where that was foolish. Drop that right out of your head, if you got any sense."

"Well?" the old man asked patiently, submissively.

"Here's what we do. We wait for the crack of dawn. Then we ride down across the hills and we plant our boys straddlin' the throats of them two valleys. We plant 'em where there's easy hidin'. I take one half of the boys. And The Lamb, here, he takes the other half." His eyes kindled as he looked across at The Lamb.

The old man nodded and struck his hand upon his knee. "I see it," he said.

"Of course you do," grunted Jimmy. "It's pretty clear now."

"You're between the house and the range," Monty said slowly.

"That's it," broke in The Lamb. "And when the boys come drifting in from the range, they're swallowed one by one. And if there should have to be a shot or two fired, here and there, it wouldn't amount to nothing. The wind would blow the noise away from the Loring house, mostly, and if it didn't, why then they would only think that one of the boys was coming in and was taking a crack at a coyote or a wolf, maybe."

Jimmy smiled with content. "You see what I mean?" he said.

The dusk was gathering through the room, the sordid, swift evening of the winter day. It turned the corners black, and the air seemed stained with soot, through which the firelight struggled and made a yellow glow.

"I see what you mean," said Montague. "And maybe you're right. I've been at the head of things pretty near too long." He was silent for a moment. Then he jerked up his head. "If you was to work this right, Jimmy, I'd step down . . . I'd take a trip to Denver, or some place like that, maybe, and I'd let you have the runnin' of things from this time forward."

"If I'd had the runnin' a long time ago," Jimmy said, "it would've been a sight better for you, and me, and everybody else. You've dragged things out. You're old."

"Aye," his grandfather said, and sighed. "I'm old. There ain't any denyin' of that. I'm pretty old."

The room fell into another thoughtful silence. For all of them were seeing those hills, white with the winter, and the battle that before long might choke the very throats of the two distant valleys.

"You ain't said much, kid," Montague said at last.

"He don't have to talk. He can do something much better than talk," Jimmy said. His voice rose into a sudden exultant booming. "I'll tell you what. He can do better than talk. And if he won't be a fool, if he won't be a darn' fool . . . if he'll work for me and with me . . . I'll take in the whole range, here. I'll swallow it all. I'll make him rich. Him and me . . . we could clean up the whole range. We could swallow it!"

"Maybe you will," said Monty Montague. "I like to hear you young kids talk. Me, I've just broke the ground. Lemme see what you're gonna plant in it."

Chapter Twenty-Nine

Now that the strategy of the camp of Montague had been revealed, The Lamb was in haste to get the news to his friends. No time had as yet been fixed for the raid. Perhaps it would come the very next morning, and if he could place the information in the hands of Colonel Pete Loring, the hunters would be caught in their own trap.

He left the house after supper, and walked out into the night. He found the sky had cleared through the zenith. A broad, white moon was up. The world was one of black and silver. Just east of him he looked at the broad back of the mountain from which he had promised the colonel he would send his signal. No doubt that eyes were straining from the Loring camp, this night, to make out the glow of the double fire.

The Lamb drew his belt tighter, making up his mind to start. He pulled out his watch. The moonlight was sufficiently bright to show him that it was only 7:30 p.m., which would give him ample time to get to the mountain and send the signal, and even confer with the colonel, yet return in time to be in bed at an hour so seasonable that no questions would be asked. He nodded to himself, and dropped the watch back—not into the secure watch pocket, but into the larger pocket at the side of his coat. His mind was traveling too far before him to be troubled by details.

The door slammed, and the voice of Milligan came up behind him.

"You done a great job today, kid. You got yourself a home here, by what you done. What about it? You ain't sorry that you came over, eh?"

The Lamb did not answer. He merely said, after a moment: "The old mountain looks pretty cold, eh?"

"With the moon on the snow," admitted Milligan. "When spring comes up this way, it ain't so bad."

"No, I guess it wouldn't be. The boys still ride that trail even in this weather, don't they?"

"They gotta. Look at the way some of the old cows will work uphill in the snow. They know that somewhere or other they're gonna find a place where the snow has slipped, and that'll give 'em easy feeding."

"I never thought of that."

"You ain't a 'puncher, kid, or you'd know that."

"Maybe. It's a twister, that trail."

"Sure it is," Milligan said. "But it ain't bad going."

"Ain't it? But even in good weather, with no snow on the ground, one of your boys took a tumble off of it last year."

"You mean Will Dunstan?"

"I guess that was his name. I dunno."

"Sure, he took a tumble. I dunno how that happened. Will wasn't a drinkin' kind of a gent. But the best horse will stumble goin' down a trail, and the best 'puncher will sometimes sit too loose in the saddle."

"Where'd he fall?"

"Oh, along there where the trees thin out. You see . . . where the black of the trees thins out a little." He pointed. "The poor fellow, he done a real Brodie. He went down about five hundred feet and hit a nest of black rocks."

"I think I've noticed them. Big fellows!"

"They are. Bad as shark's teeth to fall into. That's where Dunstan dropped."

The Lamb was quiet for a moment, and then he said in rather a hushed voice: "We all gotta find trail's end. We all gotta come to it. Dunstan was his name, was it?"

"It was. He was a good kid. Young. Eighteen, or not much more, I guess. Everybody liked him. Even Jimmy took to him. Jimmy was away, when the accident happened. He took on quite a bit, for him, when he came back and heard the news."

"Wouldn't seem like Jimmy would be much busted up by anything, would it?"

"No, it wouldn't. But I heard him say that Dunstan was the makin's of the best cowboy that ever rode on this here range. Which is talkin' pretty wide and high, when you come down to it, because we got some men around here."

Milligan moved off toward the stable.

The Lamb turned out of the house yard, across the bridge, and hastily swung away through the snow. It was hard going down the hillside. He had to balance as though on skates, for every now and then the snow crust would quiver, and then lunge away from beneath his feet. But when he came to the valley, the going was very good. The crust of the snow held him up, and he could make good time across the hollow and to the rising land beyond. So he started the ascent of the mountain.

Here he kept to the trail. The surface of it had been badly chopped by the hoofs of horses, and the split toes of cattle, and the churned snow had frozen hard again in the most difficult shapes for a pedestrian to cover. Nevertheless, he stuck to the trail, for there alone the sign he left behind him might not be noticed.

He passed the naked region, where only black heads of brush here and there jutted up above the surface of the snow. He entered the region of scattering trees, and a steer heaved up from its bedding down place and stood snorting, puffing out its breath in white clouds of alarm.

So he came to the verge of the solid pine woods, and then he paused. The trail jerked here about a corner of the mountain's shoulder, and he looked down on a bristling mass of dark rocks beneath him. At this point, then, Will Dunstan's horse had stumbled, and Dunstan himself had been cast from the saddle and rolled down to his death. There was no question about the violence of the fall, since it was a very steep shelving slope—so steep that an expert hardly could have climbed it.

The Lamb sighed. Then, absently, he kicked a tuft of frozen snow from before him. The lump rolled straight over the brim and went bounding down with enough violence to start a small current of snow dust behind it. When it came to the midway point, it turned to the right. The snow dust turned to the right, also, and dropped down to the level beneath with a flash of powdered silver.

The Lamb looked after it blankly. Then he started, as a thought drove home in his mind. He caught up a fifty-pound rock whose nose rose above the snow on one side of the trail, and tumbled this down the slope in turn, aiming it with the greatest precision at the group of black rocks beneath. The bulk of this stone broke through the crust of the snow on the slope and started a small slide. Before his eyes The Lamb saw the stone bound to the right, and the sliding snow split and turned to either the right or the left. A moment later, he heard the stone strike with an audible thud, well to the right of the black rocks. The snow crunched down to either side. The black rocks had not been touched by either snow or stone.

At this, The Lamb looked up to the sky with suddenly set teeth, and then looked down again at the slope. However, he was not yet sure. He went a little above the bend and immediately below it, and tried pitching and rolling weights down the hill. In no case would they reach the black rocks. The conformation of the slope just above was such that it acted as the prow of a ship acts on water, turning it deftly to one side or the other. And yet the angles were so gradual that the thing was not apparent to the naked eye.

The Lamb returned to the very point of the bend and there he folded his arms behind his back and stared fixedly down. He was quite certain of one thing, now. No matter how Will Dunstan had died, he had not perished by falling from this point upon the black rocks beneath. He *could* not have fallen upon them, had he chosen to leap out into the air with all his might, bent upon destroying himself. How had he come to die upon those rocks, then? In what manner had he slipped upon them?

From above, he could not have fallen, except from the trail. And yet there he had been found, his head crushed, dead from the fall.

The Lamb turned and looked darkly toward the house of Montague, which arose above the trees in the distance, looking like a black hand that was raised in signal of arrest.

Then he went up the trail, and into the black of

the pine woods. When he had rounded the shoulder of the mountain, the house of Montague was straight behind him, and thoroughly well hidden. Straight before him, although he could not begin to see it, he knew the house of Colonel Loring stood. Therefore, he descended through the woods until he came to a partial clearing. Then he made a fire. It took a good deal of work to raise a bright flame, but he managed it with patience, searching out dried bits of bark, and furnishing himself very largely with the inside rind from the stump of a tree. In this manner he worked up two small fires, with a little space between them. He allowed them to burn for a scant two or three minutes, during which time he remained in the shelter of the woods.

He grew nervous. He pulled out his watch, glanced at it, and made out that it was 8:30. One hour ago he had left the house, and this was very fair progress.

He returned to the fires, extinguished them thoroughly with snow, and then went straight down the side of the mountain toward the valley. It was difficult work. Only here and there the moon gave him good light. He was continually slipping, and crashing into the wet sides of trees. When he reached the valley floor beneath, he was in a very bad temper indeed, but he scarcely had issued into the open when he saw a horseman coming toward him.

The colonel it was, beyond a doubt, but The Lamb slipped back into shelter to make sure.

The rider came straight on across the snow, his horse hanging in its stride, now and again, as its feet slipped, but when he had come very close, the man halted and remained for a moment looking fixedly up the mountainside, in the direction from which the fires could have been seen.

He raised a hand, pushed back his hat, and scratched his head as if in perplexity, and so the moon had a chance to shine fair and full upon the face of Jack McGuire.

Chapter Thirty

But McGuire did not linger. After that moment's inspection, he pulled the head of his horse about, pointed it down the valley toward the house of Montague, and disappeared. From behind him, The Lamb most grimly watched his departure, fingering a Colt the while.

Of all the men in the house of Montague, there was none who he liked so little as Jack McGuire. The man was a brute, with the sign of his brutality stamped broadly and deeply upon his face. Moreover, McGuire hated him, and had shown it plainly. Great uneasiness possessed The Lamb. He bit his lip and shook his head. He would dread greatly returning to the house of Montague and facing the inspection of McGuire, and of other eyes.

How could he explain the condition of his boots, or the bark stains that undoubtedly would be on his coat? He would have to trust to the night, the lateness of the hour, the indifference of the sleepy men, to cover these details, and pray that he might come in for no lasting inspection.

In the meantime, another rider came out of the woods on the far side of the valley, halted for an instant, and then came on with his horse at a trot—a long-legged horse, and a short, heavily built rider. This surely was the colonel, on one of his well-bred horses.

And the colonel it was. The Lamb hailed him before he stepped out from the shadow of the trees. Colonel Loring swung quickly to the ground and advanced with hand outstretched.

"I'm damned glad to see you here, young man," he said. "I have never seen a face that meant more to me."

"Hold on," murmured The Lamb. "You thought that I'd double-crossed you today, when I met Fargo for them?"

"What else was I to think?" asked the colonel.

"And that I'd lit those two fires sort of to draw you in?"

"It might have looked that way. I knew that Montague would pay a good price for me."

"Of course he would," agreed The Lamb. "But not to me. As for Fargo, suppose you look at it this way. It's hard to train a dog not to eat raw meat."

"Fargo was an old enemy. I heard that . . . afterward."

"How is he?"

"Living, thank goodness, but pretty sick."

"Does he blame his horse?"

"He blames his horse, of course. He says that the cards beat him, and not the play. But let Fargo go. I hope he lives. If he doesn't . . . he's been taking his chances, and he's been paid for it in cash, as much as he asked."

In the moonlight, the boy could see the colonel's wry face, and by that he could judge that the price had been very high indeed.

Loring went on: "When I had the chance to get Fargo, I thought I'd better. I figured that maybe he was the man to get rid of Jimmy Montague for me. Then you'd come back to me. And no matter what the Montagues tried, with Jimmy gone, and with you and Fargo working for me, we'd clean 'em off the range."

"Is that what you want?"

The colonel snorted like a horse. "Nothin' else," he assured the boy. "They've hounded me . . . give me a chance to hound them."

The Lamb shrugged his shoulders.

"And when we make up the final accounts,

kid, you'll get your share of the pickings!" the colonel exclaimed warmly.

"Let that drop. I'll pay myself," The Lamb said bitterly. "Suppose you tell me about the way the boys are holding up?"

The colonel hesitated. Then he said: "I'll keep nothin' from you. They're pretty sick. Shorty and Muldoon will fight the thing through with me, but the rest of the boys are pretty sick. They lost most of their heart today, when Fargo went down. We all thought that Fargo couldn't be beaten. He had that sort of a reputation."

"Aye," murmured The Lamb, "the best of 'em drop when the cards are wrong. The others want to quit?"

"They want to quit bad. They're hunting around for excuses. They whine about everything. They growl at the sort of horses they gotta ride. They growl at the sort of chuck they gotta eat. All that any of them want is a chance to exchange a couple of pretty mean words with me, so's they'll have an excuse to quit me cold."

"Leave Muldoon to handle 'em, and you stay close."

"I tried that. They raise the dickens then because they say that I take it easy, while the ranch goes along short-handed. They're pretty sour. They're as sour as vinegar," the poor colonel said. Then he added hastily: "If we can do something quick, kid, there's a chance. They

229

still got the shame of men inside of 'em. They'll fight if they're crowded into it."

"Can they hold off a week?"

"Not more than three days. They'll bust loose on me almost any time. Muldoon lies and swears and promises, but he ain't got any heart in what he says, and they can see that he's only talking through his hat. Kid, you sent for me. Do you find things right at Montague's place?"

"They figure that they got you cooked, and salted, and buttered for swallowing!"

"They got reason for that idea, too."

"They're going to start for you some break of day."

"The house?"

"They'll not tackle the house, they say. Jimmy has a better idea. They'll slide in and get the heads of the passes between the hills, and then they'll bag your gents as they come in off of the range."

The rancher exclaimed in surprise. "Aye, that's an idea," he said.

"You could stop that."

"Sure. By keeping a boy on the top of the Black Hills, day and night, to send out smoke or fire signals to call in the men. But even then, they'd be between us and the house."

"They can't do a thing to you. Scatter your gents in the rocks and the brush, and the Montagues will never run you out into the open."

The colonel sighed. "I wish I could have you for that time," he said.

"You'll have me for that time, I hope," said the boy. "There's only one thing that keeps me hanging about the Montague place, and that's my own business."

"Your own business?" echoed the colonel.

"Why, it's a sort of a little matter about a dead man. That's all there is to it."

The colonel hesitated. But his own affairs were too pressingly important to allow him to diverge from them for any length of time. He said: "What day, kid?"

"I dunno. *Pronto,* though."

"Tomorrow morning?"

"Maybe."

"It cuts me short," said the colonel bitterly. "But I'll do what I can. I'll stand the watch myself till morning."

"Put your boys to sleep and go to sleep yourself," The Lamb assured him. "There isn't going to be a step taken toward your place until the early part of the dawn. It may not be tomorrow. It might be next month. But I don't reckon on that long."

"But suppose," the colonel asked softly, "that we was to round 'em up between the mouth of the valleys and the house, and pepper 'em from both sides?"

"Then," said the boy calmly, "there'd be only a

lot of dead Montagues left under our noses, and a lot of live Montagues running like scared dogs down the valley."

The colonel drew in a very long and slow breath. "I can sort of taste it," he said huskily. Then he began to laugh, and there was also a husky noise beneath that laughter that made the boy think of the sound a dog makes in his throat when its teeth are fixed in the flesh of an enemy. "I've had it a long, long time," explained the colonel, ashamed. "They've had their knives in me. If I only had a chance to get back at 'em. . . ."

"Work steady, and mind the law," The Lamb said. "That's the best way, I take it."

"What care have they for the law?"

"Not much. But always to play safe."

The colonel jerked up his head. "It stands this way . . . if they do what you tell me they'll do, I'm gonna bag 'em, and make them remember this day. And then . . . you and me will have something to talk about together, son."

"That's the finish," The Lamb said. "I'm due back."

"Does anybody suspect you there?"

"They've all been suspecting me. But there's only one that still won't believe that I'm with them. That's Jack McGuire."

"Be careful. Be mighty careful of that 'breed," said the colonel.

"You know him?"

"Oh, I know him . . . but a long ways back. He's a cross between a carrion buzzard and a bloodhound. There never was a better man on the trail, son . . . keep him off of yours."

The Lamb touched the handles of his Colt instinctively. "Thanks," he said. "I'll keep that in mind, Colonel."

"If they get a doubt about you," explained the colonel, "you're dead. And I'm ruined. If you can keep the wool over their eyes until they tackle me in the way they've planned, then we'll bucket 'em to pieces without any trouble at all."

"It'll be a barbecue," said The Lamb.

"Then good night, son."

"Good night," The Lamb said. He paused and added: "You couldn't drop a word in the ear of Muldoon, could you? He's pretty hard on me, just now."

"There's nothing I'd rather do. If he and the rest of the boys knew that you were down there working for me, they'd be greatly bucked up. But as sure as one of 'em knew, the rest would all know, and as sure as they all knew, then the word would get straight down to the Montagues."

The Lamb agreed. They parted at once, and, as the colonel started back for his ranch, The Lamb turned up the valley, keeping close to the edge of the trees, where their steep shadows would cover him. However, he saw nothing in the open, and he came straight back to the Montague house without hearing human sound. He crossed the bridge unchallenged, only at the rear door of the house a voice barked out of the darkness suddenly, and Jack McGuire stood beside him.

Chapter Thirty-One

The warning that the colonel had given him fitted exactly with The Lamb's own sense of things, and, therefore, he did not doubt a most pointed danger from McGuire. Moreover, from the first, he felt an absolute repulsion for this dark-browed fellow.

"Where've you been?" from McGuire.

"Walking,"

"Walkin' where?"

"Where I felt like going."

"Is that any answer?"

"It's all you'll get."

From the hand of McGuire a flare of light sprang into the face of The Lamb. Then the lantern was slowly lowered, so that it shone on the clothes of the wanderer. "You've been in the brush," said McGuire.

"Of course I have."

"What for?"

"Walking the idea of Lefty Fargo out of my head."

"Hey?"

"You wouldn't understand. Pork and beans is about as far as you could get. I had Fargo on my mind. I wanted to walk him out of it, so's I could get some sleep."

"Bah!" McGuire said. "That's likely, ain't it?"

"What's likely?"

"That you'd be nervous about anything. There ain't any nerves in you."

"Are you through?" The Lamb asked suddenly. "Because if you ain't, I am."

"I'm night watch," said Jack McGuire, and he grinned with triumphant pleasure.

"You're crazy," The Lamb said.

"Am I?" answered McGuire. "I'm the crazy kind that's gonna toast you on the coals, kid. I'm tellin' you that. Go on in. I'm tired of talkin' to you."

With that, The Lamb was released, and he went into the house with a gloomy and downward head. All was far from what he could have wished it to be.

The door of the big dining room was open. He saw blue wisps of cigarette smoke mixed with heavy clouds from many pipes. Some of the boys were in there talking over the day, and he paused to listen, for he had an idea that he might hear something of importance about himself.

A drawling, nasal voice was saying: "She was about a four-year-old. She was layin' down in a bare path, and the heat of her belly was turnin' the dirt to mud under her feet. The snow and the sleet was caked across the hollows of her back and I seen that her vitals would be freezin', the first thing she knew. I was dead fagged . . . I'd been tailin' 'em up all day till my arms was about pulled out at the sockets. My pony was gettin' a little smoky, too. There'd been several pairs of horns throwed his way, that day.

"But I got down and got after that old fool of a cow. I worked like the dickens. Her tail cracked . . . I thought I was pullin' it in two. But, finally, with her bawlin' her head off, I heaved up the rear end of her. She stumbled onto her feet, and swung around on me. That spilled her down on her knees ag'in. But she was so ornery mean and mad that she come up ag'in and after me. I dived for the pinto. Dog-gone' him, but he side-stepped me, and then bolted. I lit out for the next tree. It was about five miles off, seemed to me, and that dog-gone' cow run like a greyhound after me. I was more greyhounder than her, though. I got so all-fired light that just her breath was enough to blow me along ahead of her. I didn't weigh no more than a dead leaf. So when I come under that tree, I heaved myself up and caught hold of a branch about thirty feet off'n the ground, just as the critter's horns split the seat of my trousers.

"The bawlin' that cow done then was more'n I ever heard the like of before. She horned the tree. Her bellowin' shook the snow off the branches. But pretty soon the pinto come wanderin' along that way, pawin' off the crust of the snow and chawin' at the grass. He seen me and started laughin', and when the cow seen him with his mouth open, she hilted her tail and tore after him. I climbed down out of the tree and started for . . ."

"I remember a time when I was down in the Big Bend," broke in another voice, "and while I was there, I met up with a gent by name of Cozy Dolan."

"Was that Dolan of the Double Bar Y?"

"Naw, that was his cousin. This gent had a broken nose. Come to think of it, Fargo was the gent that busted his nose. Dropped him, and then stepped on his face. Polite, was Fargo."

"He ain't gonna use no more bad manners."

"Nope. The Lamb seen to that when he wrapped the barrel of that Colt around his head. I seen it sink right in. If Fargo ain't brained, his skull is made of India rubber."

"Why didn't the kid blow the roof off'n his head?"

"Why? I dunno."

"Aw, I do. You take The Lamb . . . suppose he was to chaw up all the fightin' men on the range, what'd there be left for him to do? Nothin'! He'd have to sit around and twiddle his thumbs. He'd have to go out bare-handed and jump into a cave full of rattlers, or sashay up and bat a grizzly mama on the nose. So he's savin' up the good men on the range. You get a good book and you can afford to read it twice over, can't you? He's got that idea. Keep workin' on the gunmen, till the scars begin to sort of overlap. The Lamb says . . . 'A scar beside a scar is neighborly . . . but a scar on top of a scar is damn' beggarly.' "

The Lamb moved on. There was a rough friendliness in this conversation that was all that he could ask. So he went to his room, lit the lamp, and sat down on the edge of his bed, to think. The crisis was gradually approaching, now. In this one day, he had met and beaten Lefty Fargo and had thereby established himself in the esteem of the Montagues. He had heard the careful plans of big Jimmy for the attack. He had told those plans to Colonel Loring. But, most of all, he had learned that Will Dunstan had not fallen to the black rocks in the manner by which he was supposed to have met his death. Yet report had it that the body had been found there, and the horse of Dunstan had been discovered grazing along the edge of the trail above just as if nothing had happened.

It seemed a perfect deduction that Dunstan had been bucked from the saddle, or in some manner lost his seat, and then had fallen to the big rocks below. That deduction was wrong, as The Lamb had proved. And even if Will Dunstan had leaped with all his might from the trail straight out into the air, his falling body must have struck the bank and shelved either to the right or to the left.

The Lamb pondered upon the mystery gravely. But there was one inevitable conclusion that seemed to stare him in the face. If Dunstan could not have fallen there from the trail, then either he had fallen to some other place and been dragged there, or else he had fallen from his horse upon the rocks, and the horse afterward had gone grazing up the mountain to the trail just above the accident.

But that hypothesis was not tenable by any except the wildest chance. The slope was sheer. The way around to the trail was both long and difficult, leading up through thick trees at the end, and it was asking too much of the most agreeable imagination to think that it could see the pony climbing of its own will.

The remaining deduction was the most interesting of all. If the horse did not get up to the trail of its own volition, then it was led there by some human hand. And it would not have been placed there except to cover murder. Murder had been done, and Will Dunstan had died by the hand of some man.

The Lamb stood up straight and glared fiercely before him. Then, mastering himself, he began to undress, pulling off coat and shirt automatically, frowning all the while. His wet boots stuck to his socks, but at last, after much soft swearing, he was ready for bed, and picked up his coat to take his watch out and wind it—the last act of every day.

The coat felt a shade light to his touch—and the watch was not in the watch pocket. He tried the side pocket. It was not there. With an exclamation of annoyance, he began a systematic search through his trouser pockets, through his coat and vest, even the shirt breast pocket in which he kept his sack of tobacco.

The watch was not there, and suddenly The Lamb's eyes widened and filled with fear. He shook his shoulders, like a dog getting out of water, then he rolled a smoke and took a turn up and down the room, whistling noiselessly, forcing his thoughts to other things. Only when the cigarette was finished, he sat down again, folded his arms, and looked straight before him with a piercing concentration. And with all this direct effort, he could recall nothing, except that he had noted the time in the woods on the mountainside.

He picked up his clothes to dress again, but then dropped them. After all, he dared not risk another expedition into the night, when the first one had been performed at such extreme cost of danger. When he had determined upon this, he brushed the affair from his mind, rolled himself in his blankets, and stretched upon the bed.

Sleep came slowly down upon him. He heard

the creaking of the old house in the wind; he heard the voice of the wind itself in a lonely monologue that passed continually from the north to the south. And still from time to time the electric spark leaped in his mind—Will Dunstan had been murdered, foully murdered, and only he, of all men in the world, knew it.

At last, the darkness of sleep closed over his mind, and not a dream visited him from that moment until the full light of the day dropped in through his window. It was no very strong light. The sky was sheeted across, again. The snow fell slowly, wavering down in almost perpendicular lines. And when he looked out the window, the lightest puff of wind was strong enough to raise a white cloud, like a cloud of dust, and drive it far away. The woods smoked with that flying snow powder, and all the hills were pure and soft with new white. He dressed in haste. He was overdue, he felt, on the mountainside.

Overdue, indeed, for Jack McGuire was long before him at that post.

Chapter Thirty-Two

To Jack McGuire had been given the one talent that he despised. He could follow a trail almost like a wild animal. If the nose of a dog and the sight of a hawk had been combined, that union hardly would have produced more flawless work upon the trail than was exhibited by McGuire.

But he knew that the Indian is in this respect incomparably beyond the white. He knew that his own talent was directly derived from his Indian ancestry, and he felt that every exhibition of skill that he made upon the trail really was a confes-sion of the baser mixture in his blood.

Therefore, he refused to do work that required a continual exhibition of his special talent. It was only on special occasions that he would draw upon his peculiar skill, as he drew upon it now. For McGuire had learned to hate The Lamb, as inferior and spiteful natures are bound to hate those who are above them. The half-breed usually inherits the faults of the races that are united in him. And, whatever may be his other virtues, he never is magnanimous.

So it was with Jack McGuire.

He had to dress the wound on his head once a day, and the time he chose for that work was naturally the morning. So that every day was given a bitterly unpleasant beginning. He never lay down at night or rose in the morning without promising to himself a cruel and a lasting satis-faction for the wrong that The Lamb had worked upon him.

Sometimes, in the earlier days, he had told himself that when he could take The Lamb at a serious disadvantage, then, with knife, rope, or gun, he would attack him and destroy him, and gain both glory and sweet revenge by that action. But after he witnessed the fall of Lefty Fargo, he confessed that the man was beyond his reach.

It was malice deeply felt for The Lamb that awakened McGuire long before the dawn began on this morning. The pain of that envious hatred throbbed in his heart, and he got up half stifled from his bed and sat in the dark, smoking a cigarette, and scowling as the glow of the fire ate up the tobacco to the butt. Then he pinched out the coal, and, looking through the window, he saw the first pencil stroke of gray in the east. Or, rather, he saw what the mountains had turned to a more visible blackness.

When he was sure of this, McGuire went outdoors, where it was easier to breathe. Houses were to him prisons. The fullest arch of the sky was necessary to enable him to be his best.

It was long, long before the day's work would begin. He scowled at the thought. And then he remembered how he had seen the double eye of fire upon the side of the mountain the night before, and how that double eye had suddenly gone out.

Utter malice against The Lamb had roused him so early. Mere chance sent him out to examine the fires. But how his heart would have leaped, had he guessed that the two impulses were working together to the end that he prized most dearly.

He went to the corral. Most of the horses were up. The last of those who remained lying, now pitched to their feet and lurched around the enclosure, while he spread his loop. He roped a gray that belonged in the string of Milligan, first of all. Finally he caught a tough little roan, his proper horse, and, saddling that wicked mustang, he led him into the open, then mounted. The roan was full of kinks, and they had to be worked out, but Jack McGuire could have ridden a mountain lion without a saddle, and he warmed up the roan with whip and spur in the semi-darkness of the dawn. Then he rode out across the bridge and journeyed down to the valley.

The snow was beginning to fall slowly, fluttering down so softly, indeed, that it felt like the touch of feathers on his leathery face, on his hands. McGuire hated it. It was covering up any trail.

He went straight to the point at which he first had seen the two bright eyes of the fire. Then he worked into the woods. The dimness was altered. The gray morning was there, and although the light was not good, still it was sufficient for the half-breed to begin his work. Just as an eager scholar strains his eyes late in the evening, too intensely drawn on to pause and make a light.

McGuire scouted up the valley and down a little way. Then he entered the woods, leaving the horse with thrown reins in the open. He moved in a little circle, scanning the snow, the trunks of the trees, the branches around him. He worked slowly, for the light was insufficient, but he worked with all his senses.

His step was as light as the step of a hunting cat. His foot came down toe first, in a gliding movement, and now and again he paused, while his dark, bright eyes flashed from side to side. He was smiling. In the intense joy that this occupation gave him, every faculty was aroused to a tingling delight, so that the dark ugliness of McGuire left him, and he appeared beautiful.

He stole through the first circle. He went half-way through the third when, under the verge of the trees, he found tracks in the snow. He dropped upon his heels instantly, and leaned above them. The fresh snow almost had filled the hollows. He blew, and the white fluff was driven out. The impression that remained was wonderfully fresh and clear, with the snow crumbling a little at the upper edges, as a mold in coarse sand will do. The delight of the half-breed in this discovery was such that he stretched out his hands to it, like a miser over his gold, like a frozen man to the heat, like a child to a pet.

Then he saw that this was the impression made by a man's foot, and that the foot was clad in a cowboy's boot, that the boot was new—because of the crispness of the pattern of the heel—that the boot was equipped with spurs, and that the spurs had small rowels.

He sat back a little, and smiled again, and swallowed, as though he were tasting and retasting his pleasure. Then he stood up and made a stride, bringing his foot down parallel with the imprint in the snow. He took another and another. Then he went back and had regard to the corresponding series of impressions left in the snow by the stranger. He could make other deductions—that this man was of more than middle height and that he was in weight probably between a hundred and seventy and a hundred and eighty pounds. Unless his stride was longer or shorter than his inches suggested. He was a young man, too. For a youth lets his weight rest longer, springing on the toes, while an older man keeps the heel down more, and does not use the spring of the toe so much.

McGuire discovered these things. Then he went on the forward trail far enough to make sure that the pedestrian had gone straight on down the valley. At the end of that valley the half-breed saw the house of Montague rising up darkly against the blossoming eastern sky.

That home trail could be followed at leisure, at another time. But now he turned back and made a cut for sign in a big loop. Straightway, he found his own tracks, where he had ridden home the night before, and crossing them, at a slight angle, those of a rider coming, and a rider going. He dismounted. The same horse had made those prints, he discovered when he had blown the newly fallen snow out of the sign. There was a bar across the left fore shoe for proof that he was right. Someone, then, had ridden across his line down the valley. When? And had he anything to do with the pedestrian? Or was it the same person —who had, perhaps, thrown the reins off his horse on the edge of the woods?

He compared, carefully, the trail of his own horse with that of the trail that crossed it, and he made sure that the two must have been made at almost the same time.

This was a small point. But he was overlooking nothing. In the composition of a trail story, the details are not picked and assembled beforehand. Out of a thousand incoherent and trifling things, two or three may point in a significant direction.

He followed the line of the horse trail close to the woods. There the horse had halted for a little while. The man had not dismounted. That was proved, because if he had done so, the horse either would have stood motionlessly, or else it would have ranged a little to one side or another. Probably it would have edged in toward the trees to nibble at the brush.

However, instead of this, he found that the hoof prints were scattered close together, as though the animal had shifted from leg to leg, restlessly, as a horse will do, when there is a weight in the saddle. At length, it had swerved sharply around, the snow was scuffed deeply away where the forehoofs had rested last—and the horse had gone off across the hills—in what direction?

The half-breed followed for a little distance—far enough to see that the general line of the rider extended toward the house of Colonel Loring. However, as he had failed to follow up the trail of the pedestrian, so he failed to follow up the trail of the horseman. He had made sure that they were not the same. Now he wanted to learn, if he could, why they had met, since met they had, to judge by the thick swarm of footmarks near where the horse had been held immobile.

And did either of these men have anything to do with the double fire, which, like the eyes of a great, angry snake, had glared out through the dark woods at Jack McGuire the night before?

He mustered his information, ran over it in his mind, made sure that it was all lodged securely in his memory, and then he went forward into the woods, carefully following, in the growing light, the back track of the pedestrian, into the trees. It was perfectly simple for McGuire. The light was quite clear now, and he was able to take the track back to a point high up on the side of the mountain, where he found that the trail spread again, and left many footmarks in a small clearing. From that clearing, he could look out over the heads of the trees, and, so doing, he was able to make up his mind that it was at about this point that he had seen the fires glowing.

However, there should be ways to make sure. The surface of the snow looked regularly crusted, except that toward the center there was a slight depression. He leaned and touched it— behold, the snow was soft and unjoined. He dipped his hand deeper, and withdrew it with a smear of soot upon the tips of the fingers.

Chapter Thirty-Three

Having first touched the telltale soot of the fire, McGuire straightway removed the upper surface of the snow and laid bare the fire level. It was small. There were only a few charred sticks. That would have been enough for most searchers, but McGuire was not content.

He began to move again over the surface of the snow, patting it with his hands, until it gave way a trifle. At that point he worked again, and uncovered another fire site, exactly like the first, for the last heat of the embers had slightly melted the snow that had been heaped upon them and the roof of the little cavern gave way under the weight of his hand.

He had found the two fires that had gleamed at

him the night before, and a certain peace fell upon the soul of Jack McGuire. For this had been the sole task that he had set himself in leaving the house. It was now time to return, if he were to get to the Montague place in time for breakfast and the start of work.

But still he lingered, for there was much that he wanted to do. For one thing, it would have satisfied the very cockles of his heart to know the identity of the man who had laid this fire. There was already no hope of tracing him down the valley, because the fall of the snow had by this time covered every trace of a footfall. However, he kicked at random in the snow about the fires, in the hope of turning up something of interest, and presently his toe connected with something that flew away in a yellow-gleaming arc and struck the trunk of a tree with a slight crash.

He followed, almost over-awed by such luck, and picked up a thin, gold watch. The crash had smashed the glass covering the face to bits, but the blow that his toe had given the watch had started it running again. He held it to his ears. At first, in his excitement, he could not hear a sound. But presently he made out the clicking of the smooth and perfectly balanced escapement, softly muffled by the skill of the maker.

The half-breed grinned with joy. Keen as his senses were, cunning as his hands could be, there was a patient and wise craft represented by this watch that his strong fingers, or the fingers of all his race never could have rivaled. He held it on the hard palm of his hand, smiling down at it, rejoiced. It was as though he expected that small voice to spell out to him the name of its owner.

He saw the second hand turning with a rhythmic flow; he marked that the watch face told the hour of half past eight. But, most of all, the dainty workmanship of the second, the minute, and the hour hands fascinated him. So odd did it seem to him that human wits could have found such splinters—that human patience and craft could have shaped each tiny morsel to an arrowhead. Let those arrows point him, then, to the owner of the watch!

The watch said 8:30, though it had been stopped for a long time. Having been plunged into the snow, perhaps the intense cold had stopped it—by congealing the oil—in a very short time. The hands now marked, therefore, the approximate hour at which the owner had dropped his watch, and had built these fires. In fact, McGuire could distinctly remember that he had seen the gleaming of the double eye at about that time.

When he was reassured about this, he put the watch inside a twist of paper, arranging it so that there was no pressure against the hands, and when he had done this, he put it carefully into his pocket. Then he started up the back trail from the fire.

It led onto the trail above him, where it angled around the mountainside. The trees successfully shut away the snow up to that point; on the trail itself, the footmarks disappeared, but they seemed to have turned off from the lower side, as though the walker had been climbing the hill.

McGuire sighed. There would have been much interest in pursuing those tracks in the snow, but at that moment there was a downward flurry so thick and white that it was like the waving of dense moth wings about him, and he knew that one such moment as that would be enough to obscure the deepest of tracks.

This thick rush of snow faded. He could look again over the tops of the trees and down to the white of the valley with its border of black pines. In that valley he saw a horseman coming from the direction of the Montague place. He looked again, and knew that this was the great black stallion that had been the pride of Jimmy— that now was the property of The Lamb.

The bitter heart of the half-breed swelled again with fury and envy. He even reached for his rifle, and a question leaped instinctively into his mind: What was this idler doing abroad, so early in the morning, and why had he come there?

It was not that he immediately connected The Lamb with what he had found. For the moment he had even forgotten the details of the return of The Lamb the night before. Only deep, bitter malice kept McGuire watching, until he saw the rifle of the lonely rider uncased, flashing like a sword in his hand, then tipping to his shoulder.

Cowering for an instant in dread, the half-breed stared upward. Certainly a rifle would reach to him—but, no, the rifle barrel—he could tell at even that distance—was not pointed at him, but at some loftier object.

He saw neither spurt of fire nor tuft of smoke. But he did mark the wide-ranged flight of a hawk, tipping smoothly into the teeth of the wind, and he saw that hawk drop suddenly over to one side and turn clumsily in mid-air like a creature of the pedestrian earth, and then hurtle downward—a mere lump of flesh and feathers.

The Lamb was practicing his hand. And, with a swift guess, McGuire estimated the distance to the hawk from the boy, and shuddered. To him, there was something miraculous in the swift and accurate shot. It did not occur to him that there was any large element of luck or of chance in such shooting, but he told himself that The Lamb could strike what he pleased. Skill and magic lived in the magazine of his rifle.

With that in his mind, McGuire was seized with dread lest the boy should encounter him alone in the wilderness. He could remember, now, the insolence with which he had spoken to this destroyer of men the night before, and the fear that fell upon him was colder than the cold that is pressed against the face of the earth by the accumulated weight of the winter snows.

Down the side of the mountain he scurried as a squirrel scurries, frantically crossing a clearing among the trees when it dreads lest the yellow eye of the lynx be concealed among the brush. He gained the bottom of the slope and there found that his horse was waiting heedless of the brush before him, where he might have nibbled here and there, but with downward head, glazed eyes, hanging lip, completing the sleep from which its master had roused it this morning.

The half-breed sprang into the saddle, and roused the mustang to full gallop at the same moment. He angled the swift little horse straight up the valley under the lee of the trees, then pulled him across the flat, with the snow flying up in clotted lumps and thin mists above his head, and drove into the verge of the pines on the farther side.

There he paused, chilled to the marrow of his bones. And again and again the picture of the death of the hawk sprang back into his mind, made clearer, and magnified with dreadfulness, until it seemed it had been his own winged soul that had been smitten in the midst of the snow-streaked sky and brought tumbling down through the air.

But no great black horse came up the valley. McGuire bit his lip with relief, and his blood began to stir again, stimulated with the old malice, the old hatred, which is the most potent mover of the heart. The valley was empty and his way home was secured.

Yet he chose to enter into the woods and there work his path, snake-like, among the trees, weaving constantly back and back toward the Montague house.

At last he felt that he was sufficiently past the danger point at which he had seen The Lamb to come to the edge of the trees again and look out. When he did so, he still saw nothing except the wide, flat face of the valley.

Then, far up the mountainside, he saw the beginning of a small snowslide, widening from a narrow trail to a broadening front, cutting down to the blackness of the mountainside. It struck a belt of strong trees, and the movement was at once extinguished there.

That was all the half-breed saw, before he turned the head of the mustang definitely toward the ranch house, and rode fast for home, and for breakfast.

Chapter Thirty-Four

The half-breed had lost all sight of The Lamb because the latter had turned straight aside from the floor of the valley and gone into the trees.

He was not urged to this change of direction

because he wanted to escape from the fall of the snow. His skin was not perhaps as leathery as that of the half-breed, but now he was on a trail the pursuit of which excited him so much that he forgot such paltry details as the weather.

He went steadily up through the pines, the ground rising gradually before him, until he came to that point where the downward sweep of the mountainside definitely joined the more gradual lift of the valley floor. And there he found the big, black rocks that he had noted from the trail above the day before.

It was not actually a clearing, but the trees were sparse, here—growing more thinly than on the edges of the valley or than higher up the slope of the mountain itself. And the reason for this thinness was simply the continual downward-brushing hands of the snowslides, and the shower of great boulders that, from time to time, thundered down the mountain and heaped themselves along its foot.

In such a spot as this, where the rocks broke down and kept back the trees, there was sure to be a good deal of grass growing in thick, rich lines and ridges, here and there. And the wise cowboy would have to look into such corners for strays from his herd. He looked up the slope, and he made out that the bulge of the mountain side above the rocks, almost imperceptible from above, was absolutely indistinguishable from below. At this sight, his heart quickened a little, for it was a notable confirmation and reënforcement of his theory.

Suppose, then, that Will Dunstan had been murdered by a blow—a blow from behind as he rode by these rocks. Then the murderer, glancing up, would see the trail above him—for there was the trail in plain sight, a narrow shoulder stretched across the white of the mountain side. Surely there was nothing more natural than for a man to put two and two together. There was the trail, here were the rocks. The dead man had perished, therefore, by a fall from the trail. How many have died in the same way before him.

And with that thought the killer arranges the body among the rocks—makes sure that blood appears upon one surface—tears the clothes as though rocks had rent them on the descent—throws dust and pebbles upon the prostrate form—places it in a crushed and limp position, as though the weight of the fall might have broken many bones and brought instant death. Then the destroyer takes the dead man's horse, winding back with it to the foot of the trail, and climbs up to the point above. There he leaves it, with thrown reins. The thrown reins will keep it there, and yet they might have been thrown unconsciously by the hand of a man pitched suddenly from the saddle.

Now and then, there is a degree of certainty

that comes to one like the solution of a proposition in geometry. It is not only felt to be the truth, but the ocular demonstration of the truth is here before the eyes.

With such a perfect conviction, then, The Lamb regarded his surprise. But still he wished to make surety doubly sure. He dismounted. There was the stump of a tree nearby, rotted in the center, surrounded as always by a rim of hard, sound wood. A slab of that rim he tore away, and, using it for a shovel, he removed the snow that extended before the front of the rocks. He discovered, at once, that there was a healthy thickness of grass beneath, growing in the interstices of a species of soft soapstone, as it seemed to him, which came to the surface.

He cleaned away a considerable surface until he came, at length, to the imprint of a horse's hoof. He paused to admire the distinctness of the imprint in that yielding rock surface. He even could make out two or three of the nail holes in the shoe. He could tell that it was a hoof for the off forefoot, as well. Idly analyzing the mark, he made sure that few ordinary cow ponies could have left that sign. They had not hoofs of such a size; they had not the bulk to stamp such a mark in the rock, soft though it was.

He leaned above it, still half idle in his interest. The Lamb was no miracle worker, no Jack McGuire of the trail. There was a tiny spot of red in the indentation that the shoe of the horse had made. It was like a blood stain, and the blood had been shed here.

He straightened with a sudden shudder, and a sickness at the heart, and glanced over his shoulder into the woods. Then he returned to the mark of the hoof. For it seemed to him that the red stain had a mysterious meaning—though, of course, blood of the last autumn it could not be.

He scratched at the red, and the color crumbled to nothing beneath his touch, but there came away on the nail of his finger the tough fiber of a leaf. It was a bit of autumn leaf, then, that had been imprisoned there on the rock by the stamp of a horse. Then he remembered that the girl had told him the death of Will Dunstan occurred when the autumn leaves had begun to fall. And the imprint of this hoof had been made at that very season of the year. It was the horse that Dunstan rode that had made the mark, then, or the horse of one of those who had found the missing body, or else it was the horse of the murderer that had made this mark.

One thing at least The Lamb could do. It was true that many horses wore shoes of almost the same size, but usually there was a slight difference between one and the other. This shoe, for instance, was certainly of a big spread and a heavy make. And he could reasonably hope that if he found the horse that had made such a mark upon the ground, the rider of that horse would have been one of the cowpunchers who had found the body, or else Dunstan himself, or the murderer.

And, at that last hope, the heart of The Lamb rose in him. He took from his pocket an old envelope, opened it, and made a tracing of the shoe. So perfect was the imprint in the rock that the tracery came out clear and perfect, also. He folded the envelope, so that the tracery might be on the inside of it, and then he carefully restored it to his pocket.

He continued to clear away the snow, but he found nothing else of importance. Here and there the surface of the yielding soapstone seemed to have been scarred, but he could not find anything that could be called a distinguishing mark.

When he determined that it was useless to hunt here any longer for sign, he took the trouble to shovel the snow roughly back in place, with the assurance that the present downfall would soon cover all the remaining signs of his presence at the spot.

That was an item of some importance, for the murderer might still live near—he might even be on the Montague place. And, if that were the case, a morbid curiosity would perhaps bring him back to the spot again and again. What if the man returned and found such evidence?

The Lamb remounted the black stallion and rode out from the trees, turning up the valley. He went on until he came to the spot at which he had left the woods, after lighting and extinguishing the fires. Then he left the stallion and climbed up to the site of the fires, for he was reasonably sure that it was there he last had looked at his watch, and it was there he might find it again, in the snow.

In the clearing, the snow had covered everything over with a fine, thick powder. It was very dry with cold. A mere breath lifted it into the air again. And through this he scuffed about here and there.

In a few moments, he began to realize that it was a hopeless task. And he retired to the side of the clearing, like an actor from the center of the stage, in order to think for a moment, and make some sort of a plan, if he could, before resuming the search. To go over the snow inch by inch would take hours. Perhaps even then the search would fail, for he could not be sure that he actually had lost the timepiece here. He must remember when he looked at it last.

He sighed. Like most thoughtful men, he looked down, and upon the crisp surface of the snow at his feet he saw a neat little round impression. It was the very size of his lost watch. And if a watch were dropped here, just such an impression it would be apt to make upon the crusted surface, for here the thickly spreading branches of the pine tree sheltered the ground from any precipitation, except that which might be blown or drifted beneath it. And the windless fall of this morning fluttered straight down to the ground.

He leaned to peer at the spot, and then, just behind it, he saw something glittering in the dull morning light even more brightly than the crystals of the snow surface. He touched them, and prickles of sharp glass came away, clinging to his fingertip. Then, greatly excited, he swept into his palm all the broken shards that he could find. One fragment was a quarter of an inch wide and from this he could make sure that it was in fact a watch crystal.

This was beyond any human doubt a relic of his watch, and yet he could have sworn that nothing he had done could have broken the timepiece. Certainly a fall into the snow would not have been sufficient.

There was a footprint not a foot from the spot where the watch had fallen. He made one of his own beside it, and instantly his heart leaped into his throat, half choking him. For that footmark was not his own. It was a shorter shoe, a broader toe, a heavier heel that had driven into the snow here. And, in that instant, The Lamb knew that he had been followed to this spot, and that his watch must surely have been found, and broken, and carried away.

He went sick with the knowledge of it, for he

understood most surely that the bearer of that watch could easily learn from it his identity— the identity of The Lamb himself. And once that was known, perhaps the Montague Ranch would be no safer to him than a den of rattlesnakes.

He stumbled down to the edge of the trees, and the sight of the black horse was more to him than a safe conduct signed by a king or twenty sheriffs of the Wild West. For the stallion meant secure flight, and the whole panic-stricken heart of The Lamb yearned suddenly to swing into the saddle, and ride, and ride, in a straight line, away from the curse that lay on these mountains, and into some other region where the air was freer and purer. He even grasped the withers, sprang up to the saddle, and turned the head of the stallion away.

And then he remembered. He remembered Colonel Loring's fat ugly face, and the invincible good humor of the rancher's spirit, his courage, his gentleness, his peculiar wisdom. And he had devoted himself to that cause. But the other and the greater impulse that drew him back was the cause of Will Dunstan, who had been murdered, surely, there by the black rocks. So, fighting against himself, his better nature slowly conquering the worse, he turned the head of the big horse again.

At this, the ears of the black flicked forward, as though he well knew the road toward him. He whinnied softly, and pressed at a half canter against the bit. The Lamb let him have his head. And forward they flew up the valley, with the clots of snow leaping up, and hanging for a moment like small white birds above their heads. The wind of that gallop made the falling snow whip at the face of The Lamb. This roused his blood, and it raised his heart, and so he came on a sweating horse into the stable yard of the Montague place.

Ray Milligan, with his smiling lips and his bright, unsmiling eyes, met him. "Hey, where have you been this time of day, sleepy?"

"Working some of the belly off of the horse," The Lamb returned carelessly, and went on into the stable without looking back. But he did not like that question, nor the penetrating glance of Milligan that he could feel behind him, probing at his back.

Chapter Thirty-Five

Breakfast was a silent meal. The room was dark, for the windowpane was clotted with the light, newly fallen snow, and yet there was no lamp. There was no needless expenditure of oil in the house of Montague. So they ate in the dimness, consuming beans, porridge, hot cakes and molasses, coffee, bacon. They had quantities of food. They devoured it in dark discontent, their eyes clouded with sleep, their faces bent over their plates, so that one looked up and down the table at a long double row of tousled heads. From them issued harsh, guttural voices, like the talk of Indians.

"Gimme some salt."

"Sling the beans down this way."

"Chuck a lumpa bread across here."

They finished with an elbow on the table, a fist propped against a cheekbone, a tin cup of black coffee clutched in the other hand. This powerful nerve poison they took joyously, as a far-gone victim takes his cocaine. They felt the stimulant working in them, and they were roused, not to cheerfulness, but to angry interest in life and in the world about them. They glared at one another with baleful eyes. They snatched at the food before them. But like savage dogs that have felt the teeth of one another before, they kept their surliness within certain bounds.

At the head of the table, old Monty Montague kept watch, looking here and there, drinking coffee, tasting no food, hating the others for their youth and their appetites, but glorying also in their strength, as in the sharpness of so many swords.

Then in came the half-breed, Jack McGuire, and the old man scowled and smiled upon him at the same time. He was ashamed of having introduced bad blood into his household, but the qualities of the half-breed were so valuable, at times, that he would not have dreamed of sending him away. McGuire took a place, lowered his head a little more than the others, and began to feed with a wolfish rapidity. He was by far the last to sit down, but he was by no means the last to rise. And this quality also the head of the house admired with all his heart.

But the last of the lingerers were finished, finally. The cook came and leaned in the doorway, with a wreath of evil-smelling kitchen smoke about him. "It's clearin' off," he announced.

"The coffee's like mud," answered old Montague.

"Is it?" said the cook. He picked up the nearest cup from the table and swallowed the cold dregs he found in it. "That ain't bad," he said. "It's too good for them, of course. But if you want better coffee, buy it. Fire and water won't tell you lies about what it's worth. Where's The Lamb? He ain't showed up."

"Are you givin' me the news?" Montague asked. "Ain't I been watchin' for him?"

"I ain't gonna pamper nobody in this house," said the cook. "I got my job to do. I've waited food for him before. This here is the last time, I tell you. I'm through with it!" He scooped up an armful of dishes from the table. And just at this strategic moment, The Lamb appeared. The cook

266

glared at him, looked at Monty, and then he burst out: "You're too late, kid. You get no chuck this mornin'."

"Aw, I didn't come in for chuck," The Lamb said.

"Nor no coffee, neither."

"I can get along without coffee, too," The Lamb said.

"Then whatcha want here?"

"I wanna have a chat with you," The Lamb said.

"The boys is turnin' out for work," said the other. "You could go and chat with them."

He grew more insolent, seeing that Montague made no remark during this dialogue.

The Lamb made a cigarette in his usual dexterous manner, and sat down at his ease, crossing his legs as he lit the smoke. "The way a gent overloads his stomach is something terrible," he said.

"Aye," said the cook grimly, "there ain't any lie in what you say there."

"Look!" said The Lamb. He gestured toward the great platters that had been heaped and now were empty, and only streaked here with beans, there with cold bacon grease. "Enough chuck there to feed ten horses."

"If horses would eat meat," said the cook.

"They will," The Lamb said.

"What?" The cook paused, a great stack of

dishes upon one arm, the other greasy fist planted upon his hip. "A horse eat meat?" he repeated challengingly, and he looked to old Montague, as though inviting him to be a witness to this absurdity.

"I disremember where it was," The Lamb began, "but there came a time when I was sort of tired of hearing the yammering and the chattering and the noise of folks, and I figured that I'd go off and have a time alone in the hills."

"The chatterin' of guns didn't have nothin' to do with helpin' you to make up your mind?" suggested the cook with a sour grin.

"I disremember all the details," the boy said with perfect good nature. "I tell you what. Sort of a longing to get away from the trails was on me. I hankered for still places more than a dog ever hankered after a bone."

"You might have tried a jail," the sour cook said.

"I did," answered The Lamb, nodding genially.

"Hey?"

"I tried a jail, but there was a couple of doors with squeaking hinges in that there jail."

The cook was silent, grinning in pure expectancy now.

"So I took off them doors, one night," said the boy. "I figured on oiling 'em. But then I remembered that I didn't have any oil. So I left the jail, and went out to get some oil. But it was late at night, and all the stores were closed. Dog-gone' absent-minded, I am."

"Sure," said the cook. He laughed. "I bet you forgot to come back to the jail, even."

"Well, sir," The Lamb said, "you sure are a mind-reader, partner. That's exactly what happened. Which I dunno how you come to guess it."

"Was that the night your horse ate meat?"

"Nope. I borrowed back my horse from the sheriff and took a ride off to sort of enjoy the cool look of the moon on the snow, because it was this time of the year. We went along for a couple of days . . ."

"Enjoyin' the moon, all the time?" put in the cook sagely.

"And the silence. And pretty soon a couple of posses rode along to find out what for I'd took down them doors and not put 'em back? But I was in that kind of a frame of mind, I sure hated conversation. So I rode on. They give me an eight-day run, off and on. They came so close to me a couple of times that they scared the nap off of my hat. And I got right down low in food. There was plenty of water, or snow that would do for water, but there wasn't much chuck, except a lot of jerked beef that I'd got off a rancher that was willing to loan it to me. And for three days I dined off of my belt, and tough chewing I found it. And I fed that horse, four times a day, little chunks of the dried meat. He was plumb skinny. His hips looked like the hips of a ten-year-old cow in February. But dog-gone' me if he didn't keep a lot of his strength."

"Is that a fact?" the cook murmured, his eyes staring.

"There's a couple of sheriffs that'll tell you how that mare of mine come through the chase. They had some pretty close views of her . . . all from the rear."

"Damn my eyes!" cried the cook. "That's the outbeatin'est thing I ever heard tell of."

"I thought you'd like to know about it," The Lamb said. "Time might come along when you'd get tired of other gents and want to take a trip yourself and avoid all kind of talk, even with sheriffs."

The cook laughed deeply. "I dunno but I might," he said. "That horse didn't get sick, did he?"

"No. And a delicate, high-bred mare she was, at that."

"Aye, aye! It was her, was it?"

"It was," The Lamb said, and sighed. "But every horse and every man has gotta come to the end of the trail."

"They do," agreed the cook grimly. "I remember even old Jeff Parker, he went down, at last. Him that I thought never would break or rust. Wait a minute till I hustle up some chuck and we'll have breakfast together. You know Jeff Parker?"

"Him? I was in the Panhandle with him!"

"You was there?"

"Sure."

"At the time he fought Buck Marston?"

"I was about fifty feet off."

"The dickens! I always thought there was nobody else there."

"Sure, they say that. I wasn't writing for the newspapers in them days."

"I'll be back in ten shakes!" cried the cook. "Wait a minute, kid! Dog-gone' me if I wouldn't pay a hundred in gold to hear the facts about that fight." Then he disappeared, the kitchen door slamming after him as a great clattering of pans began in the kitchen.

Montague asked: "You really was a friend of Parker?"

"I never heard of him before."

Monty smiled, and The Lamb smiled back, and a sweet understanding passed between the two of them.

"He'll carve you up small, if he finds out you're lying," Montague commented.

"A man can't live forever . . . not even Jeff Parker," said The Lamb.

And the old man laughed in his rasping way. "You was put together so's you could have your own way . . . even into a snake's hole," he said. "I'm glad that I got you here with us."

"Thanks," said The Lamb.

Then the patriarch leaned across the table. "But if you was to try to outsmart *me,* son," he said, "heaven help you, because no man would be of much use to you."

Chapter Thirty-Six

As the cook had announced, the sky had cleared. After the rather involuntary breakfast, The Lamb walked out into a dazzling world. There was not air enough to flutter away the snow that his walking knocked up. There was not air enough to make the tips of the pine trees tremble. It was not the wind but their own weight that caused little streams of crystal fineness to slip from the loaded branches and glimmer to the ground.

The Lamb's step was silent, as though he moved upon feathers. Or at the most, there was only the faintest of whispers as he strode forward.

A very pleasant and bright day it was. To look down into the level floor of the valley was to be blinded with the reflected light. And even the forest was seamed and streaked with gashes of the most startling white. Snow was king. It threatened to heap over everything in another day. The cook was beginning to shovel out a great trench behind the kitchen door.

The Lamb drank in this cheerfulness with head

thrown high and with eyes almost closed, but he kept moving at a brisk pace, for the cold was extreme. His breath came forth as white clouds of steam, which almost instantly was converted into a haze of suspended ice crystals. Moving briskly, he came out through the trees at almost the same point where he had met and talked with Louise Patten before, and here he found her again, and His Lordship, leaping and floundering through the snow.

He warned her hastily: "You'd better take him in. This cold will get at his lungs, most likely."

"I'm only giving him a breath of air. I'll take him in before the cold drives into him," she said. "It's a lovely morning."

She glowed with beauty and high health. The Lamb turned in beside her, and they went on a few steps, with His Lordship diving through the drifts and plunging above them like a porpoise gamboling before the prow of a ship.

The Lamb began to feel absurdly happy and wonderfully alone with her. He had a strong sense of possession, of superior age, of vaster experience. He wanted to kick the snow from before her and clear her way. He wanted to help her over the inequalities of the path. Then he knew, suddenly, that he was in love, and that admission passed through him warmly, and with a sudden weakness, so that he felt his strength was disintegrating. He swore beneath his breath, and looked up to find her regarding him gravely. He apologized.

"I've been used to sashaying around mostly with horses and mules," said The Lamb. "Out here in this part of the world, the animals wouldn't understand you were talking at all, if you didn't cuss a little. So it gets into your brain, y'understand?"

She nodded. She understood perfectly. But why should he swear now? At the snow?

"At myself," said The Lamb, "for being more foolish than a six-months' calf. Here I am walking along with you in the top of the morning and getting dizzier than measles and jaundice rolled together."

"About what?" she asked. "Is the snow bothering your eyes?"

"You bother my eyes," said The Lamb bluntly. She looked straight at him, without answering. He continued to explain. "I get taken this way, once in a while. It don't mean anything. I'm harmless. Usually I don't even talk about it. But for a couple of nights it keeps me awake, and gets me moony in the daytime. A miserable feeling it is."

She was as grave as could be. "I've heard that it is," she said.

"You never was in love?" he asked impersonally.

"No. Not really."

"It's a cross," he said, "between sea-sickness and a pitching horse, when he fishes for the sun, and your heart jumps higher than the horse wants to go. Food doesn't have any taste. A gent feels like the way that a cow sounds when her calf has been fetched away from her and turned into veal."

Louise Patten, listening to this singular exposition, laughed and nodded.

"You don't mind me talking?" he asked.

"No. Not a bit," she said. "I'll never hear another man talk like this, I know."

"You won't," he agreed with her. "Mostly they're took sudden . . . cowpunchers. But they take themselves pretty serious. They begin to propose. Sometimes I've known it to last out more'n a week of miserableness. There isn't anything more foolish than love."

"I don't suppose there is," she said.

"There isn't," he insisted needlessly. "There'll be a spell now for a few days when thinking about you will plumb make me ache, and every minute I'll have you in the back of my mind. Unless I can talk you out."

"No doubt you can," she said, and she smiled at him with such a friendly manner that The Lamb gasped. His grim face contorted.

"Don't do that ag'in," he said.

"What?" she asked him, perturbed.

"It's like this," he explained to her carefully. "A

275

girl looks pretty mysterious and high-in-the-air to a 'puncher. There is no more writing on her face than there is on the face of a stone, and so, a poor cowboy, he turns her out dressed up in his best ideas. Look at me. I'm spraining my eyes and my brain to look high enough up to see you, and the next minute I'm on the edge of asking you in to work in my kitchen, and roll biscuits for me, and patch my duds, and all of that. There isn't any sense in a man, when he's taken this way. But it's a sort of a fever."

"Is it?" she said as one willing to be instructed.

"It is," he repeated. "Thank goodness that the crisis comes pretty quick and the temperature goes down with a slam. Whiskey is a pretty good way of breaking it. Whiskey has cured a lot of colds and love affairs for me, only that here on this job I can't drink. All I can do is to talk. If you don't mind?"

She laughed cheerfully at him. "Every cow-puncher under sixty," she said, "doesn't feel polite unless he asks a girl to marry him. It's his way of making conversation."

The Lamb stopped and touched her arm. "D'you think that this is conversation?" he asked her darkly.

Her eyes opened a little at him. "Oh no," she said. And she repeated it breathlessly. "Oh no! I don't think that about you."

He resumed his walk beside her. "I'm glad

you don't," he said. "Because we'd better leave action out and stick to words. Suppose we change the subject. There's the barn. Let's go in and speak to the horse."

She went obediently beside him, and this ready yielding to his suggestion caused the heart of The Lamb to soften more than before. He was aware of a decided shortness of breath, and an odd unsteadiness of lip, so that he grinned like an idiot at nothingness.

They reached the stall of the black stallion. He was at his manger, burrowing his head into a great feed of hay, but at the first word of his new master, he whirled lightly about.

"Great heavens," said the girl, "what a cat he is on his feet."

"Keep back your dog, or he'll put a hoof through His Lordship."

"Down," said the girl. "Down, silly boy."

The bull terrier sat down, with her hand upon his head, and he pricked his ears and canted his head wistfully to one side with a bull terrier's own stupid hungering after trouble and after love. For the bull terrier is the knight of errant dogs. He is as useless as any knight in plate armor, and he is as glorious and as true.

"What have you done to that great black demon?" asked the girl as the stallion nibbled at the hand of The Lamb with tenderly mischievous eyes.

"Oh, I haven't done a thing to him."

"And yet you've made him safe?"

"Why, safe enough for me."

"I don't think that he'd hurt a soul," she said, and straightway she laid her hand between the stallion's eyes.

"Great guns," breathed The Lamb, and struck her arm away just as the great teeth of the horse flashed and clicked like a steel machine.

"It's only for you, then?" asked the girl. She had not changed color. She merely seemed curious and interested by this display of tigerish ferocity.

The Lamb took her hand in his, and held it to the muzzle of the stallion. "This isn't an apple, you old fool," he said. "This here is a friend. Understand?"

With flattened ears, with flaring nostrils, the great horse sniffed. Then he turned with a jerk of his head and went back to his hay.

"We'll try again, later on," said The Lamb. "The old fellow is mean today."

"But he loves you," the girl said, and she smiled at him with melting eyes.

"He's only a horse," The Lamb said brusquely to her.

He led the way out of the stable, gloomy, preoccupied. For he felt that her gentle ways, and her friendly manner, and the intimate trust of her glance were by no means making his way an easy one. However, he hardly could teach her how she should treat him.

He determined to go back to the house at once, and so he would have done, had not His Lordship, at that unlucky instant, sighted something in the snow—or was it only a flurry in the snow itself, at the verge of the ledge? Away he went with a shrilling yelp, a white thunderbolt.

On the verge of the danger he swerved and tried to save himself, but the stiff crust of the day before now was replaced with a stuff as unstable as feathers. That light surface snow gave instantly beneath him, and His Lordship toppled over the edge of the cliff and disappeared.

Chapter Thirty-Seven

The girl did not cry out, but she ran like a deer for the edge of the cliff. The Lamb passed her, and he had to dig his heels to keep from being thrust over the edge by his own impetus. He saw beneath him a dizzy drop—not a sheer fall, but a gradual outward swoop of twenty feet. At the bottom of this, the cliff face dropped in a straight line to boulders beneath, and close to the beginning of the vertical drop the terrier, in brave silence, was digging furiously at the snow, fighting for his life, though all the time he was gradually slipping back toward the fall. The

Lamb heard a moan from the girl beside him, and he looked suddenly at her—a grim, piercing glance at her helpless grief and wonder.

Then action followed more swiftly than words. The Lamb smashed away the rim of the snow with his heel, and, dropping suddenly, he clung by his hands to the rocky ledge that he had uncovered. The girl had cried out above him, urging him in a piercing voice to come back. But he threw one glance over his shoulder and then launched himself down the slope. Fifteen feet below him there was a bush jutting outward, and at this he aimed, digging in with hands and toes to slow up his motion.

Yet it was impossible to retard his slide greatly, for the loose surface snow yielded and scooped away beneath him. Worst of all, a smother of white rose before his face, blinded him. Through that cloud, he clutched with both hands, and suddenly his grip was fixed upon the bush. The pull of the right hand ripped away the branch that he held, and the left-hand branch ripped, gave, but then held precariously, while he dangled from beneath the waist over emptiness.

He heard the cry of the girl, relief, and a sickness of terror, half choking her. She would go for a rope. . . . But the dog would be lost long before that time could come. The Lamb drew himself up gingerly, then slued his whole body to the side. In that manner, his left leg came within reach of the scrambling terrier and the dog's digging forepaws instantly were upon it. A second later, it had scrambled over the man's body and lay on the snow on The Lamb's shoulder. It gave the side of his face a wet flurry of gratitude, then it lay with head depressed and tongue hanging out while the hammering of its heart kept jerking its ribs against the cheek of the man.

But they hung by the least sure of holds. Twice he freshened his hold upon the branch of the vine that had held, but twice he felt it slipping. The first violent pull had apparently snapped the tap root. Now the lateral roots were giving away slowly, steadily and he could hear them popping beneath the snow.

Into that snow he kicked with his toes and scraped with his hands, but he could not get a purchase. He listened and wondered why the girl had not cried out for help. Then there came a crunching in the snow above him, and the long, lithe shadow of a rope dropped over his head.

"Find a rock," he gasped to her, "and get a purchase on it."

She disappeared behind the ledge. Then: "Ready!" rang her voice down at him.

He passed the rope under his shoulders at the same moment that the bush at last gave way and slid down beneath him. The bull terrier was firmly astraddle of his neck. And in five seconds he had climbed up the rope, hand over hand, and saw His Lordship leap wildly into the arms of his mistress.

The Lamb, grown oddly weak and shaky, disentangled himself from the rope and automatically began to coil it. Tiny black spots swarmed before his eyes. The snow surface rose and fell like waves at sea, and all the tall pines were in motion.

A hand took his arm firmly. "You'd better come over with me," said the voice of the girl.

But he could only see a dim silhouette of her, as though they were standing in the thickest midnight. He followed obediently. Then she pushed him down on the stump of a tree.

"I'll have some men here in a minute to help you into the house," she began.

"Don't do that," he pleaded. "I'll be all right again in a second. I'm mighty sorry. It never happened to me before. It's this here cold air, I guess," The Lamb apologized. Then a red-hot wave of shame went over him. Suddenly he could see, and as his senses came back to him, he knew that he had been reeling back and forth, swaying even as he sat on the stump. The mist was snatched from before his eyes and he could see the girl. Crimson painted the face of The Lamb—a deep, hot crimson.

"I got a little dizzy," he finally said.

"Of course you did," said the girl.

He stood up. Agony possessed him. "You'll think I'm a pretty poor kind of a gent," he said. "Getting shaky like this. I dunno what happened. I . . . maybe there's something wrong with my insides. . . . Well, so long." He started for the barn door, cursing his knees, for they sagged dreadfully, trying to hold his head high. But the girl came beside him swiftly. "I'm gonna be all right," he told her.

"Of course you are," she said. "You'd better come to the house with me."

"Nope. I'll be all right. Must've pulled a ligament . . . seem sort of lame and . . ."

Oh, a poor lie was that to excuse the manner in which he was reeling. She drew his right arm over her shoulders, and when he looked down, he saw that her face was stern—or was it sheer disgust?

"You'll come straight to the house!" she commanded.

He started to withdraw the arm of which she had taken possession, but discovered that he could not do so. She mastered him with her child's strength. And when he drew away, his muscles twitched oddly and refused to react.

"You'll come straight to the house," she repeated.

He could not resist. She was drawing him forward, and he gasped in the agony of his heart: "Don't do it. Lord knows I deserve it . . .

but if a man was to see me like this. Lemme get to the barn . . . I'm pretty near finished. Help me to the barn . . . and then laugh at me. I'm a sack of bran . . . I'm no good . . . but don't let the gents see me."

"Ah, is that it?" he heard her murmur.

She was bringing him steadily on toward the barn. She put an arm around him, and his weight lopped down onto her shoulders and his knees gave sickeningly.

Then the sweet, warm air of the barn was about him. They passed a narrow door, and she lowered him toward a pile of sacks. Heavily he fell upon it, inert.

"All right, thanks," said The Lamb.

She darted away, but she was back again while he still lay stretched in a strange valley of shadow that closed over his head and rose and closed again. She raised his head in the circle of her arm. The bull terrier licked his face assiduously and yet he had not the energy to push the dog away. Women, and even dogs, could pity him, now.

Suddenly he wished with all his might that the bush had not held, but that he had dropped to swift destruction before the eyes of man or beast should have seen him in this pitiable condition, but he could not resist the arm that supported his head. Against his lips the mouth of a flask was pressed, and stinging brandy flowed hurriedly down his throat. He coughed, shook his head, and lay back against the side of the big feed box. He closed his eyes, then, for he did not wish to see her face; he could only wonder that she disguised her contempt for him so perfectly.

"Are you a little better?"

"I'm gonna be all right," he told her.

"I'll open your shirt."

"No," he said.

Her quick fingers already had performed the task. He heard her cry out sharply, then she was silent.

At last he said: "I'm well enough, now. That brandy . . . that's the stuff. I wish you'd let me be, now. My gosh," murmured The Lamb, "I never knew I was a yellow dog."

And the greatness of his horror made him open his eyes and look up into her face. She was white, and her eyes stared wildly back at him, but she was shaking her head and trying to smile at his words.

"You don't understand, but I do," she said. "It's the shock that's upset you. You'll be as well as ever in five minutes. Your pulse is a lot better now." Aye, she was holding his wrist with cool fingers. "The shock," she said. "That was it. I've seen it happen before. Are you afraid that I think you're a coward? You?" She laughed, and the laughter broke. "Ask His Lordship," she said. "He'll tell you."

The terrier, hearing his name, pressed in

between them and licked the face of The Lamb, then whined, as though eager to be of use.

The Lamb reached for the brandy flask, and drank from it again. It gave a quick, hot strength all through his body, and he thrust himself up to a sitting posture on arms that were suddenly restored to vigor. "You're making things easy for me," he said.

"Do you doubt that I've never seen a man do such a thing?" she cried at him. "Or a man that would dream of such a thing, even? Except one man alone . . . and why do you wear his picture around your neck? Ah, will you tell me that?"

He fumbled at his breast and neck until his fingers touched a thin chain and down the chain to a small locket. True—she had opened his shirt to give him air, and all at once the last weakness was stripped from him. He rose to his feet and faced her grimly.

"You knew the face, eh?" he asked her.

"It's the face of Will Dunstan," she told him.

"Go up to the house and tell 'em that you found me wearing this picture of him. There'll be someone there that'll be interested, I'm thinking."

"I've been here these weeks that have seemed like years," she said, "trying to find out how it was that he lay where they found him. If you are his friend, do you think that I'd be able to breathe a word of it? But what was he to you?"

"My brother," The Lamb said.

Chapter Thirty-Eight

She looked at him with bewilderment, with utter astonishment, and then with a flush of pleasure.

"You are Will's brother?"

"You wouldn't think it," he admitted, "by the look of me. I never had any face like Will's, and what I've had, has been shot crooked by kind friends. And now that we're talking, what were you to Will?"

She hesitated, her eyes wandering a little.

"Will was fond of you, eh?" he asked her sharply. She nodded. "And you of him?" he persisted.

"And I of him," she said softly. "But . . . differently. He wasn't very old, you know."

"And how old are you?" he asked her harshly.

"I'm twenty," she said.

"As old as that?" he asked her almost sourly.

"Yes. Nearly as old as Will."

"Older," he said.

"He was twenty-one," she said.

"He was nineteen," said the brother.

"But he told me . . ."

"He lied to you. He knew that you wouldn't be doing any cradle robbing, so he lied to you."

She stared at him. "You couldn't be wrong, of course," she admitted.

"About him?" He laughed fiercely. "I couldn't be wrong about him."

She was silent, watching him, for it was plain that his mind was deep in the past, working here and there like a mole, underground.

"He was like brother and son to me," said The Lamb. "I was his mother, and I was his father."

"And how old are you?" she quickly asked.

"I'm old enough," he said. "I got wages when I was twelve . . . I kept the kid in school." At this, her eyes filled with tears, but he said to her harshly: "What difference did it make about me? Why, no difference at all. I was headed wrong from the start. Window-busting and nose-punching was my idea of a party since the time I could crawl. There wasn't any good in me. So why shouldn't I hit the range and have my fun?"

She wiped her eyes. Then, with her lips steadier, she watched him again rather dimly, as though she were seeing something with her mind's eye, other than his face.

"He went to school. He did fine . . . maybe you disremember how slick he could talk?" asked The Lamb.

"No, no."

"As slick as you," The Lamb said defiantly.

"He knew a thousand times more than I."

"He was gonna start college last fall," The Lamb said thoughtfully. "That was what I'd got him up to. College!" He added: "There've been Dunstans in college before. Me, I'm the wrong one. I never did any good with books. I never cottoned to 'em none. But the kid was different. He took to 'em like a calf to bunch grass. You've never seen anything like it. The way he'd eat up a book, I mean. He could tell 'em out to you by the hour, what he knew. I used to listen. It didn't hurt any to listen to the kid when he was talking, did it?"

"No," said the girl, still looking past him, as though there was another person in the room.

"I got him up and ready for college," said The Lamb. "I kept him out of the West and off the range. When he was in high school, he used to be writing me letters . . . he wondered how could I make so much money out of the little bunch of cows that I had." The Lamb laughed.

"And how could you? Enough to keep a boy in school . . . no matter how poorly."

"Poorly?" The Lamb cried savagely. "There wasn't nothing poor about the way that he was turned out. I'm telling you that he was done up proper. He was slicked out in fine togs. He had about five suits, I mean to say, and a horse that was a high-stepper . . . you would've laughed to see how fine he looked on a horse. You've never seen anything like it!"

"And you could manage all that?" she asked.

"Why not?" he snapped at her. "I was sashaying

around the range. You pick up a good deal of cash out of poker games, now and then. And you pick up more sometimes, at the talking end of a Colt!" He scowled sternly at her. "I'm not a Sunday school superintendent," he assured her. She nodded. "And the kid was my bank. I sent the cash to him. He used to live pretty prime, the kid did." Then he sighed, remembering. "He was the captain of his football team . . . he was on the debating team. He was a streak of greased lightning to run. You've never seen anything like that, either. They used to write to me about him . . . I mean, his teachers. They used to write to me. One time his football coach wrote to me, too." He rubbed his hands slowly together, laughing softly to himself. "So sometimes, I'd just run in on him. There never was anything that he wouldn't drop when he saw me around. We were thick, is what I mean to say. We were that close together. You would've laughed to see him stand up and box with me, too. There wasn't anything yellow about the kid. He used to wade into me and those big shoulders of his, they used to work and pump the gloves at me, I'll tell a man!" His head thrown back, he dreamed joyously. "You would've laughed to see him. He'd work in and slam me on the jaw. That's what he used to do." He laughed, as he had advised her to do. "Once he slammed me right up ag'in' the wall. He comes in quick and grabs me beneath the arms to hold me up. He says that he hopes he hasn't hurt me.

"'Stand away or I'll knock your block off,' I said to him. "And I did it, too. And he took it, too. He was that straight. He was that clean. There was no whimper in Will," said The Lamb. Dexterously he jerked a cigarette together, lit it, inhaled, and then talked rapidly on, the smoke crowding from his mouth, from his nose.

"He would've made something in the ring," The Lamb finally continued. "I thought of going in for the ring myself. It was big money. It was quick money. But suppose when the kid was a high-faluting doctor, or lawyer, or senator, or something like that . . . suppose that somebody had said . . . 'Where did he get his start? Why, his brother was Al Dunstan, the prize fighter.' That would've sounded pretty good, I guess not." He paused, then said to her: "I'm sort of stringing this along."

"I want to hear," she whispered.

"I got him the money, and he never knew how I got it. I mean, that he never knew for a long time. Till a dirty rat, he got the low-down on me, and he wrote to the kid just before last summer's vacation, and the kid came right out, hardly waiting to pass his last examinations at the top of his class. He came sashaying out. He said to me . . . 'Is it true that you're The Doctor of Denver, and The Lonesome Kid of Nevada? Is it

291

true that they call you Texas in Idaho, and Montana in Texas?'

"It took me quick and it took me hard, like getting a straight right to the wind, when you expect it at the head. I tried to lie, but I must've turned pretty green, because he sat down and looked at me, white, and sick, and still. Gosh . . . ," said The Lamb, and closed his eyes.

After a moment, he continued: "The kid wouldn't stand for anything. He would work for what he got. I pretty near went down on my knees to him. No, he was gonna work for a whole year, and when he'd got his year's pay, then he'd start in for college. He wouldn't use any spoiled money. It was spoiled if it was dug out of a poker game, y'understand?"

"Yes, yes," whispered the girl.

"Well, he went to work. He wouldn't work for me. He said that he would go off and work by himself, where he'd get no favors. That was the way he was. He was clean. He was a straight one," The Lamb said.

"He was," said the girl.

"If you had known him the way that I knew him," said The Lamb, "you would've loved him, too."

"I did love him," said the girl.

"Aye, and did you, then?" The Lamb said gently. He laid a hand on her shoulder. "You're right," he said. "There isn't anything but rightness about you. But I used to get letters from him. He used to tell me about the work, and about getting his share of spills from the bronc's . . . a darn' tough bronc' it would've taken to drop him, though. And then he wrote to me about meeting up with a fine girl, by the name of Louise Patten. He wasn't so hot about going back to college, then. He thought that maybe the best thing for him was to start to work and make a home. Y'understand?"

"Yes," said the girl.

"But he didn't make any home," The Lamb said slowly. "No, and he didn't go back to college, either. But he was to come to his finish lying on the rocks, dead. He was to come by his death by murder, if you know what I mean."

She caught her breath. "You've thought that, too?"

"I've proved it," The Lamb said quietly. "But the years of his life, they come to an end, like all men have got to come. Only sometimes it sort of seems to me like he might've had his chance to stand up before the world, and that I could've been out there in the crowd, nobody knowing, and heard what the folks had to say about him. But he never had any chance," murmured The Lamb.

He was silent, and then he saw that tears were running down the face of the girl. "Aye," The Lamb said gently, "I understand. I'm sorry that I made you cry for him."

"Ah, no," said the girl, "but for you."

Chapter Thirty-Nine

She left him, while he still was fumbling at the meaning that her last words might have held. Then he hurried to the door of the barn with a strange lightness of heart, but she was gone from his sight, and he leaned against the edge of the door, looking down, partly in thought, partly to keep the glare of the brilliant snow out of his eyes.

Rain and snow-soaked, battered by long usage, the lower boards of the tread way that led up to the barn floor were a pulp, soft and impressionable, where the hoofs of every horse inside the barn had often been printed, but to the side The Lamb's attention was now held by a larger print than ordinary—the big, round, deeply stamped mark of a shoe. After that first glance, all memory of Louise Patten was scattered from the brain of The Lamb.

He dropped upon his knees and took the envelope from his pocket. There was no doubt. That print was identical with the print of the horse that he had copied from the soapstone near the black rocks, and that horse was now in the barn!

What horse, then, could it be? He swore that he would examine the hoofs of every mustang on the place until he found the right one, and in the meantime he passed them in a steady drift before his eyes.

But here he was puzzled. Only the huge, sleek animals that Jimmy Montague rode could po- sibly have made such marks, but which one of them all had forehoofs so beautifully rounded? He gasped as the truth jumped into his mind, and, turning, he ran straight back to the box stall of the black stallion, entered, and made the big fellow put his forehoof upon the sheet. All doubt vanished as soon as he examined the print that had been made. It was the black that had made that sign!

And, at this, other thoughts instantly were brought in line with a dizzy speed of succession. For in those days, only Jimmy had ridden the black. Upon the stallion Jimmy must have been when that mark was made in the soapstone. But Jimmy was away from the house at that time. Away, certainly. Away from the house, and lurking for days in the hills like a wolf, ready to strike down his prey.

The sign could not have been made later, for had not Louise said that she remembered the season as that in which the leaves were falling, and the snows had begun? So by good fortune the crimson bit of leaf had been stamped into the stone to give a sign and a date to the act. The stallion had been there, and therefore, Jimmy, and the murder lay at his door.

The Lamb did not need genius to find a motive for the crime. For young Will Dunstan had simply showed his fondness for the girl, no doubt, and she had smiled back at the boy. That would have been enough for the young brutal Montague.

The Lamb began to pace up and down. The day was long. And it would be dusk, perhaps, before Jimmy returned to the house at the end of his day's work. Let it be the end of the long trail for Jimmy, forever and ever, and the end of this strange and twisted trail that The Lamb had followed, also.

He set his teeth as he thought of the time that must pass in between, and bitterly he resigned himself.

At the end of this day, out on the range, Jimmy Montague was following up the trail of a cow in the snow. Behind and beside the sign of the cow went the triple sign of three timber wolves, and Jimmy, and Jack McGuire with him, could see where she had paused, time and again, to make a stand and drive away her foes.

She was weakening. She had fallen on her knees here, and stumbled with a wide sprawl as she regained her feet, but still the gray wolves had not closed on her. As if knowing that she was doomed, they took their time, playing safe in spite of the gnawing hunger in their bellies.

They came to a steep slope, and here McGuire,

leaning to study the sign, pointed significantly before them, as though to say that they would find the tragedy acted out on the far side of the knoll.

So they dismounted, and, walking softly together through the snow, they soon heard deep snarling blown down the wind toward them. Hats off, on their knees, they raised their heads above the rim of the hill and saw the three lobos tearing the remains of the cow. No word was spoken. The half-breed took the right-hand wolf, Montague the left. Their guns spoke at the same instant. Two howls cut the air. Two lobos lay twisting and snapping on the snow. The third raced for liberty, dodging like a snipe, and though the repeating rifles chattered at him, he was soon in a patch of brush.

They made no attempt to follow. They did not even put the wounded wolves out of their misery, but only making sure that the cold of the night would surely end both the stricken animals, they looked at one another with sneering smiles of agreement. For the half-breed loved the infliction of pain no more than did his master.

The blue dusk began to pool in the valley as they went back to the horses.

"My watch has stopped," Jimmy said. "What time you got? No, I forgot. You wouldn't be carryin' a timepiece."

McGuire said: "Lemme tell you something.

There ain't a better watch on the range than what I carry."

Jimmy grinned at him. "Where you carry it? In your head?"

"Here!" cried the half-breed. And suddenly a thin gold watch lay in the palm of his hand.

The rancher looked at it in amazement, for it had the slim look of a Swiss case. "Lemme see," he said.

"What for?" fenced the half-breed.

"I ain't gonna eat it. Give it here." Jimmy snatched the watch and turned it. "Where'd you get this?" he asked.

"In town," McGuire answered.

"You lie," answered Jimmy with easy assurance. "You lie, because there ain't been a time in your life when you ever had a hundred and fifty bucks to sink into a watch."

"A hundred and fifty!" gasped the half-breed. "They ain't any watches that cost that much!"

The big man was staring at the face of the watch, and announced with satisfaction: "They make 'em for that price in Geneva, where this watch comes from. They make 'em to cost more, too. Who'd you stick up for this, eh?"

"Give it back to me," McGuire said surlily. "I ain't gonna answer no more of your questions."

"Aw, I'll give it back to you," replied the big man mildly. "I ain't gonna rob you. Only . . . you tell me."

"I'll tell you nothin'," said the half-breed. "Give it back, Montague, will you? Hey, whatcha doin' now?"

For Montague had cracked open the back of the case and was squinting at the inner panel. "A.D.," he read. "Since when was your initials A.D., McGuire?"

"I got it for a girl of mine," said the half-breed. "Them was her initials."

"Say," said the other, "you didn't even know the price of it."

"Sure I didn't," McGuire said, "if it's worth a hundred and fifty. I got it secondhand."

"Huh," grunted Montague. "There ain't any pawnbroker that don't know what a Swiss movement is worth."

"Ain't there?" growled the other. "You know a lot, don't you? You got pretty near all the information drifted into a corner of your lot."

"Your girl went by the name of A.D., did she?"

"Alice . . . er . . . Dougherty, was her name."

"Dougherty? And you give her a man's watch?"

"It looked about the right size for her."

"What did you do? Take it back from her?"

"She died," McGuire said. "And her ma gave me back the watch to remember her by."

"I never heard worse or more foolish lies," Jimmy declared.

"I'll take the watch, and you can keep your

opinion," said McGuire. "You can keep your opinion, and be hanged to it, and to you."

"Watch the way you shoot off your mouth," said the delicate Montague. "Or I'll be knockin' a few manners into you and a few teeth out."

"Montague, do I get that watch?" demanded the half-breed.

Jimmy was suddenly thoughtful. "A.D.," he said. "A.D. Dog-gone' me if the other one ain't got W.D. wrote into it." He turned suddenly upon McGuire. "Will you come home with me and lemme show you this here watch's own full brother?" he asked.

"You got one like it?"

"I have."

"That you paid a hundred and fifty bucks for?" The eyes of the half-breed glimmered with curiosity and greed.

"I paid for mine what you paid for yours, maybe," said the big man. "That was nothin' at all. I just picked it up. Where did you pick up this?"

"I'm done talkin' to you about it. Pass it over, is all I gotta say."

"You chump," said the big man. "Am I gonna rob you?"

"I ain't trustin' nobody with a hundred-and-fifty-buck watch," McGuire said stoutly.

"We'll go down together," Jimmy said. "If this here watch is what I begin to get an idea of . . . why, I'll pay you a hundred spot cash for it."

The hesitation of McGuire vanished, under the strong heat of this temptation.

"It's time to go back, anyway," he argued. "It's close on to suppertime."

So they turned the heads of their horses back down the valley and jogged them patiently, steadily through the snow toward the ranch house, curved up onto the road, and then entered across the bridge. In the stable, they unsaddled together.

The tall, lithe form of The Lamb appeared among the shadows.

"I'd like to have a couple of words with you, Jimmy," he said.

"About what?" Montague barked, dragging off his saddle.

"Something pretty important."

"Important to who?"

"Why . . . maybe to both of us," said the boy.

"I'm busy," Jimmy answered gruffly.

"It'd take only a second," urged The Lamb.

"I'll give you a second later on. Come on, Jack!" They walked out of the stable together, and at the door McGuire looked over his shoulder with a slight shudder.

"Looked like he was gonna stop you," he confided to the big man. "Dog-gone' me . . . he makes me get gooseflesh. He's a queer one, that fellow."

"He a fellow that can be handled," Jimmy said with unaffected indifference. "And I know the man to do it."

"Do you?" taunted McGuire. "I'll tell you what, Jimmy. He's too fast for you."

"Is he? I licked him once. I can do it again."

"You licked his horse . . . not him."

"Shut up," said the young Montague. "You make me tired."

They reached the house and went up to his room. It was as small and bleak as any room in the house. Surroundings made no difference to Jimmy. But he had quite a modern desk in a corner of the little chamber, and, unlocking a lower drawer of this, he presently took out a small box, and from the box he took a thin, golden watch and laid it beside McGuire's watch.

"Look!" he commanded.

The half-breed gasped. They were as like to one another as two peas!

Chapter Forty

All the thoughts of Jimmy, however, were not for the ear of his brutal companion. And when he opened the backs of both watches and placed them facedown, McGuire, looking over his shoulder, failed to see what his master was observing, and this was that while the initials were W.D. in the watch that already was in his possession, and A.D. in the watch that he had taken from McGuire, still there were other circumstances, which made the similarity more striking. It was hardly such a great mystery that two watches of the same pattern should be found, for the company that produced the watch might have turned out thousands of the same pattern, but what seemed extraordinary in the extreme was that the letters in each case were formed with exactly the same method. The Ds could not have been told apart, and the A and the W looked as though they had come from the same letter-press.

Still bent above the watches after he had closed them, Jimmy said quietly: "Jack, you got this watch where?"

"Out of a pawnshop," said Jack stubbornly.

The big man glared at him as though on the point of knocking him down, but, changing his mind, he said gravely: "Suppose I pay you down seventy-five dollars. Would you give me the watch?"

"You said it would cost a hundred and fifty," countered the half-breed.

"This here is cash," big Jimmy said in a business-like manner, and he counted upon the table two $20 gold pieces, and six half-eagles, and then added five, ponderous, massive dollars in silver.

It was the only form of wealth with which the eye of the cowpuncher was acquainted, and he could not help a flutter of his hand toward the money. "I'll take it," he said suddenly, and swept the coins in his other hand. He backed away, uncertain and a little afraid. It did not seem possible that Jimmy would resign such money in such a manner—and for the sake of a broken watch picked out of the snow.

Young Montague merely nodded and smiled. "I'm giving you that money . . . I keep the watch. There's only one thing that you gotta do for me, and that is to tell me where you picked it up."

The half-breed halted with his hand on the knob of the door. With his retreat secured, he waited there, willing to talk, the newly acquired money weighing pleasantly in his pocket. He felt that he had secured a crushing victory over the injustices of this wicked world.

"I picked it up out of the snow," he said suddenly, and he guffawed in the face of Jimmy.

"I thought you did," answered the son of the rancher. "Where?"

"On the side of the mountain, yonder."

"That's all right, Jack. I'm glad that you got it. Any sign around?"

"Why, there was sign, all right. But none that I could trace down to him that made it, I guess."

"What sort of sign?"

"I come across the hills, the other night, and there I seen a couple of fires shine all at once out of the woods on the mountain."

"Facing where?"

"Across toward the southeast. I looked at 'em. All at once they went out, and I rode on home. The next mornin' I started out bright and early. I went up the valley and there I come on sign of a gent that had walked along under the edge of the trees."

"Could you make anything out of it?"

"I would take him to be a gent as heavy as me, taller, and younger a bit."

"Go on."

"Snow was fallin' a good deal, that mornin', and I didn't lie around and wait to trail them tracks back. I turned on to the back track. First, I seen where a horse had come out of the woods and crossed the valley."

"Go on, man. A horse, eh? From where?"

"From southeast."

"Loring's direction, eh?"

"Aye, I would've said that it laid a straight line for Loring's place."

"Go on!"

"I will. Gimme time. I followed them tracks back through the woods, and in a bit of clearin', under the snow, I found the smudge of two fires that had been smothered there before they'd had a chance to get goin' real good."

"What has that got to do with a watch?"

"Over to the side, under a tree, I found the watch. I kicked it out of the snow as I was walkin' along."

Closing his eyes, Jimmy seemed to be digesting the information that he had received, and that it pleased him there could not be the slightest doubt, for he grinned in a ghastly fashion at the other now. He said: "Partner, I want you to take a good think. There wasn't any sign that you could've used to hang the job on anybody?"

"Signs like them is pretty general," said the half-breed. Then, his face wrinkling with poisonous malice, he went on: "But the other night, about half an hour after I seen those signs in the valley, in come your new man, The Lamb, as they call him, with bark stains on the shoulders of his coat, like he'd been brushin' along through the trees. He'd been walkin' in deep snow. He said that he'd had a fall in the woods. That was all. The woods here near the house, he meant. I dunno. It don't mean nothin'. I don't want The Lamb on my trail," concluded Jack McGuire.

"Sure you don't," Jimmy said soothingly, "because there ain't anything in what you've said that would ever mean anything to The Lamb. Go on along, McGuire. I'm through with you."

McGuire retreated in a good deal of haste. His

heavy footfall faded down the hall, and instantly Montague issued from his room and sought that of his grandfather.

The old man was rousing the fire with a heavy poker, and he turned, blinking his old eyes from the smoke that had rolled into them, and cursed his grandson and the world at large.

Before him, Jimmy put down the watch. He said: "You always say that The Lamb reminds you of somebody."

"Sure," Monty Montague said. "He reminds me of good luck. Because that's what he's brung to us. He's broke the back of Loring, and all that we need to do now is to cook and eat the meat. What do you mean?"

"I'm gonna tell you a little story. Then you can make up your mind."

And he told his story, and he told it with care. He had not come quite to the end with the suspicion of McGuire, when Monty Montague touched him on the shoulder to stop him.

"I seen the finish before you came to it," he said calmly. "Him that The Lamb reminds me of is Will Dunstan. What would you think of it? And why would anybody that's connected with Will Dunstan be down here packin' a wrong name, except that he wanted to make some trouble about the death of Will?"

"Aye," Jimmy said. "Why?"

The old man pointed a sudden finger at his

grandson. "You know something about the finish of Dunstan," he said.

"I killed him," answered the other with perfect calm. "Why?"

"I only wanted to know," said Monty Montague. "That was all. This here is Will Dunstan's cousin. He ain't like enough to be a brother. He's down here to find the trail of the killer. Most likely he's on it now. Those horse tracks pointed across the hills. Straight to Loring. He's still Loring's man, then."

"Aye, but he done up Fargo. That's the thing that I couldn't get past."

"He had an old grudge ag'in' Fargo . . . besides, he loves a fight better than a tiger. But wait a minute. It won't be so hard to find out what he is. Get him up here, and we'll see if he's got a watch."

And, therefore, it was that, not two minutes later, young Alfred Dunstan, more widely known under many another name, walked into the room where the two were talking softly together.

"Sit down, sit down, young fellow," said the older Montague with a hearty voice. "We're talkin' over right times for tacklin' the Loring place, son. We're even thinkin' that night might be better than day, accordin' to certain ways of thinkin'."

"I don't see how," The Lamb said.

"Hold on. What time is it now, Jimmy?"

308

"I dunno. My watch is stopped," the young Montague said.

"You blockhead!" roared the other furiously. "When you get better sense than to put castor oil into the insides of a watch, maybe you'll have a watch that'll run for you."

"How was I to know that castor oil wouldn't work?" growled Jimmy.

"Because it run a wagon, you thought it'd run a watch, you loon," snarled Montague, "both a wagon and a watch havin' wheels."

"I'll step down to the kitchen and see by the clock of the cook. Ain't you got a watch on yourself?"

"You know damn' well that I dropped it on the floor last night," said Montague.

Jimmy disappeared from the room, and the old man went into a savage paroxysm of anger, abusing the clumsiness and the stupidity of the younger generation that filled this degenerate world. In his violence, his coat button pulled through its loose buttonhole, and an expansive gesture showed the waistcoat of the old man drawn tightly across his breast by the swing of his arm—and in the lower vest pocket, in a neat circle, there was outlined the impression of the watch that it previously contained.

It was not much. Neither is the snapping of a twig in the forest, but The Lamb from that instant grew as alert as a frightened wolf in the wood. He leaned to pick a match from the floor, and when he straightened, the old man's coat was buttoned again, and his keen eyes probed anxiously at the face of The Lamb.

The glance was an additional reason to The Lamb.

A moment later, big Jimmy returned to the room.

"And what time is it, Jimmy?" asked Montague with well-assumed eagerness.

"It's late," growled Jimmy. "It's very late. Come here a minute into the hall with me while I tell you what we gotta do to that chump McGuire. . . ."

He hung in the doorway, but now The Lamb saw a strange movement of old Montague's hand. He saw it from the corner of his eye, and in that instant he leaped from his chair and got into a corner, with a Colt firm in either hand.

Jimmy sprang back through the door and slammed it. Old Montague's own hand fumbled beneath his coat, and the flash of steel disappeared.

Chapter Forty-One

Old man and young, they watched each other grimly. They heard the lock of the hall door turn with a screech from the outside.

"Are you all right, Monty?" called Jimmy from the hall.

"I'm as right as I can be," Montague said grimly. "What you plan on, Jimmy?"

"I plan on smokin' him out and havin' his hide," Jimmy said. "That's what I plan on. But before the news goes to Loring that his spy is caught, I'm gonna raid Loring right now, and when I come back from crawin' on his bones, then I'm gonna finish up with The Lamb, as he calls himself. Dunstan, you hear me talk?"

The Lamb listened to that name with a slight smile. His face was white, but he nodded and answered with perfect self-control and gravity: "I hear you, Jimmy. There's only one thing ag'in' that plan of yours. I seem to have your old grandfather in here with me. The smokin' out of me might be the smokin' out of him, too."

"It might," Jimmy agreed. "That'd be a pretty hard blow, to me."

He stamped on the floor and shouted. Presently footsteps came running up toward him, while old Monty Montague said to the youth with

311

him: "Old bones can fertilize new lands, is the idea of Jimmy. Bright, promisin' boy, is Jimmy."

"Bright murder is what he does best," commented The Lamb.

"Why, we guessed that you were lookin' into that line," said Montague. "Was he a cousin of yours? Will Dunstan, I mean?"

Under the shock of that question, The Lamb knew that all his secret purpose had been revealed. It disturbed him. He could not imagine how the truth could have come out so suddenly against him. But Montague, as though unwilling to perplex him, grated out, almost gently: "It was the findin' of your watch, son."

There was a murmur of voices in the hall. Then steps departed.

"He's gone off. He's left his guard behind him. Now, maybe he made a fool mistake, in doin' that," suggested Monty Montague. He went to the door and tapped. "Who's there?" he called.

"Me! Milligan."

"Milligan, I'm glad that it's you. Open the door for me."

Milligan laughed loudly. "I know the whole game," he said.

"Milligan," persisted the old rancher, "he'll like you no better for knowing how he put an end to his own father. He's done murder before. He'll do it ag'in."

"I'd trust a young rat rather than an old one,"

insisted Milligan. "There ain't any use of your talking with me. You can't argue me down."

"Milligan!"

"Aye?"

"There's eight thousand in cash on me this minute."

"Let it stay there. Every gambler has gotta carry a big stake," Milligan said. "This here stake may be high enough to win any hand but the one that you're playing now, old-timer."

Old Montague turned away with a shrug of his shoulders. "I'm kinda half glad that he didn't listen to me," he said to The Lamb. "I can't live forever. Sit down, kid. We'll have a chance to talk for a while before they come back and get you."

A heavy hand suddenly beat on the hall door. "Hello, Dunstan!"

"I'm here!" The Lamb called calmly.

"You dirty dog, you done me proper once, but I'm gonna be in at the last laugh," gloated Milligan.

"You're a fine fellow," said The Lamb. "Leave us be in peace. We need to talk." He turned to Monty Montague. "There's ways and ways that we might manage to get out of here," The Lamb said. "What's beyond the windows?"

"I dunno," Montague said. "Nothing but thin air that I can recollect. And nothin' above them windows that you could reach to. Set down, son, and we'll have a little yarn together."

"I was always interested to draw the fangs of a snake before I did tricks with him," The Lamb said. "Back up ag'in' that wall, and fetch your hands up over your head."

"I'm an old man, for you to be foolin' with me," said Montague. "You and me go west the same way. What more do you want out of me?"

"Your teeth!" The Lamb said impatiently. "Man, don't you irritate me none. I'll kill you as quick as I'd stamp on a snake's head coming under my door."

"Well, well," murmured Montague. "I take this kinda mean and hard, from a young man to an old." And, struggling, he forced his hands above his shoulder height, while his bright old eyes glittered venomously at The Lamb.

The latter, with professional adroitness, fanned his victim, and from that surprising veteran he took no fewer than two Colts, a small, blunt-nosed Derringer that hung by a cord from about his neck—"I should've tried a last shot at you with that," the old warrior snapped.—and then a pair of slender-bladed Italian knives, fitted for throwing, or for deadly poniard work, hand to hand.

"Nice, quiet old gent you are," The Lamb commented, looking at the formidable arsenal that he had lined up on the table. "Now sit down," he invited. "We can talk, after this."

"Listen," Montague said, and his eyes flared as he raised his hand.

314

Out of the cold night they could hear the whinnying of horses, and then a trampling on the bridge.

"They're gone," said the old man. "And luck keep Loring's watch strong and good this night . . . or else it'll be the last night he'll see, and all of his boys with him."

There was a slight rustling at one of the windows, and a quantity of the snow that was heaped and frosted tight against the pane fell away.

"The wind is changin'," the old man commented. He began to pack his pipe contentedly.

The Lamb remarked: "I can see the inside lining of your mind, old-timer."

"And what is it made of?"

"Something harder than felt," The Lamb said. "You see your way out of this."

"How come?" said old Monty. "Ain't it plain that Jimmy would rather see me dead than you free? And ain't it plain that he'll never be able to get at you before you've got at me? And ain't it plain that you'd take a pride in finishin' off me before the boys smoked you out?"

"You poison old varmint," The Lamb hissed, his lip lifting. "You know that I don't pawn the bones of old men. It isn't my style. I leave it for low-down ones like the Montagues. Is that straight with you?"

"I understand you fine," Monty Montague said.

"A damn' fine, large, an' liberal nature is yours, kid. And I got no doubt, if once I was shut of this here room and you, that I'd be able to persuade Jimmy to have better sense about you."

The Lamb smiled sourly again, and, as he did so, his mind flickered away to the picture of the naked countryside, moon-ridden, silver-bright, and the cavalcade of strong riders making across it. He could see the grim possibilities of that attack, for Loring, trusting in the report that the attack was due for the dawn, would relax every trace of vigilance in the night, in order to rest his men, short-handed as he was. And it seemed to The Lamb that he could see the train of practiced fighters making steadily across the snows toward the black, sleeping house, with the shimmer of the moon upon its dark windows. As Indians fought and slaughtered, so would those men of the Montagues. For the fiend himself could not have gathered together a primer crew of cutthroats.

There was not even the minor consolation of the vengeance the law might take afterward. Granted that some fugitive might escape, still there was very small chance that the officers of the law could get up to this far-off retreat among the snows for several weeks. The late fall of snow would render the roads impassable. And when the sheriff came, there would be a well-bolstered tale, no doubt, of a murderous attack on the part of the Loring men, a justified counter-attack—and what would the newly made law courts of the region do with the case? No more than blacken the name of the Montagues, already sufficiently besmudged.

At this point in his reflections, he heard the old man murmur: "What the dickens business is that?"

Montague, he found, was staring at the same window from which the snow had fallen away, and now The Lamb could make out a sinuous shadow swaying away into the darkness, and back again into the faint lamplight.

As for The Lamb, he understood, or thought he understood, in one leap of the heart. He stooped and swept up the rag rug that was nearest to him upon the floor, and leaped at the patriarch. Montague turned with a cry of alarm forming on his lips, but it was instantly strangled under the impact, and the jerking of the rug that was about his head.

Once the old fellow was under his fingers, The Lamb was half of a mind to contract his grip and extinguish that wicked life at once. But he delayed. The moral principles of The Lamb were undoubtedly most sketchy, but fair play was vastly important among them.

Swiftly, securely he went about the gagging and the binding of the veteran. He left him swathed with cords, and gagged almost to suffocation, then he turned to the window and pressed it up. The noose end of a rope instantly blew in against his face.

He leaned out and called softly, guardedly, cupping his hands at his lips.

And presently, from above, faint as a whisper, the voice of Louise Patten floated down to him: "I've made it fast here about the chimney. It'll hold your weight."

He jerked down heavily upon it, but it gave not a whit under the strain, and The Lamb delayed no longer, but wriggled out over the sill. He saw beneath him the sheer side of the house, the packed snow along the banks of the creek, and the dark, swift gleam of the waters of the creek itself. Then he swung himself out, and began to climb hand over hand.

Chapter Forty-Two

Cowering against the piled snow upon the roof, The Lamb found Louise near the chimney, cold and trembling, so that he had to help her up with one hand, and she went with a tottering step toward the skylight through which she had climbed up from the attic. From Jack McGuire, she had gathered enough to guess at what had happened—from him, and from Milligan on guard in the hallway. And the scheme of rescue had been thrust into her mind by the manner in which both man and dog had been saved that same day.

There was no need to tell her that, after this, the house of the Montagues would be no place for her. Jimmy had asserted his authority, even if the exercise of it were to cost the life of his grandfather, and that old man no longer would be an ameliorating influence in the house. All would be in the iron hand of Jimmy, when he returned from the expedition against Loring, and Louise Patten would be in his control among the rest.

Neither she nor The Lamb said a word of this, but when they had stolen down the attic stairs, they paused only a moment in the hallway, hearing the voice of Milligan calling, just around the corner: "Tap and be hanged! Tap and beat as loud as you like. I'll never open to you, you sneak! Shut up and keep still, or I'll smash a bullet through the door in a minute!"

Apparently old Monty had wriggled across the floor in spite of his bonds, and was now beating against the door—with his feet, perhaps—in a vain effort to make the guard open to him. It might be that he would prevail by very persistence, after a time. But, before that, The Lamb and the girl must be away.

They slipped, softly as shadows, down the stairs, and into the open again. The air of the house was like the air of a prison left behind them, and the moonlit open received them with all the purity and sweetness of the great pines.

There was no soul left on guard at the stable. Throughout the place, there was only Milligan to guard Montague in that otherwise empty room. The rest had marched to strike their blow.

The black stallion was saddled by The Lamb no quicker than the girl equipped her own slender mustang, and rode it prancing out into the snow. Then down the driveway they fled together, the bridge sounding hollow beneath the driving hoofs of their horses. Out onto the open road they scampered, giving one another one tight-lipped glance of relief. They had saved themselves, but there were other lives about which to think.

Before them, the snow had been cut and trampled by a solid cavalcade that went on for a full quarter of a mile before it turned down into the throat of the valley. Here, The Lamb checked his horse.

"I hoped that they'd take the way across country," he said. "But I couldn't hardly pray for it. They wouldn't take the open road. They were afraid that a watch was kept on it. Now, I think I can trail 'em across the valleys. But if your horse can run at all, you're sure to get to the house before Jimmy Montague and his murderers. Round up Loring, and tell him I sent you. Rouse him up, and tell him to stretch his men across the head of the two cañons. Up one of 'em,

Montague is marching . . . into a pocket, fate willing . . . and all that Loring has gotta do is to close the head of the sack. He'll have 'em."

"And who will close the bottom of the sack?" she asked him. "Do you mean?"

"Ask no questions . . . ride fast. There's a dozen lives of honest men in this." And he swung the big black about and put it down the slope so fast that the stallion slid, at last, on braced legs, knocking up a great shower of dry snow dust.

She did not attempt to follow for a further question, but The Lamb saw her horse scooting rapidly along the roadway. She had taken up her part of the burden. Now if only he could perform the thing that he saw before him. He would need speed, for one thing, and speed the stallion gave to him in abundance. Across the rolling hills, and through the crooked little snake-like ravines, the big horse carried him at breakneck force, his weight driving his hoofs through the loose snow, and biting down securely into the earth beneath.

All the while, The Lamb scanned the rims of the hills and every skyline before him. At last he saw what he wanted—a long line of dark forms mounting over a hummock, and dropping out of sight into the darkness beyond. They were filing into the ravine between the Black Hills and the Capper Hills, and the heart of The Lamb rose as he saw it, for the line began broad, with wide-spread arms, but, presently contracting, it pointed up toward the house in a narrow funnel, hardly forty feet across. There, fate willing, he would seal one end of this trap—and seal it most securely.

He looked to the magazine of his Winchester. It was filled. Two revolvers weighed down his saddle holsters, another sagged from his hip. It would go hard if he could not hold the enemy with this force of repeating weapons.

In the meantime, he needed only most careful secrecy, and a prayer that Louise should have arrived in time at the house of Loring. That she was sure to do, unless she had a fall on the way.

Jimmy took his men on slowly, with the deliberateness of one who knows that victory is in his hand and does not wish to bungle the last effort. The riders wound up the constantly narrow defile, while The Lamb drifted easily behind them, working from the cover of jutting rocks to the cover of the big brush. So he saw before him the lofty sides of the ravine in its narrowest portion—hollowed sides, eaten away by the rip of the currents that flowed here for a few days, in the middle spring when the melting of the snow was at its height.

The Lamb went on, his teeth on edge, like the teeth of a carnivorous animal, and a cold and steady fury in his heart. There was much to avenge—but in one great blow all might be done.

He dismounted. The stallion followed him like a dog—a cunning dog that saw that its master was stalking, and, therefore, went in the same manner, choosing its footsteps with care, stretching forth a lowered head as though anxious to avoid being seen. To The Lamb, looking back at the sleek, glimmering sides of the great horse, this seemed a terrible and a wonderful thing. Dumb beasts themselves seemed to wish the downfall of the Montagues.

He came into the narrow bottom of the gorge. The shadow from the eastern wall fell steeply across him. At that moment, rifles exploded at the head of the cañon, and long, wild yells rang back to The Lamb, mingled with the clangor and the echoing of the rifles. So that in an instant the gorge was filled as if with the sound of a great battle. He threw himself forward into a nest of rocks placed there by fate for him, in the very center of the ravine, with a fine, open stretch before him.

He heard the wild yelling swing about and pour back at him. Then from the tangle of rocks and brush a dozen riders broke out in one knotted clump, the leaders of the Montague retreat. Here was his time, at last.

With set teeth and grinning lips he placed his shots. Men were what he wanted, but the fall of men might not stop this rush. He picked the horses, and shot straight into the compacted center of the group. In the center, a whole cluster fell, one dropped by a bullet, others pitching over them. Next the flight split, and, with terrible yells of rage and despair, the Montagues whirled to right and to left and streamed back toward cover. On the ground lay three horses. Two men got onto hands and knees and began to drag themselves away.

The Lamb let them go. Even now he wanted battle, not brute slaughter. But the heart of The Lamb was filled with a savage joy, and a sad joy, also, for it seemed to him as though the gentle, cheerful shade of Will Dunstan went beside him, rifle in hand, and nodded approval of this work that was going ahead.

From the far end of the valley the rifle firing had ended, and a triumphant shout came down to him, continued long as one man took up the yell where the other left off. Prolonged, and magnified, and jumbled by the repeated echoes along the walls of the ravine, it came to The Lamb like the screaming of many eagles, and like eagles he wished them to come upon their prey in the throat of the hollow ravine and sweep it before them. Then he heard a great voice shouting from the scattered men of the Montagues, and he knew the hoarse, deep bellow of big Jimmy, calling to his followers that they were shrinking away from one man. And what one man could hold so many?

The Lamb smiled, still with set teeth, and as a cat peers around one side of the bush and then the other, with the feeding bird scant feet away, so The Lamb peered out from his nest of rocks, at one side of the valley and then at the other, reloading the partially emptied magazine of his rifle as he did so. For, though there was no cover for the others, at least they might work their way along the walls of the valley, where the shadow of the moon lay most deep, most like midnight— doubly deep, compared with the silver flaming edges of the cañon.

A steady blast of rifle fire began. It swept about the rocks. Sure hands held those rifles at point-blank range, and though they had no target, they were firing rapidly, putting their bullets blindly through the crevices among the rocks, in the hope of striking their man. The Lamb was showered with rock fragments, and with stinging splinters. He crushed his hat, and held it before his face, working still from side to side, like a snake, and so keeping his steady watch.

And presently, to the right, he saw a drift among the shadows, close at the edge of the cliff. Shadows cannot flow like water. He stared more intently, and saw that men were working along, on foot, trusting to the blast of the rifle fire to cover their retreat. Aye, and to the left were others.

He could recognize the brain of Jimmy, working behind this touch of battle tactics. He took steady aim to the right, gathered a dim form in the middle of his sights—and fired.

The yell of the stricken man leaped in his brain like the leap of a blindingly bright flame. He turned to the left. The shadows were scuttling back, close to the ground, but again he fired, and a gasping cry answered him. He saw a man fall; he saw the companions gather him up and half carry and half drag him back to shelter. At that, he held his fire. For he respected that touch of virtue among thieves.

The torrent of rifle bullets no longer pattered and rushed about his nest of rocks. Silence all at once covered the little ravine. There were no voices from the refugees; there were no shouts of triumph from the besieged. And one picture stood out in the darkness of The Lamb's mind, and that was the boiling wrath of Jimmy Montague, as he saw his strength and his fame so bottled, so helplessly stopped and netted.

The suspense grew, like an increasing strain on a rope that will not hold a sail long against the pressure of the wind. Then, from the right-hand upper rim of the ravine, a rifle cracked, a sound strangely far off and small, for it was not caught up by the loud echoes of the ravine. But, small though the sound was, it brought a sudden shout of consternation from the herded Montagues, gathered somewhere among the rocks. He heard them scattering, the brush snapping and crackling under their feet.

From the left-hand wall, another rifle spoke. And then The Lamb understood. With a few men, Loring was choking the upper end of the ravine. With the rest, he was lining the wall to torment the refugees with a plunging fire. No doubt he had sent one or two more far down the ravine wall to some point where they could lower themselves to the bottom, and so join The Lamb at his vital work of holding the horde.

He heard the big voice of Jimmy booming again, and he could distinguish the words.

"He's only human! We can rush him! Suppose he gets a couple of us. Most likely to get me. I'm bigger than the rest of you. But if a couple go down, the rest will surely get him and crush in his skull. He's only human, you know!"

The Lamb laughed, loud and shrill, and then he sent his voice pealing: "I'm not human, Jimmy. I'm The Lamb! Come and get me, son! Come an' get me, Jimmy boy! I'm waiting here all alone for you!"

An incredulous bellow of rage came from the young Montague, and from the rest, a groan. And The Lamb knew that nothing could persuade them, now, to trust themselves under the fire of his gun.

Another voice spoke, and this was from the left-hand wall. He recognized the great tones of Muldoon.

"Are ye there, kid?"

"Aye!" called The Lamb.

"Bless ye forever and ever. Can ye hold 'em?"

"I can. Hold 'em tighter than beer in a bottle. I got 'em corked, Muldoon!"

"Kid, it's a glorious night. Oh, we got 'em sewed up . . . if you can hold out. Not long now. Shorty and another is comin' up to brace you. And we'll help hold from the rim, here! Hey, you Montagues! Will you talk sense, now?"

"Damn you," bellowed big Jimmy, "and all your kind, and every dirty hound that runs behind Loring! We'll have no talk with you!"

But another voice called—farther off, and thin and sharp with fear—"Hello! Is it you, Muldoon?"

"Aye, it's me. Who's there?"

"McGuire! Jack McGuire!"

"Ye spalpeen! What'll you have, McGuire?"

"A chance for living, Muldoon!"

"March up to the far end of the ravine. Drop your guns, and walk out with your hands in the air. Mind you! There's boys there waitin' to take you!"

"Waitin' to fill me full of lead."

"Ye deserve it, ye dog! But Loring is a gentleman. He'll let you come safe through. There'll be no murder in this night's work, if ye'll come in free, with your hands up. He wants no blood."

"You fools!" roared Jimmy Montague. "What else would he want out of us, except our blood?"

328

"Is that you, Jimmy? You murderin' skunk!" cried Muldoon. "You are named out by Loring. We want your scalp. But the rest of 'em can come out quiet and safe. And quiet and safe they'll have to lie for a few days. Because over on your range there's dogies, and cows, and calves that Loring can use. They's nothing wrong with 'em except the brands that is wrote upon them! That's what we want. Boys, see sense, or we'll pot you like sick sheep before the mornin' ever gets pink!"

Big Jimmy kept shouting.

The Lamb could hear him arguing, almost pleading, but there was no response. And presently there was a shout from the upper end of the ravine. The Lamb needed no interpreter. The first of the pocketed rascals had come out in submission—probably Jack McGuire in person. No doubt the others would come soon, and Jimmy must have known, and known, too, that he was fighting now for his life, in the last hole.

For suddenly out of the dark of the brush, with a spitting of fire from the rocks on which they trod, came two horses, running side-by-side— one a tall gray, and the other a common mustang, with two empty saddles, and yet running as in harness, side-by-side. It was an old Indian trick. In between those running horses was the man who controlled them, of course, and that man must be Jimmy.

It was at the gray that The Lamb carefully aimed, hating his work. And the fine animal stumbled to its knees with a cough.

A shadow climbed the side of the mustang and dropped away to the farther side of it. They were very near now. Again, and again The Lamb fired, but the mustang rushed on, and straight at the nest of rocks, then reared and pitched heavily forward on the verge of them. Out of the heart of the sky, as it seemed to The Lamb upon his knees, the great form of Jimmy Montague spread-eagled down at him, with the spurt of a Colt darting from his hand in a tongue of flame.

Like a cat, The Lamb sprang to the side, but a great, massive arm caught him and hurled him down. They spun over and over, their guns knocked from their hands by the impetus of their fall, and then, by an odd chance, they staggered to their feet and faced each other, empty-handed, panting.

"And now, you dog," said Jimmy. "There's one minute of whiskey and honey left to me. I'm gonna wring your heart out. You hear me, you sneakin' spy? I killed Will Dunstan, if that's what you want to know. I bashed out his brains. And I seen him tumble like a sheep out of the saddle. Now, here's for you."

He rushed eagerly in, laughing drunkenly, and The Lamb laughed, also, if such snarling could be called laughter. Straight in at the lunging giant he sprang. The spat of his fists on the face of Jimmy was like the clapping of open palms. Then, Montague stumbled. And his gasp had more bewilderment than pain in it. He lunged, and the blinding, hard fists of The Lamb were in his eyes.

"Damn, it ain't possible," Jimmy gasped, and dropped to his knees as a straightly driven right found his chin.

But he had power still. He came to his feet, with a ragged rock in his fist, and lunged forward, and it was at that instant that little Shorty rose from behind the rearmost screen of rocks and fired. Jimmy wandered two aimless paces forward, and then slumped upon his face.

They turned him face upward. Both his hands were knotted in the last convulsion, and The Lamb turned savagely upon Shorty.

"Bad luck to you!" he cried angrily. "That was due to me."

Epilogue

But there was no bad luck for Shorty. There was no bad luck for any of Loring's men. They had not received a scratch in this fracas. Most mysteriously, there was not a dead man among the forces of the Montagues. But afterward, their name faded from the range. They were heard of no more. Except that Monty Montague, dead of a broken heart, as men said, was buried with honors in the town, and speeches were made over him.

For the rest, Colonel Loring suddenly prospered. His herds miraculously increased, but remarks about that miracle were the most unpopular words that could be spoken, and the least safe.

The law—what law there was—asked no questions. And men were chary of expressing their opinions, also. It was not safe, while Colonel Loring sat enthroned among the hills. Particularly it was not safe while one Alfred Dunstan, alias The Lamb—and alias many another famous name—ran his cows with the cows of the colonel, sat at the colonel's Sunday table, built his house upon ground donated by the colonel's large heart, and named his first son after that kind and ugly man.

Louise insisted upon that.

About the Author

Max Brand® is the best-known pen name of Frederick Faust, creator of Dr. Kildare, Destry, and many other fictional characters popular with readers and viewers worldwide. Faust wrote for a variety of audiences in many genres. His enormous output, totaling approximately thirty million words or the equivalent of five hundred thirty ordinary books, covered nearly every field: crime, fantasy, historical romance, espionage, Westerns, science fiction, adventure, animal stories, love, war, and fashionable society, big business and big medicine. Eighty motion pictures have been based on his work along with many radio and television programs. For good measure he also published four volumes of poetry. Perhaps no other author has reached more people in more different ways.

Born in Seattle in 1892, orphaned early, Faust grew up in the rural San Joaquin Valley of California. At Berkeley he became a student rebel and one-man literary movement, contributing prodigiously to all campus publications. Denied a degree because of unconventional conduct, he embarked on a series of adventures culminating in New York City where, after a period of near starvation, he received simultaneous recognition as a serious poet and successful author of fiction. Later, he traveled widely, making his home in New York, then in Florence, and finally in Los Angeles.

Once the United States entered the Second World War, Faust abandoned his lucrative writing career and his work as a screenwriter to serve as a war correspondent with the infantry in Italy, despite his fifty-one years and a bad heart. He was killed during a night attack on a hilltop village held by the German army. New books based on magazine serials or unpublished manuscripts or restored versions continue to appear so that, alive or dead, he has averaged a new book every four months for seventy-five years. Beyond this, some work by him is newly reprinted every week of every year in one or another format somewhere in the world. A great deal more about this author and his work can be found in *The Max Brand® Companion* (Greenwood Press, 1997) edited by Jon Tuska and Vicki Piekarski. His Website is www.MaxBrandOnline.com.

Center Point Large Print
600 Brooks Road / PO Box 1
Thorndike, ME 04986-0001 USA

(207) 568-3717

US & Canada:
1 800 929-9108
www.centerpointlargeprint.com